PART STAR PART DUST

A Novel

L. M. VALIRAM

Copyright © 2018 L. M. Valiram

Edited by Emily James & Scott Pack
Book Interior Layout & Proofreading by The Inspiration Hub
Cover Design by Ampersand Cover Designs

The moral right of the author has been asserted.

Apart from any fair dealing for the purposes of research or private study, or criticism or review, as permitted under the Copyright, Designs and Patents Act 1988, this publication may only be reproduced, stored or transmitted, in any form or by any means, with the prior permission in writing of the publishers, or in the case of reprographic reproduction in accordance with the terms of licences issued by the Copyright Licensing Agency. Enquiries concerning reproduction outside those terms should be sent to the publishers.

Matador
9 Priory Business Park,
Wistow Road, Kibworth Beauchamp,
Leicestershire. LE8 0RX
Tel: 0116 279 2299
Email: books@troubador.co.uk
Web: www.troubador.co.uk/matador
Twitter: @matadorbooks

ISBN 978 1788038 973

British Library Cataloguing in Publication Data.
A catalogue record for this book is available from the British Library.

Printed and bound in Great Britain by 4edge Limited

Matador is an imprint of Troubador Publishing Ltd

I AM YOUR NARRATOR

We are more intimate than you care to appreciate, as intimate as your every breath and the beating of your heart. I happen to you as I happen to everything and everyone else. You reside within me and this is how you have a past to reflect upon, a present to enjoy, and a future to anticipate.

Still, I am rarely understood. But that is just part of my charm. The minds that have tried, the brilliant unyielding ones, to define or explain or even imprison me, failed miserably. All they came up with is calendars. Yes, calendars that can be flipped so that moments and experience have some sort of order, some reason and sequence. They cut me into neat little squares on paper and numbered me in days and months and years to gain some perspective, to make sense of life, to give themselves points of reference.

But here is the secret—I am the grandest of illusions, unstoppable and beyond the bounds of imprisonment.

I am also your most reliable storyteller because everything that happens to you happens inside of me. It rises, unfolds and perishes in my bosom alone.

Your stories are my lovers. I have thousands, millions of them for each moment that passes.

So what stories shall I tell you today?

I could tell you the stories of the countless suns in the universe, of each star in the vast sky, of every breathing being, of every flower or every leaf. I could tell you about the dynasties that lived or the empires fallen, about revolutionaries that changed the landscape of humanity and martyrs that spilled blood for their beliefs. But I choose to tell you none of these. Instead, I will tell you stories of choice. Because what is life if not a series of choices? And what is destiny if not a consequence of those very choices?

A millionaire, a widow, and a monk.

None of them knew that the tickets they held for flight VA4625, scheduled to depart for Delhi at 1225hrs, were tickets to an altogether alternate destination. Oh, there were subtle omens, so many; the smog-filled sky, the blanket of grey that engulfed the city, the three flat tires, the forgotten passports, the choking highway. And then there were also the clouds. Clouds that curdled like thick, impenetrable cream just outside Bombay airspace, clouds whose intentions were less than honourable.

But I am getting ahead of myself again. Let us begin at the beginning.

PART I
RADHA

CHAPTER ONE

5th October, 1985, Bombay

Moti and his mistress were on their routine evening walk on Tilak Road. They had just turned the corner from the row of fruit stalls and Mrs Kamalnath was still thinking about the ridiculous price of watermelons. Moti began to jerk and pull Mrs Kamalnath toward the dumpster. She scrunched her face in irritation and reprimanded him with a hard tug and a nice loud scolding,

"Moti *chalo*, it is late. Dirty fellow, get your nose out of that junk."

But Moti was adamant and he would not budge even an inch. Mrs Kamalnath skirted closer to the stinking mess to see what it was that had captivated her otherwise compliant dog into disobedience.

Gingerly, she pinched her nostrils shut, leaned in and

studied the pile. She heard a faint whimper from within the mound. Oh no, not another dog. Or cat. Lord no, she wouldn't know what to do with a cat. What if it was a whole litter?

She tugged at the leash again.

"Come on Moti, let's go. Leave it now."

She started to walk away. Moti whined and followed. But something very strange happened. Her feet grew enormously heavy, as though transformed to stone. And her heart, dear God, at her age people died from a heart that raced this fast. She trotted along but this discomfort in her chest would not go away. She finally recognised it as a familiar one: it was guilt, the exact same guilt she felt each time she tried to turn away yet another orphan.

Fine, she thought, just fine. She would turn around and have a look after all, just so this wicked fluttering inside her would stop. She couldn't afford this kind of anxiety, she needed her sleep and a clear conscience.

So then, if she found kittens, she would just leave them there, she decided. There was no way she could breed cats with Moti around. If it was puppies, she would take them back, put them in a box and feed them, and then in a few days she would hand them over to the animal welfare people. There. That was that and in her head it was all sorted.

She burrowed through fruit peels, soiled newspapers, spoiled food, dirty wrappers, and other varieties of unidentifiable but revolting items. Finally, she came upon the source of the whimpering. Her hands touched something, only one thing, wiggly, warm and alive. She worked through the gunky sticky pile to fully get to it.

Nothing prepared her for what she found, for she had never before seen a human this small, not even a newborn. This child, bless its sorry soul, had most certainly been born before the full nine months. It was red and shrivelled like the pink prawns in the Sunday fish market. A girl, a she, loosely wrapped in a ratty rag, caked in dried blood the colour of rotten eggplants and scrawnier than Moti had looked when he had wandered into the orphanage. The baby's breaths were shallow, barely there. Mrs Kamalnath marvelled at the survival instincts of the creature and its ability in its pathetic condition to mewl and squeal for attention.

When Mrs Kamalnath arrived home, her husband, Mr Kamalnath was in the kitchen. "I hope you bought the loaf of bread I asked you to," he called out as he stirred the simmering curry on the stove.

"No I forgot but there is something else I brought. I really think you should come out and take a look at this."

"Bring it in here. These potatoes are already beginning to stick to the bottom of the pan. And why didn't you just buy what I asked for? You know nothing goes better with potato curry than…"

Mr Kamalnath was forced to pause mid-sentence because his wife had entered the kitchen and with her came a faint gurgling from the bundle in her arms. He dropped the ladle and moved closer to get a better look. "Not another one!

Now where did this come from? We can't manage anymore than the ones we already have. And this one is so..." his voice dropped, "small. She's barely alive."

The potatoes did stick to the bottom of the pot and the curry scorched and stank up the kitchen while Mr Kamalnath made the troublesome but obvious call to Doctor Ghosh.

The good doctor came to the house immediately. "What luck," he marvelled, "of all people, to be found by the caretakers of an orphanage. Had she been left like that, unfed and undiscovered for even a few hours more, this baby would surely have died. We must act fast, she needs to be hospitalised, immunised and we have to put her on a drip immediately," the doctor spoke firmly as he lifted the little one's arm and turned it over, squinting and inspecting the skin all around. He tut-tutted, "she needs to go under the light; she has jaundice."

He scribbled a note and handed it to Mr Kamalnath who rushed to the hospital and had the child admitted immediately. What a relief that was for him. Neither he nor his noble wife had any energy to care for yet another child, let alone an infant. The matter was duly resolved and the baby was off his hands and he didn't think very much about her at all.

So when the phone rang some eight days later, Mr Kamalnath was unpleasantly surprised. It was the hospital calling to inform him that his baby was ready to be discharged, and could he please come and pick her up. He started to reply, to tell them that this was not his child, this was not his problem—not his responsibility. But to his own surprise, he found that he did not say any of these things.

Instead, he went to the hospital, bundled her up in a warm blanket and brought her home.

Thus, the population of the orphanage grew for the third time that year. There weren't any other babies at Seva Dham. All the children were between the ages of seven and seventeen and they came there from the streets, the slums and the villages. They were children whose parents had disappeared into drugs, delinquency or death.

The arrival of a baby caused quite a stir amongst the children. Expectedly, Moti had issues of insecurity as he adjusted to the division of attention. He sulked plenty when the older ones took turns to hold the bottle and feed her, when the younger ones practiced their counting on her little toes and fingers and when Mrs Kamalnath gushed as she tickled her tummy.

She was named Radha, not for any profound reason, such as it being the name of the devoted consort of the Blue God, Krishna. But merely because it happened to be the name on the tag of the blanket in which she came home: Radha Textiles and Mills. Polyester Cotton. Hand Wash Only. Made In India.

Since her unlikely discovery and her even unlikelier survival, she has recovered well. For a four-year-old, she is of satisfactory height and average weight. She has hair the colour of charcoal and her eyes are a tone darker. She talks with a slight lisp and tends to end her words in a squeak.

She lives in a large and sparse room with rows upon rows of rickety steel frames with thin mattresses atop creaking slat platforms. When Seva Dham Memorial Orphanage For The Destitute is uninhabited during school hours, this room can be as distressful and depressing as a communal prison or a military hospital ward whose inmates are in recess. The floor is cold concrete, uneven but buffed so the children that run over it do not cut themselves. The walls are bare and mottled with grey water stains resembling storm clouds. Six washbasins made with cold metal mount the wall like a row of tin guards.

The forty-seven orphans who reside here are as happy as children can be. Their ages are tender and their minds simple. They do not grasp yet the profundity of their misfortunes. They are not completely cognizant of their low status. Ignorance—only sometimes—can truly be bliss.

These children are never hungry or dirty, they are well looked after by their wardens. Sure, they argue with each other over a toy or a game, but most of the time they love each other. If you came here on any school night when the lights are out and they are supposed to be asleep, you would hear secrets being whispered, fluttering laughter, and fairy tales aplenty.

Every morning, they leave here in washed uniforms and carrying overfull school bags. On Saturdays, they stay on the premises, they play, and complete their school work. On Sundays, they have a lesson in the dining hall where their housemaster and housemistress, Mr and Mrs Kamalnath, tell them stories about noble and honest people. They love these stories; they listen with rapt attention to the nonviolent struggle of Mahatma Gandhi, the compassionate work of Mother Teresa, the spiritualism of Vivekananda. They hear tales of mythology, of demons of demigods, of battles and of weapons, of good defeating evil.

Mr and Mrs Kamalnath, both retired schoolteachers in their sixties, have managed Seva Dham with sincere love and impassioned zeal for fifteen years. They draw a humble salary from the Trust for their services.

Radha is the youngest child here. She is also one of the quietest. Today, she sits on her corner bunk by herself while all the other children are away at school. Well, she is not exactly by herself. She has for company her closest friend, Roma, a ragged doll that has been handed down to her after being used rather roughly by other children who have outgrown her. Roma is missing a hand and a patch of hair on her scalp. Other than that she is beautiful and Radha loves her very much.

"The fairy will give you new clothes," Radha murmurs lovingly. "And she will fix your hand and your hair."

She tells Roma that the fairy lives in a palace up in the clouds and her hair is made from strings of silver and her eyes glitter like diamonds.

"Yes, Roma, you will walk and talk and be just like me."

The fairy will float in on her translucent wings from the window tonight after the moon rises, and she will tap them on the arm or the leg or even the head with her jewelled staff. And they will sprout wings, real ones, ones that flap and ones that can make them fly high up into the sky where they will enter the huge palace. Everyone in the palace has magical powers and every girl is a princess who combs her silver hair for a hundred strokes.

"These are four-legged horses, Roma. Real ones. Not like Bunty. He is just a three-legged horse and he is made of wood. Bunty is a toy and if Gopi hadn't rocked him so hard then he would still be ok to ride. But he is still a toy. He can't fly."

All the children eat sweet sticky *mithai* and spongy, syrupy, round *rasgolla* for breakfast, lunch, and dinner, Radha explains to the inanimate doll.

"It is not like here. No it is not. Up there, we won't have to wait for uncles and aunties to bring treats because there they are giving them away all the time. Sweets grow on trees, and if they don't pluck the candy leaves and the fudge apples then it will all get spoilt and go to waste. *Kulfi* grows, and *barfi* and *jalebi* and *ladoos*. We won't have to make do with just one piece. Understand Roma?"

The gate creaks loudly. Radha jumps off the bed, runs to the window and peeps out. Surely the fairy will not come through the gate. That is not how fairies arrive. She will fly through the window. Perhaps she wants to meet Uncle and Aunty because they are so nice. Maybe she will turn them into fairies too.

Radha worries. If Uncle and Aunty become fairies

and fly away, then who will mind the rest of the children? Imagine everyone's shock and horror when they return from school to find her, Aunty and Uncle gone!

This morning after Radha had washed herself, she waited for Gauri, her twelve-year-old bunkmate to come and help her put on her uniform. But Gauri hadn't come. Instead Aunty had. And she'd said, "Today you stay home, we are expecting a special guest who wants to meet you."

This is how Radha has come to the conclusion that today is the day of the fairy's arrival. But now she thinks she will want her friends to go with her too. She can't leave Manish, who always plays "It" in Blind Man's Buff. If he goes with her, the fairy will give him eyes and he will be able see everyone. He won't need to fumble with his food and trip over toys. And Janki has to come too. The fairy can give Janki back her leg so she can play catchers and she will no longer have to hobble around anymore.

Radha cranes her neck and squints into the sunlight. She sees a man, younger than Uncle Kamalanathan. There is a woman with him and her hair is black, not white like Aunty's. No, these strangers are not fairies she decides, because she can't see any wings.

Aunty stands at the threshold, her eyes moist and full. A solitary tear trickles down her cheek, glistening like a jewel in the beam of sunshine that shoots through the window. She enters the room and sits down in front of Radha.

"Why are you sad?" Radha cups Aunty's face in her small hands and touches her cheek to check if the shining streak is real. "Don't cry, Aunty." Radha climbs into her lap, wraps her arms around her neck and kisses her cheek. "She will come."

"Who will come?"

"The fairy godmother."

Aunty breaks into a smile and brushes aside a stray hair from Radha's forehead. "The fairy godmother is here and the godfather too."

"Where?"

Aunty points out the window. The young couple is walking past the pile of toys and into the office with Uncle.

"They're not fairies, they have no wings."

"There are different types of fairies. Many come in disguise and they hide their wings on the inside."

Radha cocks her head upward and examines Aunty's face with suspicion. "How can you have wings inside?"

"The wings grow on their hearts."

"So they can't fly? But fairies fly."

Aunty holds Radha tightly in her arms. "Their hearts fly high my darling. High above the clouds, and they scatter stardust on special people like you."

"The stardust is magical?"

"The stardust is love."

Radha crinkles her nose. "But what about magic?"

"It *is* magic my dear. Love is magic."

The office at Seva Dham is located at the side of the building. It is cluttered with well-worn manila folders stacked high over iron cabinets. Two oversized work desks and three wooden chairs for guests cram the small space.

Ledgers are balanced here, bills filed monthly, receipts stored, letters typed. It is a simple system. There is file for every child, opened when the child is first admitted to Seva Dham. A standard form is filled out with any and all information known: date of birth; date, height and weight of admittance; hospital and immunisation records; photographs; known or presumed family history, race, and religion.

Radha's file lies open on the table. Mr Kamalnath is reviewing it while the two guests seated across from him wait anxiously. He checks that all papers are in order. He has already made a copy for them.

The couple rise to their feet as Mrs Kamalnath enters the room.

The lady guest bites her lip nervously, searching for Radha because Mrs Kamalnath appears to be alone. Disappointment spreads over her face like a dark shadow. She hangs her head. She has been waiting to see Radha all week. She has missed her so very much.

It has been ten days since she laid eyes on the girl. Ten long days since she stood inside this very same office and peeped from a crack in the door while Radha played with an older boy. He was making shapes by stretching a rubber band between his fingers, and Radha was trying to do the same.

Over the course of the last two months, Champa has visited the orphanage and observed Radha from afar every week. And every week she has fallen deeper, she has loved stronger, she has been surer. Her husband Mohan is happy; this day could not have come soon enough. This morning, he has stopped at the temple before coming to Seva Dham and offered a hefty donation as gratitude to the gods.

He nudges Champa and gestures with his eyes. Champa tilts her head to the side and catches a glimpse of the girl cowering behind Mrs. Kamalnath. She looks as beautiful and innocent as ever, even more angelic than Champa remembers. But she also looks so very afraid. What have they told her?

Champa steps forward slowly, careful not to upset her. She kneels before Radha and offers her a smile, at first quivering but then warm.

Radha blinks and furrows her brows. She clings closer to Mrs. Kamalnath. Then she whispers soft and timid, "Are you the fairy godmother?"

"I am not a fairy godmother. I am just a mother. I am your mother." The words leave Champa's lips like little sparrows set free. She has waited to say them. She has waited since the very first day she visited the orphanage and saw Radha. Not one cell did she have in common with this stranger, but not one beat of heart wanted to understand that. Because what, after all, has love to do with body or birth?

Mrs Kamalnath too kneels in spite of her muscles and tendons protesting. She opens her bony arms and envelops Radha within them, whispering in her ear, "These nice people here are going to buy you some ice cream, and then they are going to take you and get you a nice pretty dress, just like the one in the story book about the princess. Would you like that?"

"And ribbons?"

"Yes, ribbons too." She pulls back, looks Radha in her eyes and speaks with exaggerated excitement, "And do you know what else? You can even try and find a dress for your Roma because Roma can go with you."

Champa hesitates at first but then decides to chime in, adding delicately, "And you can stay with us for a few days. Do you like toys?"

Radha nods.

"They have bubbles in the toy shop near our house, and balloons. There are bicycles too."

Radha looks to Mrs. Kamalnath, who nods her approval. Radha doesn't move. The lump in Champa's throat grows as Radha deliberates.

The girl finally speaks. "Can we get vanilla? One scoop for me and one for Roma?"

CHAPTER TWO

7th December, 1986

"Such wide eyes,"

"I love her eyelashes, they're so long,"

"Is she your first?"

"Oh she is beautiful, she looks just like you,"

Both friends and strangers often pass such remarks to Champa. Her response is always the same; a smile of acknowledgment with carefully hidden pride beneath. Her heart overflows as she agrees with them.

Yes, she does look like me. She does have my eyes. Yes, she is my firstborn. We are alike. So alike.

She has almost forgotten that she and Radha are not bound by blood. After all, it is such a minute detail, negligible, irrelevant. For parents are not created by bonds as perfunctory as genealogy. No, those bonds are made of flesh and bones and marrow and blood, all physical and transient. Parents do not become parents by giving *a* life to their child. They become parents by giving their life to *their* child.

Champa and Mohan have raised the young orphan as though she was cast from their own bodies. There is no distinction and no impediment in their love for her. On the contrary, they value her with more intensity than the best of biological parents. She did not come easy like the rest, she is not the mere by-product of pleasurable lovemaking. Radha is the child nature never meant for them to have. She is the anomaly, the blessing conferred by unknown benefactors.

In their earlier years together, the couple had imagined a house full of children. Champa wanted one daughter but secretly hoped for at least two. Mohan is from a loud and large family of four boys and a girl. He could not imagine anything less for himself. It had never crossed either of their minds that life would turn out any different. After all, children were the natural progression of marriage. They happen to everyone. Life is a simple sequence, isn't it? Fall in love, marry, have children.

They did fall in love. Madly. It swept over them root and branch. Within a month of laying eyes on each other in the summer of 1978, they plunged themselves into marriage. They were both twenty-three.

It was Champa's love for music and art that drove her to the city of Varanasi after her graduation to study classical music under the auspices of famed teachers at the most prestigious musical institute in the country. At the time, Mohan was based out of Bombay, interning as a chemical engineer by weekdays and fulfilling his wanderlust as a freelance photographer on the weekends.

And it was in this capacity that he travelled to Varanasi alongside a rather snobbish English writer from *OurPlanet* monthly magazine. He was to take photographs and assist the Englishman with translations. They were to visit the Ganges river, several temples, some embankments and lastly they were to go to the oldest music school in the country.

The trip to the music school was to be on their final day and the arrangement was that the Englishman would first interview the head of the school and then attend a performance by the students.

Mohan was instructed to take some natural shots of the musicians and their traditional instruments in the majestic open-air auditorium. He stood at the back of the hall swivelling his zoom lens left to right as the musicians presented themselves on stage in a row. They filed in and settled down one by one over their instruments; *tablas* and *sitars*, flutes and harmoniums. Mohan could tell you even now, without looking at the photographs that Champa was second from right in the front row. He could tell you that four minutes into the performance her fingers paused their dance over the keys of the harmonium for she had to pin a stray lock of hair that tickled her nose causing her to sneeze.

He never received fair payment for that Varanasi job because he could not explain why three expensive rolls of film were spent on photos of the slender young woman in the sky-coloured sari. There were no shots of the facade of the school, none of the intricately carved pillars or the stone sculptures of celebrated musicians.

Love blossomed with compelling urgency. They decided to marry and live in Bombay. She wanted to start a small tuition centre and teach music. He secured a generous package at Yuva Biotech, the subsidiary of a large multinational firm, Zinmac Industries.

The desire for progeny arose like a ripple in the calm lake of their lives. Every month they waited, and every month they were disheartened. These ripples soon turned to torrents and their peaceful co-existence started to fray.

Then one day, when they were on the verge of losing all hope, Mohan suggested they see a doctor. It was time, he said, for medical intervention. She wanted to resist, to refuse. What if it was her? She was sure it was her. But he persisted and tests were carried out on them both.

"I am sorry," Mohan said that night in bed, "it is unfair on you. You should not have to remain childless I just want you to know that I love you very much and I will be okay if you choose another path. You deserve better than me."

"Another path?"

"You had a dream. It is a dream I cannot fulfill. I have failed. You are still young and so beautiful. You deserve an undamaged life."

She placed a finger over his lips. "Shhh . . ." she choked,

"whenever I have had that dream, you have been in it. We have been in it together."

Days later, the decision was made. They would adopt. And this was how they ended up at Seva Dham.

That first night Radha was brought home, Mohan had slept in the guest room and Champa in the master bedroom with Radha. They lay in bed, new mother and new daughter, shoulders touching.

"Aunty," Radha whispered into the pillow.

The word hung heavy, unfamiliar, like an unwanted guest. Champa hadn't anticipated the insurmountable gulf that needed to be quelled. Of course it would take time.

Why had she expected to be called Mama right away? What gave her the right to even want it from this child? What if her motherhood would never grow on Radha? What if she failed to win the little girl's heart? What if Radha was going to start crying now?

"Yes, dear," she answered, trying her best to keep her voice from shaking.

"When can I go home?"

Home? This was home. This being together. This being a mother. This placing their heads on the same pillow. This was home.

There had been six dishes at dinner, cakes and pastries for desserts, a room full of dolls and a sea of toys at Radha's disposal. Then why was she saying this now? Was it all a big mistake? But how could Champa turn back? There was nothing to turn back to. How could she ever be anything but Radha's mother again?

"Aunty?"

There was that word again, pricking her like a thousand thorns all at once.

Mohan. What would he have replied? She battled the paralysis in her body and slipped her hand under the blanket. She found Radha's hand, held it tight, and then moved a little closer and whispered.

"I think your dolly Roma wants to hear a story. I know a really nice one about a fairy. You like fairies don't you? Shall I tell it to you?"

"Can the fairy fly?"

"Yes, she most certainly can. And she can sing too. Would you like to hear the song she sings when she flies high in the blue sky?"

"Yes."

Champa began to hum.

Love in the song that the birds do sing

Love in the summer, Love in the spring

Love in the rays the sunshine brings

Love Love Love in everything

Love in the morning, Love at night

Love makes everything shine so bright

Love in the rays the sunshine brings

Love Love Love in everything

Radha's breaths slowed, her body relaxed against Champa's. She fell silently, comfortably, peacefully into the arms of sleep.

There are more songs and more stories every day. They are told at mealtimes and before bed. Sometimes it is Champa who tells them and at other times it is Mohan. Radha says Mama can sing the songs better than Papa. But Papa makes the best sound effects especially when he roars like Simbaa the lion and makes her cower and giggle all at the same time.

On weekends, they go on road trips. They visit the beach or the zoo or the carnival if there is one in town. Mohan clicks photos of her; licking an ice cream cone, peeking out of the trees, crinkling up her nose, kissing Champa. Roll after roll is Radha, Radha and more Radha.

When they go to the park, Mohan will push her on the swings. They blow soap water bubbles in the bath. She helps Champa knead the dough for *chapatis*. They play Snakes and Ladders or Ludo after dinner. She has to watch Papa closely or he cheats! Mama is no good at the game at all. She always gives up. Radha always wins everything.

Radha goes to a new school now. It is nearer their home and there are less children in every class. The teachers are nicer and Radha gets to go to the toilet whenever she needs to, even if it is in the middle of the class. But she has to ask the teacher first. This is fine by her, because the teacher never says no.

It has been a year since she has been with Champa and Mohan. Love has done what love does best. It has united.

"Good girl. Now that we are nice and clean, let's eat." Champa wipes Radha's dripping hands with a tea towel and prods her alongside out the kitchen into the dining room.

She lifts Radha by her tiny waist. She does not need to. Radha is all grown up. *I am five*, she exclaims proudly when anyone asks, holding all five fingers up for them to count.

"Ready? What story does the princess want to hear today?"

"Tell me the story of the elephant and the mouse," Radha says. Champa plates her lunch and sets it before her.

"There was once a big, fat elephant by the name of Raghu." She spoons a bite and brings it close to Radha's mouth.

Radha purses her lips tight, crosses her arms and shakes her head vehemently.

"Now what happened?"

"It doesn't look good. It is brown colour and it looks mushy."

"It is mince, come, open your mouth please. Mama has to go. Uncle Lakshman has come already. If you don't finish your lunch than he will have to wait and that is not nice. Mama can't be late for her own class. Please," she pleads with the girl.

Radha half opens her mouth. Her lips quiver and a big fat tear starts to crawl down her cheek. She pulls her head back and repels the spoon. "What is mince made of?"

"Mince is mince, my dear."

She crinkles her nose and wipes her eyes with the back of her hand. "But what is it?"

"Mince is lamb. Why so many questions?"

"Lamb is an animal? *Mary had a little lamb*, its feet was white as snow," Radha starts to sing, tears still flowing, voice shaking.

"Ok, shhh, darling. Don't cry. Mama is not forcing you. And it's fleece, not feet; *its fleece was white as snow*."

"What is fleece?"

"Fleece is like hair. It is the covering on the lamb's skin."

"But this is brown. How did the lamb become brown? It was white as snow."

"It is brown because we took off the fleece before cooking it, my dear."

"You cooked it on the fire?"

"Yes, my darling, come on now, my clever girl *chalo chalo*, eat."

"Did it cry?"

"No it didn't because it was not alive."

"How did it die?"

"Because the butcher..." Champa hesitates here. "Because the butcher killed it and cut it."

Radha pouts and frowns.

"But why did he kill the lamb? What did the lamb do?"

"It didn't do anything. We have to eat it—that is why we had to kill it."

"But Mama, why must we kill animals? Why can't we eat apples? Animals should not die. They should live and play. Like in the zoo."

Champa takes a deep breath. There is nothing she can think to say. She clears the mince from the table and instead heats up the leftover peas and rice from last night's dinner. "How about this? It is not an animal. And peas make you strong."

To Champa's relief, Radha picks up the spoon and starts to eat on her own.

CHAPTER THREE

24th February, 1990

You can tell a lot by looking at children. Watch the child that is reverently quiet, the one that listens and does not speak, the one that dances alone with his thoughts. Watch the one that is assertive, the one that must be heard at all costs, even if he hasn't much to say. Watch the one with a streak of meanness, the bully that rejoices in domination. Watch the one that compensates with a joke; the clown, the earnest, the sincere, the happy, the coy, the insecure. You can see the shade of their personality clearly forming, you can see them unfolding and becoming. You can almost see their future.

~~~

Mrs. Shukla is the English teacher at CM Memorial School. She reveres Wordsworth, Tagore, and Shakespeare. She sits at her desk by the window in the staff room and chews her cheese, tomato, and cucumber sandwich. The school is in recess and she has a direct view of the playground; she watches.

A group of children by the hopscotch stand in a circle deep in an animated discussion. It is a mute one as far as she is concerned, because their voices don't carry. She guesses they are in disagreement about something trivial like whose turn it is or who is out or who cheated. Nine-year-old Radha is among them and is speaking. Mrs. Shukla observes with great interest how Radha waves her arms about, how she gestures earnestly, how her sincere eyes express themselves.

This is just what Mrs Shukla has been looking for. Radha is exactly what she needs. She becomes so excited that she puts her sandwich down on the desk and leaves the staff room immediately.

She approaches the group and they cower at the sight of the steel-tempered face behind thick rimmed glasses. "What is going on here?"

Clearly some of them are at fault and making mischief because no one replies; instead they skitter away, dispersing like a bunch of rabbits.

"Not you, Radha," Mrs Shukla says in a soft tone of voice, completely uncharacteristic of the dragon teacher. "Come with me."

Radha's friends see her being led to the benches, dreadful Shukla in front and Radha following behind, her head bowed. They whisper with anxiety. What will become of their friend? Will Shukla make Radha stand on the bench, make her hold her ears through recess? Worse, will she cane her for all the school to see? To their surprise and even Radha's, she invites her to sit beside her on the bench. She then starts to state the case. She ends with, "In my opinion, you would be absolutely perfect."

That afternoon, Radha comes home and tells her mother everything, every single word. "And she said that she has been looking for a long long time but never found anyone as perfect as me. She said I must ask you because I may need to stay after school."

Champa all but jumps off the sofa. She hugs Radha a little too tight and showers many kisses on her cheeks. "Of course you can stay after school and you absolutely should say yes to your teacher. You will make a splendid princess Jasmine."

And that is how Radha becomes involved in the school performance of Aladdin. It is also how she will make acquaintance with both fear and exhilaration for the first time in her life.

Radha rehearses after school for days at a stretch. There are twenty-two children participating, only five with major roles, and Radha is one of them. Every day when classes are over, Champa arrives at the school auditorium with a tetra pack of mango juice and a tiffin containing after school snacks, sitting with the other parents while she waits for her daughter to finish practice.

Everyone compliments Radha on her fine delivery of dialogue. She is doing exceptionally well and it is plain to see that she will be the jewel of the production. Even Amit, who plays Aladdin, pales in comparison. He keeps forgetting his lines.

As the day of the performance nears, the rehearsals veer from school into the home. Radha stands in front of the mirror in her room every spare moment she has.

How dare you? All of you? Standing around deciding my future as if I am a prize to be won.

Who are you? Tell me the truth.

Does Abu have anything else to say?

Goodnight, my handsome Prince.

It is as though the girl is born to act. The allure of being able to summon the personality of another, to pretend to be someone else, to experiment with her own consciousness becomes a sort of addiction. How intriguing it is to her, to become more than one person.

On the day of the performance, Radha's heart races as she steps on to the stage. She cannot see Amit even though he is standing right in front of her. She cannot see Ranjit dressed as the Sultan in his dopey turban. She only sees the million-headed monster with its countless pairs of glaring eyes. It waits as one unified body, expectantly in the darkness, to devour her whole.

Her face turns pale as wax; her bladder grows threateningly full; her limbs freeze and her teeth chatter. She opens her mouth, but the lines that were memorised to perfection now escape like thieves in the night.

The lump in her throat threatens to explode into a hiccupping sob.

And then, just as she is clenching her legs tight to keep from wetting her purple sequined harem pants, a familiar voice from the corner of the stage calls out in a loud whisper, "Radha, don't be afraid."

She turns her quivering head to the side and sees the face of her mother, smiling, blowing kisses that travel straight into her heart. It responds instantly by slowing down.

"Mama," she mutters. A pin mike turns her tiny voice into a thundering reverberation through the auditorium. The monster can hear her.

"You can do it," Champa mouths. "Just pretend you're a princess. You're Jasmine."

Radha believes her mother. Radha is a princess. Radha is Jasmine. The monster melts away and words begin to tumble out of her mouth. She prances the stage delivering line after line. She pretends to laugh and pretends to cry, she kneels on her knees and speaks to the Genie, she dances with Aladdin and rides the magic carpet that for her is afloat in the sky.

The monster arises from its multitude of seats and claps with its infinite hands. The applause echoes from the unpadded walls and high ceilings. The very same heart that raced with fear now throbs with exhilaration.

Radha learns many lessons this day.

She learns she is not one person. She can be anybody. She can be everybody. She is not trapped, she is free. She also learns that her mother is a fairy after all, with magical powers that chase away dread better than any make-believe genie.

Her biggest learning is that this is what she wants to do for the rest of her life. She wants to act; she wants to play with personalities. She wants to be different people and feel what they feel, think what they think, do what they do, even if it is only for a short time. It is not the escape from her own mind that appeals to her, but the ability to have a phantom mind enter hers.

CHAPTER FOUR

5th October, 1997

She sits on the ledge of the terrace with a day-old newspaper between her buttocks and the concrete. Her shoulder-length hair blows in the wind, her legs dangle carefree ten floors above the bustling city. Her hand is comfortable and warm in Varun's. He holds it with the ease and lightness he handled the flowers that sit beside her now.

"You made them so pretty today, you're getting good at this" Radha fingers the purple freesias within stems of silver eucalyptus.

"Handmade especially for you. How many boys would do that for you? You know I thought real hard about this one, about which flowers will go with which," Varun says with a proud smirk.

He is a fatherless boy, not rich in wealth but good in

heart. His mother has raised him with difficulty, toiling ten hours a day at a flower shop. He works there after school and has come to be a favourite employee of the lady owner, Mira, also a widow. Mira often tells Varun's mother that he has a gift for knowing flowers, that he arranges them in the most inventive of combinations; yellow snapdragons with pink Sweet Williams, white fuji mums with lavender roses, purple butterfly asters with sun kissed carnations. He has a full-time job at Blooms & Blossoms waiting for him anytime he is ready.

The classmates sit, hand in teenage hand, and watch the city throb beneath them. Cars, bicycles, carts and every other thing on wheels snake through congested lanes and avenues. People crawl, busy as ants in the nooks and alleys. This hurrying, bursting, overcrowded place is no longer called Bombay. It has been rechristened Mumbai, the ruling government's effort in ridding the country of its colonial past. The Indians are asserting their independence from the Portuguese and the British Raj. If only it was that easy to free oneself of slavery. For we may free ourselves from one master only to surrender to another. We may remove the foreigners only to discover the shackles that bind us are within.

Radha has allowed herself to fall in love with this flower boy, although she sometimes suspects it is out of curiosity. Half of the girls in her class have boyfriends that they think people don't know about, even though they have told their secret to everybody and made them promise to tell nobody.

Varun and Radha have been together almost a year.

When Varun asked her out, she hesitated because she was afraid to ask her parents if it was acceptable that she go out with a boy. She mulled over it for some days and then gave in to his advances, choosing instead not to tell her parents at all. That, she decided, would slip her into the safe place of neither having lied nor having disobeyed.

She has not gone all the way, like two of the girls at school have; she knows they have because the boys have told. She hasn't admitted him into her body. He has asked more than once. He says she is beautiful, he says he wants to be one with her. But she wants to know love for the sake of love first. She wants to know it without the corruption of sex or lust. Sometimes she gets weak and allows him to touch her in places. But it doesn't feel very good. She has often been troubled by this.

She read an article a few weeks ago in *Women's Era* about asexuality. It is a relatively new concept, the magazine said, a term coined by western psychologists for people who are happy with romance or cuddling, holding hands and taking long walks, but do not feel the need to have sex. She thinks she just may be asexual. But she has decided that she will never know unless she tries, so she has given herself a deadline. It starts today, on her sixteenth birthday.

Varun does not know of her intentions, but if he did, oh will he be ecstatic. He will know exactly where to go. He will probably get up and grab her by the hand and take her there right now.

He turns to her as though reading her thoughts and

sweeps a coil of hair away from her cheek. She loops her arm around his tighter, drawing him even closer. He shifts a little and reaches into his pocket, pulling out a small box. It is covered in velvet, like the ones her mother has in the drawers of her cupboard.

When Radha was younger and Champa would be getting ready in front of the mirror for a performance or a dinner, she would ask Radha to get the boxes out for her. There were many, all different—big, small, royal blue, and ruby red. Radha would tiptoe and reach into the drawer, then carry them one by one and hand them to her mother. Inside them were pieces of jewellery in handcrafted *kundan*, delicately uncut multi-coloured gemstones set in a base of silver with hand-painted enamel designs on the reverse side.

There were *jhumkas* that dangled like little bells from the ears, intricate nose rings with thin chains that travelled to the back of the ear or could be pinned into the hair. There were necklaces, heavy and elaborate with multiple tiers. These were all inherited pieces from Champa's mother. Some were made with artificial gemstones but many, especially the smaller pieces, were real. She knew because those were reserved for special, smaller events. Radha would insist she try them on before Champa wore them and her mother would place them around Radha's neck, ears, and fingers. She would then prop Radha on her lap and together the women would take in their reflection in the mirror, faces shining and glittering in the adorned jewellery.

"When you marry, you will wear all of this," Champa

would say.

"I don't want to marry," Radha would reply every time.

Now she holds Varun's gift in her hand and wonders why she said that. Wasn't it every little girl's dream to marry?

"Open it," Varun says.

The box is the size of a lemon, small enough to hold nothing more than a ring. Her heart races. *It cannot be,* she thinks.

She clicks it open with shaking fingers and breathes a silent breath of relief. Inside is a half heart in silver with a ridged edge, as though it has been broken. What a sad gift. A broken heart with a thin silver chain looped around the top of the pendant.

She says nothing and gazes at him with wrinkled brows.

"Wait, I will show you." He unbuttons the two top buttons of his shirt to reveal the other matching half of the heart. It shines bright against the tanned skin of his chest.

"Happy birthday to my other half." He pulls her close and kisses her on the lips. He then places a hand on her shoulder and turns her around, taking the necklace out of the box and clasps it around her neck.

"There, we are complete now."

She is flattered by the sweetness and thoughtfulness of his gift. She is happy, touched—but no, she doesn't feel in any way complete. And she does not feel like his other half.

"It is beautiful," she says convincingly, then kisses him

beneath the greying sky and above the muffled sounds of the city.

She must go though, because there is a party at home tonight. All the family are coming over to celebrate her sweet sixteenth. Even Aunt Rimi is coming all the way from Poona, which is only a few hours' drive, but still it makes her feel special. And her favourite Aunt Uma is flying in all the way from Delhi. Her flight would have arrived three hours ago; she must be home by now.

"Thank you for making my birthday super special," she says.

"Hey, a special girl like you must have a special birthday."

"Must be expensive." She holds up the pendant and examines its jagged edge with her finger, it is polished smooth.

"Not really, it is nothing." He shrugs.

"I should go, they all must have arrived."

"What time does this big birthday party start? It's never too late to invite me you know," he teases.

"I can't even imagine that, how excruciating to explain you to everyone."

"Oh come on, I am sure your parents know by now."

She sighs, "I hate to admit it but I think they kind of do."

"But they haven't asked you?"

"They're not like that." She feels a tinge of guilt at

keeping it from them. They must suspect. They've seen her drop her voice to a whisper if they appear while she is on the phone. They've watched her fumble for words if she's asked where she's been.

She will tell them; they won't object. In fact she is not quite sure why she hasn't told them yet, they have been open-minded about most things thus far. When she told them she wanted to sign up for acting classes at the institute, they were supportive even though the course was expensive. Most other parents she knows would raise an objection to such a pursuit. Acting is not readily considered a respectable profession for most daughters.

The sun's fiery disc has set. Crows fly from here to there and there to here in a V-shaped formation. Lights appear like dragonflies in the windows of surrounding buildings. The air grows still and ready for the quiet of night.

She pecks his cheek. "Shall we?" She jumps off the ledge into the terrace and pulls him along, her hand not letting go of his.

"If you insist." He slaps the dust and grit off his jeans, picks up her flowers and hands them to her.

She inhales their scent and smiles at him. "And how do you propose I explain these?"

"I told you, I can come to your party and we can do the grand reveal."

She slaps his arm. "Please take the stairs down in case anyone sees us together."

"How will they even know where I am coming from or whether I am with you? I will just be a guy in the lift, I will stand in the other corner with my eyes downcast but peeking at you."

"You will never be just a guy in the lift. You will be noticed because you are so very handsome. Come now, let's go already." She pulls his arm and they make their way through the potted plants, over the pipes, around the wired fences and buckets reserved by residents for when there are water cuts.

She presses for the lift, he pecks her cheek. She can hear him whistle a tune as he runs down the stairs to make his way home.

Their voices are faint but familiar as they chatter over each other, everyone drowning everyone else out. Radha is not able to make out what they say, but she recognises the sound as the chaotic coming together of her exceptionally large family. This is how they communicate, so loud and boisterous that she can hear them even before the doors of the lift open on the 5th floor.

She cringes as she passes Mrs Chawla's unit, 5D. The old grouch's visitation at their doorstep tonight is certain. She will show up in her housecoat and hair rollers and whine about the "unbearable" noise levels. Her mongrel, heaven knows what breed, will whimper at her feet in agreement.

Mrs Chawla rarely leaves the house but when she does, it is almost always to call on a neighbour and register an unhappy complaint about something they are doing that is turning her "life into a living hell"—like hanging their clothes out the side balcony where she can see them, or the smell of frying fish that is making her nauseous, or their children spoiling the corridor tiles with their bicycles. One time she accused someone in the building society of spying on her, which is preposterous, Radha thinks, because why would anyone want to observe anything this old grouch did. She led the most uninteresting life and she wore the strangest clothes.

None knew what exactly was under that housecoat. You could see a loose and long floral blouse under some kind of parka or a mini kaftan over a long skirt and a lacy hem, perhaps a slip, dangling from beneath it. It was hard to establish where one layer of clothes ended and the other began. And heaven forbid anyone end up trapped in the lift with her, because oh, that breath was enough to bring kingdoms to their knees.

Except for Mrs Chawla and that creepy Baman from the eighth floor who leers at Radha as though she is a piece of sugarcane he wants to dig his teeth into, she doesn't much mind living in this building. It is a far more convenient arrangement than their previous house; transport is easier because there is always a rickshaw around the corner waiting. There are friends in other blocks that she can stop and chat with in the compound, and of course the safety. The building has a large guardhouse at its entrance and visitors must register before being given permission to enter.

Their old neighbourhood had, over time, become a

dangerous place to live. Odd characters had started to appear on the streets, boys with noisy bikes and filthy tongues. Their numbers and varieties grew over the months. They loitered about, wearing t-shirts with fierce graphics and chain smoked cigarettes leaving unsightly butts littered on the floor everywhere. Their presence started to encroach on valuable personal freedoms of the residents. People were careful to draw shut the curtains as evening fell, they no longer left their doors unlatched even in the day. Soon, there came stories of catcalling and worse as womenfolk walked out of their homes to go to the shops or to the bus stop. Mohan forbade both Champa and Radha from going out alone after dark.

He made discreet attempts at investigating who exactly these vagrants were and why they had colonised the area. Some, it seemed, were children of unknown neighbours that curiously enough had morphed into gangsters. The rest were likely birds of a feather. But you couldn't tell who was who, and by the time Mohan made it to the police station to lodge a formal complaint, there were already too many. The police were of no use anyway. No action could be taken, as there could be no charges brought; there were no tangible crimes to speak of.

Until the day of the robbery at Mrs Hamsa's.

Thieves broke in in broad daylight. Poor Mrs Hamsa was on the potty wearing nothing but her brassiere. They picked the lock of the main door and then kicked the door of the bathroom open, dragging the terror-stricken soul out into the hall, where they tied her up and taped her mouth. They took everything, even her new Onida flat screen TV.

But even this did not bring much change, and no one was ever implicated because Mrs Hamsa refused to go to the station to identify the robbers. Too much shock and fear.

Finally, Mohan decided enough was enough. If the hoodlums weren't going to leave, then he would. "We have a young girl in the house, Champa, and you are often alone at home. What this Lakshman will do if these scoundrels force entry?" He made his lips as though blowing a candle, "One *phoo* they will do and he will fly off like a feather."

And so, five years ago, amid a particularly punishing season of monsoons, the family readily moved into Shireen Society, Block A, flat 5E.

Radha took to it immediately. Their flat is big, with three spacious bedrooms, three bathrooms and a modest balcony she can sit in and watch the sun rise and set.

Where to keep the Paneer? That is Karuna Chachi on the other side of the door inside her house. Her father's eldest brother's wife has the hands of a magician. Radha's mouth starts to water just thinking about the Butter Paneer, its tomato gravy rich and creamy spiced delicately enough to tantalise. And the cubes of cheese immersed in it are so soft, so supple that they melt like clouds on the tongue.

She rings the doorbell.

Her mother answers the door, frazzled and rushed, flour dust sprinkled like smoke over the purple of her sari and one hand cupped, catching thick drops of yellow batter dripping from the other's fingers.

"Where have you been? Come in quickly. Everyone is here already. Please see to them *na*, ask them what they want to drink. Ice, please get the ice out of the freezer and don't use the old bucket, use that new one Papa bought. It is in the cupboard above the stove," she says, and scurries away out of sight.

Radha exhales in relief; the bouquet, surprisingly, has gone unnoticed. A pang of guilt runs through her, she will tell her mother about Varun tonight, after everyone has left. She places the flowers on the cabinet in the passageway, out of sight of the living room filled with relatives. She can see and hear Mohan's three brothers, their wives and children inside.

She starts toward them and all goes blank as her body is swallowed into a soft cushiony bosom. Aunt Rimi. Mohan's only sister.

"Happy Birthday!"

"Aunty, I can't breathe!" Radha's voice muffles within the layers of the saffron-smelling body and she knows she is going to get *kheer* for dessert tonight, thick and sweet and milky with almonds and cardamom.

"Ok, ok." Aunt Rimi releases her. A speck of glittering gold peeps through the corner of her smile. "Every time I see you, you are prettier and prettier. Haiya look at that, make up and all you are wearing. Young lady you have become."

"Aunty, you just saw me four months ago!" Radha laughs.

"Absolutely positively correct thing you have said. But look how I have come all the way for your birthday. Now come inside, everyone is waiting to see the birthday girl."

As soon as she appears in the living room, Radha is greeted with a round of applause and hugs from them all. She thanks them, serves up drinks, and helps the women in the kitchen heat dinner.

"Where is Aunt Uma?" she asks as Champa strains the golden crisp samosas out of the bubbling oil. "You said she was arriving this afternoon. Is her flight delayed?"

Uma is not really related; she is not Champa's real sister. They were roommates for a time. Uma still lives in Delhi. She never married. She is a teacher in the very same college Champa and her went to, where they first met and became friends.

When Uma heard Champa had had Radha, she took the first flight to Bombay to see her new niece.

Radha still remembers when she was five or six and she had come to visit. She brought her a present inside a box so large that all three of them—Champa, Mohan, and Uma—had to carry it together to the table. It was wrapped in gift paper the colour of silvery stars with a big puffy yellow bow.

Radha tore the wrapper open. Inside was an elegant two-storey dollhouse; a pink and white little building complete with a manual elevator installed. Its little plastic doors opened and closed at the press of a button. There was also a small blond-haired doll in a light blue frilly dress. You could place the doll and her bunny rabbit in the elevator, press the button and with a push of your finger, she'd arrive at the upper deck where you could lay out rooftop furniture: a sundeck chair, a barbecue pit, and a dainty pink dining set.

Unlike Roma, this doll was smaller and was in one piece with a full head of wavy golden hair. Roma was too big for the tea parties so every time Radha played, Roma sat outside like a God, her head towering above the playset. Radha loved her present and played with it every day. She had never seen anything as elaborate before. Many nights she dreamed herself in the dollhouse, sitting elegantly at the dining table and sipping milk from the teacups.

In the months that followed, Aunt Uma sent her more accessories; there was a crib and a baby doll, different dresses, a vanity set, and even a pet dog on a leash that reminded her of a dog named Moti, whose memories are now faded and unclear.

"Uma called last week, she can't come. I didn't want to tell you then, I knew how unhappy it would make you."

"Why mama? Why did she cancel?" The disappointment and hurt are clear in her voice.

"Now don't feel bad. See how many have come. What to do, I tried to force her but she has a friend from Bombay visiting. I even told her to meet her friend Mira here, and that she is welcome to join us tonight. But Mira's son is going to college in Delhi and there was some paperwork there to be done." Champa holds Radha's chin in her doughy hands. "She said she will plan a trip and we will go on a holiday for your birthday."

"Mama, eeks! All this is on my face." Radha washes the gunk off in the kitchen sink.

After dinner, dessert is served and the cake is rolled out; butter sponge with chocolate cream icing and seventeen candles. Sixteen are for her years on this earth and one is symbolic of a long life ahead.

The guests leave, save for Aunt Rimi who is staying with them, but she has had a long day on the road driving in from Poona and retires as soon as the last of the family is out the door. Radha starts to clear the dishes from the table. Champa grips her arm. "Sit down, child."

Her tone is solemn, the kind she uses when she wants to "talk about something." Those conversations rarely go well. Violated curfews, a foul word used, slamming the door in a temper tantrum, rude backtalk. That is what these kind of conversations were about. Radha's senses scramble as she realises what will be discussed now. They must have found out about Varun. But she was sure, very sure that they would not condemn dating. Maybe they will want to know who he is, or where he is from and what they do when they're together. She sits, heart in mouth, breath in throat. She should have told them a long time ago.

Mohan takes a seat across from her and Champa settles by his side. Radha faces her stern and serious parents; their disposition is that of someone about to deliver devastating news, like a doctor about to inform a patient that he has a terminal illness. The house is steeped in a strange uncomfortable silence, disorienting and contrary to just half an hour ago when everyone laughed their goodbyes.

Uneasiness surges through her as her father fidgets, picking on the skin of his cuticles. Her mother is silent, eyes downcast. Radha is perplexed. She did not expect a strong reaction as this. Teenagers date in today's India. It is not such a big deal. She thought her parents were open-minded, then why…?

She is about to part her lips, to open her mouth to say that she was going to tell them, and there was no need be to upset, and she would never dishonour them in any way. But before she can do any such thing, her father speaks.

"There is something we would like to tell you."

Her mother's lips quiver. She has never seen her father like this, his voice is unfamiliar, barely above a whisper.

He places a white envelope on the table between them.

"You had asked us when you were young," he says.

Intuitively, she knows. She now knows why her mother's frame is shrunken, why a teardrop is rolling down her cheek, why she refuses to meet her eyes.

"Papa," Radha protests.

Mohan holds his hand up and shuts his eyes tight, his voice shaking. "Please."

The memory floods through her. She was nine. It was in school, in the classroom. She sat at her desk; the teacher hadn't arrived yet. She busied herself with the sketch of a house with a chimney and with trees, their tops in circular squiggles, little bobs as apples growing within. V shapes flying above in the sky and a quarter of the sun peeking out from the corner of the page. She remembers which part she was on when she heard them; she was shading alternate bricks of the roof of the house with her pencil. And she knew when she finished that she would draw stick figures holding hands outside by the tree. Three in total. Two would be tall and one, her, would be short and standing in the middle. But she never got to that because of the voices behind her. Children can be so very cruel.

It is true. My mama told me she is not her mama and papa's real daughter.

Means?

Means she is not their daughter. They found her on the road.

Really?

Ya. She was a beggar. Their car was passing and she knocked on their window for food. You know how you see the beggar children in the road at the traffic light?

Silence. They were behind her, she could feel their eyes claw into her back.

My mama says I cannot be Radha's friend because nobody knows who her real parents are. And when she was found she was dirty and hungry and she was not wearing clothes. I am not allowed to talk to her.

Radha knew this story was not true. She had memories,

faint as they were, of Seva Dham and Mrs Kamalnath, of Moti the dog, of friends on crutches and in wheelchairs, of playing hide and seek. And Roma was proof, Roma still slept beside her even though she had better dolls with full heads of hair and all limbs intact.

She came home from school that day and cried to Champa. She cried because even though she already knew she was not their child, she didn't know others knew. She cried because she was not a beggar, she was not dirty and naked. They were all liars, every single one of them. But most of all, she cried because she wanted to know who her mother was.

Papa says I am a gift from an angel. It is not true. He only says it to make me happy. Everybody has a real Mama.

Champa held her and they rocked back and forth together, sobbing into each other's arms.

I am your Mama.

No you are not. I came from somewhere else.

This is that last thing Radha remembers saying. The rest she knows she has blocked from her memory, banished it out of her mind like unwanted demons forever. The next thing she remembers is waking up beside her mother in her bed.

She hears a sniffle. Champa wipes her cheek. Radha considers the envelope between them. Nothing written on it, no clue or hint. What is inside will answer a question that has long stopped haunting her, a question she never had the heart to ask again. But now, with only silence as distance between them and nothing in the way of her knowing, she is tempted.

Mohan speaks. "Take it, please. We waited till you were old enough, and many times we talked about when is the right time. Today you are sixteen. We both think you are ready to know what we know.

"We brought you to our house from a lovely place called Seva Dham. You were four. You were well-loved and happy. Your caretakers were kind people. You were found by the warden of the orphanage as a baby. A woman, presumably your mother, left you on a footpath. I know this must be painful for you to hear. But the truth is what we are here to tell you and we shall. We owe at least this much to you for all the joy you have brought us.

I am sure the poor woman had her reasons, it is not a kind world. But she did come back a few days later, she came looking for you. A man, I think a hawker or tea seller, told her you were taken by the old lady from the orphanage. He knew, you see, because the warden walked her dog every day on the same road and the hawker traded in the same spot every day. Your mother—your real mother—then went to the orphanage and looked for you. But she could not take you with her. She was very afraid. The warden told us she was not even willing to tell them her name. But the warden insisted, in return for the promise of looking after you. So she told them her name and she left them an address, in case anything untoward should ever happen to you."

Mohan slides the envelope closer to Radha. But the

moment of weakness has passed. Her blood rushes to her temples and she clenches her fists in anger. How can a mother leave her baby to die on the street? That woman is not her mother. These here, these people who have loved her with every fibre of their being, with every ounce of their soul, with every drop of their existence, these are her parents.

She gets up from the table and wraps her arms around Champa, kisses her cheek, and says, "This is my mother."

Her father's shoulders jerk with the torrent of sobs that come. She hugs him into calm. "You are my father."

CHAPTER FIVE

19th March, 1999

Everything is determined, the beginning as well as the end, by forces over which we have no control. It is determined for the insect, as well as for the star. Human beings, vegetables, or cosmic dust, we all dance to a mysterious tune, intoned in the distance by an invisible piper.

Albert Einstein said that. He is better known for his genius in scientific discovery than his quotes of wisdom. Oh, but he was wise. Very wise. Because wisdom comes from knowledge, and knowledge comes from curiosity, and Mr. Einstein was profoundly curious, especially about me, Time. Most people stop thinking about things once they get too complicated. It is easier to let sleeping dogs lie. But not Mr Einstein. If there be a concept that tickled and teased his intellect, there was no rest until a satisfactory answer was found. Curiosity is a good thing, it breeds genius.

Radha is curious. The question in Radha's mind at this moment is mundane but rather urgent; how long will she have to walk before she gets to the riverfront? She is starting to feel a burning in the balls of her feet. She has been walking these ancient streets since...she looks at her watch...over an hour. It is almost seven a.m.

These are the convoluted, maze-like roads of the oldest inhabited city in the world, so old that at different times it has had different names: Kashi, Benares, and now Varanasi.

It is the land of temples, priests, pilgrims, the Buddha, the Shiva, the holy city. It is the city of immortality and liberation, Moksha. It is where people come and learn to live, where they study arts and philosophy and meditation. It is also where they choose to die, where the Gods are said to welcome the bodies of the deceased on the banks of the River Ganges.

But importantly, it is where Champa and Mohan first met when he was a young man tagging alongside a foreign journalist with his archaic clunky Nikon that is now stored away at the top shelf of his cupboard. He uses a digital camera these days, and his Dell sends the images directly to a printer. The world has changed. His camera has changed. But his heart hasn't.

It will be twenty years to the day this month that he has been the husband of his wife. And this year, he does not want to celebrate the anniversary of their wedding. Instead, he wants to celebrate having first laid eyes on her. A few weeks ago, he had come home with three sets of return tickets and two hotel vouchers. His eyes were soft and hopeful, like a man proposing marriage, when he told his beloved wife what his plans were for them.

I want to take you back in time. And I want to be young again. I want to walk along the banks of the river with you as the pilgrims chant and the holy men bathe. I want to do it all over again. And this time, there will not be two but three of us. A complete family.

The city is steeped in grey. Radha walks alone, her parents sound asleep at the hotel. She has never been to Varanasi before but has read about it in History when she was at school. Archaeological evidence dates it back to the eleventh or twelfth century BC, but it is said to be even older, founded by none other than Shiva himself. She can smell the riverfront as she weaves through the narrow winding alleyways. It is a thick sweet aroma of incense burned by the hundreds, perhaps thousands of pilgrims that line the banks every evening. And she inhales the fragrance of remnants of the flowers offered to the unseen forces of Creation. But there is also a hint of death in the smell of hundreds of corpses burned atop piles of sandalwood and sprinkled with rose water.

It is as though she has gone back five hundred, a thousand years in time. These maze-like alleys are short; one leads to another and then another like a never-ending labyrinth. She is like a rat caught in a maze. But these roads will end. She knows because Girish, the trainee at the concierge counter at The Palm Hotel had told her so.

Don't worry, Madam. Varanasi is best seen on foot. Cars don't even fit through the lanes. Only bicycle or legs. Madam, have you heard of Mark Twain? He visited the holy city in 1898. He had said that Benares is older than history, older than tradition, older even than legend, and looks twice as old as all of them put together. It is old madam, very old. The lanes are narrow and may seem confusing but they all lead to the river. You walk walk walk, you just keep walking. It does not matter if you turn left or right. The alleys all open up to the steps, we call them ghats, leading to the riverfront of the Ganges. There are more than eighty ghats and you are sure to end up on one. When you reach one you will see the steps clearly and you just climb down; the boatmen are all there. You must bargain, madam. They will take you out into the river and you can see the sunrise from the boat. It is very beautiful, Madam.

At the end of every short street, Radha makes a perfectly random choice of turning left or right. The saying, "All roads lead to Rome" comes to her mind. Her pace quickens as she wonders if Girish was wrong. What if she becomes irretrievably lost, scuttling through these roads and alleys in search of the sunrise forever?

On either side there are grey shutters pulled down against blocks of short buildings painted in pink, green, red, and yellow. Sign boards hang crooked, bent, rusted; Ganga Tailoring (full Punjabi suit stitching one hour only), Ramesh *Lassi* and Fruit Juice (best in the world), Sri Silks (discount for foreigner), Star Telecom (repair for Nokia and Ericson, new and used handset available.)

Her heart is starting to race as the sky is beginning to turn. She shuffles with urgency. She set out this morning to chase the sun, to catch the sunrise she has seen in the photo albums of her father, with the fireball suspended like a glowing giant tangerine in a flaming sky above a river of liquid gold. Now she considers turning around, but her chances of getting back to the hotel are direr than finding the river, so she moves along.

Minutes later, the alley widens to a platform and the river is before her. It has been worth it. The river is glorious, vast, everywhere all at once, shimmering and trembling, sacred. Worshippers scatter along the steps. There are old *sadhus* in orange, pilgrims in white dhotis with their sacred thread across their torsos, swamis whose beards reach their navels, women in groups of four and five in simple austere saris.

There are stray dogs roaming, cows lazily resting, crows pecking. Some people sit in silence, some whisper their chants as they turn their rosaries. Many are dipping themselves in the holy waters in the hope that the river, as promised by the Vedas and scripture, will wash away their sins.

Few boats glide in the waters, boatmen paddling lazily into the bruised skies that are quickly turning a deep hue of orange.

Radha races down the steps, she must find a boatman who will take her out into the river that she has heard stories about in her childhood when she was seven, eight, nine. And now, seeing it lay splendidly ahead, she feels like a child again; she can feel Champa's breath on her cheek; she can hear her whisper; about the war between the demigods and the demons, the sage that swallowed the ocean, the defeat of the demons, the desperation of the people who had no water, Goddess Ganga flowing from the tip of Shiva's matted locks, the earth having water again, Ganga saving all of creation.

Radha is almost at the edge of the banks, hurrying, moving faster than she should to approach a young bare-chested boatman, when the sky begins to swim and the waters rise upwards. The world blots and starts to fade into a blurry greyness. Her knees lose their rigidity, her head cannot hold itself up, her body crumples to the floor, and she rolls down. Her body bumps and tosses over the rocky steps, downward till it lies at the banks, bruised. But fortunately, she is in no pain—she is already in the arms of darkness.

॰ೞ॰

Radha squints into the light of the sun. She lays on a bed that is not her own; it is hard and unfamiliar. Above her, the yellowed blades of a creaking fan spin lazily. The room is small, its walls painted light green, chipped, stained, old. She has never been here before, she is bewildered, uneasy.

She tries to sit up. Her body feels stiff and foreign, little it did when she'd come out of the appendix operation all those years ago. She becomes abruptly aware of a sharp pain in her left temple and brings a hand to her forehead, but her fingertips do not feel her skin. They touch a warm coarseness; gauze or fabric of some kind. It is damp. She rubs her fingers together and blood smears between them.

She struggles out of the bed, her limbs sore and uncooperative. There is an ache in her legs, more specifically in her right knee. She hopes she has not broken any bones, but more importantly, she worries that she has been taken against her will and is being held captive. Her last memory is that of looking out into the horizon, and then, then… nothing.

Hot fear gushes like lava into her chest, where it turns to stone. Her breaths come shallow. She climbs off the bed and hobbles toward the open door; best to attempt escape before her captor returns. But her body is different; her knee fails her, and she falls to the ground. She lays helpless, sprawled on her back. A fly buzzes over her right ear and then around the tip of her nose.

She twists her body to the side, biting her lip as the pain lashes through her leg. She wriggles to her feet with caution and balances her weight on her left leg. She must find her purse, she had a purse. Her anxious eyes flit across the bedroom and rest at the bedside table, both surprised and relieved to see it lay by a jug and glass. She limps toward it, picks it up and checks its contents. Her phone is in there. The tension in her body eases, because this to her means that whoever brought here has no intention of keeping her against her will. She presses a button and the device lights up. The display flickers dimly, indicating a battery life that will expire at any moment. It is 7.23 a.m., 19th March, the same day and not even an hour since she thinks she blacked out.

Four unread messages. She opens them.

Papa 6.21 a.m. : Sleeping?

Mama 6.45 a.m. : Called your room no ans.

Varun 6,52 a.m. : Mrng. How's the trip? Washed away your sins yet?

Papa : 7.11 a.m. : We are gng down for brkfst. Call when up.

She dials her father. The recorded voice of an operator informs her in pure Hindi that the number she is dialling is out of coverage. She tries her mother, knowing fully well that her mother will most likely not even have switched on her phone. To her surprise, she gets a ringtone. After the first ring, Radha's phone dies.

She replaces it and inspects the contents of her purse. Her hotel room key, her tube of lip gloss, her packet of tissues and a box of mints are all there. Her money is there too, untouched, all three hundred and twenty-eight rupees.

She hangs the strap over her shoulder and starts toward the door. It is unlocked and leads her into a small living room, sparse, large enough for a single rattan chair, a desk and shelving with kitchen utensils. A one-burner stove is on the floor. Beside it are a tin of oil, some cans, jars of pickles and spices, and plastic packets of different pulses.

The latch easily slides across the wooden double doors; she pushes them to open, but they don't. They are padlocked from the outside. She starts to panic, takes out her phone and presses the power button. Nothing.

She looks around the living room for another door, but there is none. But there is a small window, high above the shelving. The sun shines in thick slabs through the iron bars that are going make her escape impossible. Plus, she will have to climb on top of the shelving to access it. But how will she manage that when her knee is trembling in pain? And how will she loosen those bars? It is futile.

Perhaps she must arm herself. She kneels with excruciating pain and searches behind the jars, the tins, the packets. She finds some steel plates, pots and pans, small bowls, ladles. But no knife, not a fork even. There is a plate of food, covered with a mesh lid; rice and green vegetables. Her mouth waters. She hasn't eaten since early dinner the previous night.

She hears footsteps coming from the outside, drawing nearer and nearer. Her breath halts and she gets up from the floor and retreats until her back is against the wall. The door screeches, she slams her eyes shut and prays with all her strength.

Two men stand before her, neither look dangerous. One is dressed in saffron robes. The other wears a doctor's coat, he is wiry thin and painfully old.

"You are awake." The monk's forehead is anointed with sandalwood in the shape of a crescent. "I have brought doctor sahib to take a look."

The old doctor approaches with caution and gently asks that she please sit down on the bed but Radha remains where she is, her body still and her eyes darting from monk to doctor, doctor to monk.

"You should let him take a look at that before you go," the monk says kindly.

Radha does as told. She feels safe but not entirely at ease. She does want the pain in her leg and the throbbing in her head to stop. The doctor waits for the monk to leave before firing his questions, she answers them all.

My name is Radha

Eighteen. Just turned.

No, I did not consume any alcohol or sleeping pills.

No, this hasn't happened before.

No, I am not from here.

No, I don't remember how it happened.

No, I don't have any health issues.

Yes, my family is in the hotel.

No, I haven't informed them, my phone is dead.

Yes, please I would like some painkillers.

No, I haven't eaten anything.

No, I am not hungry now.

"Your blood pressure is fine and your heart rate is normal and you don't seem to have signs of any major illness as far as I can see. Maybe you are just tired from the travel, or maybe it was the heat." His hands shake as he unravels the cloth around her forehead. He inspects the wound and wipes it with cotton wool doused in alcohol. She clenches her jaws tightly at the sting.

He kneads her kneecap with his cold bony fingers, his bushy grey eyebrows arch and frown and his deep breaths are laced with whistling sounds; it is not broken, he announces, but he tells her the tendons will need time to recover. She must use crutches if she is to leave.

He takes out a syringe and a small empty ampule from his weathered leather bag.

"What are you doing?" The curtness in her own voice is alien and she regrets it immediately. "I am afraid of needles," she adds with softness.

"I will need to check your blood for abnormalities."

Radha does not want to sound ungrateful but a lingering discomfort plagues her even though she knows these people are only trying to help her. She has not been raised to trust complete strangers, no matter how aged and lustreless, especially ones that want to stick a needle into her.

"Doctor, thank you so much, but I much rather have it done when I go back to Bombay."

She expects him to insist but he shrugs indifferently, caps his syringe and puts it away.

"You would like some painkillers?" He is clearly offended because he does not meet her eyes, instead he busies himself packing away his gadgets and gizmos.

"Yes, please." She rolls down her sleeve.

He places two bottles of pills on the side table. "Be sure to not take them on an empty stomach. One is for the pain, the other is an anti-inflammatory."

He leaves and she is alone again. She can hear the two men speaking outside.

No need for this, I cannot accept money from a holy man. Besides, you are helping someone in need. Say a prayer for me as payment.

Radha slides her legs off the bed and manages to bring herself to her feet, wincing in pain. She must leave, and she thinks of her parents. They will be worried, looking for her. She regrets not having left a note under their door. She even thought of it but decided there was no need, as she would be back before they awoke. And now, a couple of hours later, she is in a stranger's home with a knee that feels like jelly and a head that is about to explode.

The monk enters the room holding a plate. A warm smile plays on his lips. "May I offer you some breakfast?"

"I really should get going," she says. But a part of her doesn't want to leave. She wants to have a conversation with this man. A bud of strange curiosity has sprouted in her mind about people like him that she has seen before but never bothered to speak to because neither has she been in such close proximity, nor have they ever seemed this approachable.

Sadhus, swamis, yogis are not entirely commonplace in Bombay; she has spotted a few in trains and buses commuting between their caves or temples or ashrams or wherever it is that they hibernate to seek whatever it is that they are seeking: enlightenment, peace, bliss and other such vague states of being.

Here in Varanasi, there are plenty of them and they roam freely, as ordinary as any man, some wearing nothing but a loincloth, some with matted dreadlocks and ash across their forehead, some like the one that stands before her, in flaming orange robes and a string of chanting beads around his neck.

She was told stories in her childhood by her mother, of powerful sadhus both deviant and divine. Their curses could melt mountains and dry up oceans, their boons gave riches of the heavens and comforts on earth. She wonders now if these stories have any grain of truth.

This swami has salt and pepper hair and a full beard; he is not very much older than her father. His eyes are kind. He puts down the plate of rice on the table.

"Will you able to make your way to your parents by yourself? I can drop you."

"On second thoughts," Radha says as she sits at the table and picks up the spoon, "thank you for taking care of me. I don't know what happened."

"You fell down. I don't know if it was because you were rushing or if you tripped."

"I don't think I tripped. I am glad you were there to help. How shall I address you?"

The monk smiles kindly. "People know me as Babaji. I do not have a name as such."

Radha's eyebrows rise. "Everyone has a name."

"One was given to me at my birth by my parents, but I have since renounced it along with other belongings."

"A name is not a belonging."

He peers at the plate of rice and lentils and then watches her chew. "I hope it tastes alright. I tend not to put salt in my food." He picks up a small jar filled with clumpy white powder from beside the stove and places it on the table.

"It tastes fine, thanks. A name is not a belonging," she repeats.

"It is an obstacle."

"To what?"

"The bud must give up its identity to become the flower," he says casually, then gets up from the table. "If you will excuse me, I have to bring in my clothes from the veranda, they must be dry."

She eats the rest of the food, rinses the plate in a small sink, and tilts the heavy clay pitcher to pour herself a glass of water which she drinks with the pills the doctor has left her.

"Thank you," she says to the monk when he returns with his pile of orange clothes.

"You are welcome. I hope you are better soon."

She takes her purse and steps out. He shuts the door behind her. A wooden box is placed on a small table outside his door. It is clumsily made, uneven at its edges and held together by nails that jut out. There is a slit at the top, an opening like a letter box. The word, "DONATIONS" is painted in red on the front.

She reaches into her purse and pulls out her wad of notes. Twenty-eight rupees should suffice for the rickshaw ride back to her hotel, she slides the rest of the money, all three hundred rupees into the box.

Her headache has disappeared and her legs feel fluid again. *It must be the medication,* she thinks. Her heart has never been lighter. She can see the morning light come through from the end of the dark corridor. She starts walking towards it. She is smiling.

CHAPTER SIX

2nd February, 2001

In the time that it takes to compose this thought into a sentence, 300 million cells will have died in your body. My condolences. Every seven years or so, all of your body's cells replace themselves, you are not you, you are new. Now add to that a personality that keeps changing—babbling baby to self-aware child, self-aware child to school boy, school boy to grown man—and what we have is a thoroughly fluid entity that is neither the same in form nor in mind.

Some become suspicious, they ask many questions. Have you too stopped and enquired into the nature of your existence, or the mysterious concepts of life, death, salvation, identity and purpose? Have you?

~∞~

If I am in me, who is in them?

Radha sits at the dresser and looks at herself in the mirror. Her fingertips trace the contours of her jaw, her chin, they press on the flesh on her cheeks and brush over the brows of her eyes.

Who am I?

Flesh, blood, bones, skin that grow and change and transform at their own will; breasts that have come unannounced, a bloody monthly cycle that causes excruciating pain in her back, nails and hair that grow on their own. She has commanded none of these. And yet, this body that does everything it wills without consult or consent, is her.

Am I my thoughts?

A glossy red cardboard box filled with rich dark chocolates sits at the dressing table in front of her. Sid sent them. He has been sending presents every couple of weeks since the shooting of *Amaanat*, her very first full length feature film started. She is not new to the screen though, she's already been on television. Short stints, but still quite an achievement in an industry that's almost impossible to break into. She's done two advertisements (one for Purita shampoo and one for Amaze air fresheners) and six episodes of *The Lives We Lived* before her character was killed off in a car accident.

Sid, always the encouraging force in her life, pushing her forward to take on the next challenge, to try out for the next audition, to email the next director. *You can do it. You are so going to nail this. I bet this one will get the attention of the critics. I can already see you on the silver screen.*

As far as the matter of love goes, in the way Radha understands love to be, she can say without too much doubt that she loves him. More than she has loved any other man at least. He is a breath of fresh air. It is after being with him that she has discovered her preference is definitely for older men. Sid is twenty-eight so there are seven years between them, but she doesn't feel them at all. Sid fits her better than anyone ever has; Varun who grew up slower than her, Deepak who was too self-obsessed, and Fairuz who was suffocatingly possessive. Sid gets her; he is intelligent, funny, composed, mature and handsome.

She was nineteen when they met. She was drinking a peach mojito at Fizz, a popular bar with college students. She didn't know how to appreciate the smooth taste of alcohol those days, taking her whiskey with cola, her vodka with orange juice and her gin with Seven-Up.

So when the then stranger, Sid, sent over two tequilas to the table, her friend Sonia stared at the little glasses in shock. "Oh my God! He is so old, he drinks it like that," she said, perhaps too loudly.

"Shhhh... smile," Radha instructed her friend through gritted teeth. What was this man among boys doing at a bar like this?

He sat alone on a sofa, his computer on his lap, a notepad by his side. His jeans were a shade lighter than the in-fashion indigo blue, his loose-fitted white linen shirt fell over his thickly curved arms. A hippy-looking wooden beaded necklace clung to his neck – the kind you could buy on the beaches of Goa.

"Quit staring," Sonia said.

Radha self-consciously looked away. "I'm not staring. I'm just wondering who he is. Never seen him around before."

"He's not even cute. That Nishaant is better, your screen brother who you're not even interested in; you may as well introduce us already."

"If you spend five minutes with him you would gouge your own eyes out, biggest bore ever. He has no conversation except films."

"That's a good thing, isn't it? Considering you are both actors." Sonia rolls her eyes and sips her shandy.

"It's a shallow thing."

"Come off it Radha, why can't you be nineteen?"

There was a tap on Radha's shoulder. She turned and there stood Sid. He wasn't handsome in the conventional sense, but there was an unmistakable charm in that toothy smile. Wisps of unkempt hair patterned his wide forehead.

"You always study at bars?" his eyes drifted from her face to her Introduction to *Psychology* textbook.

"You always talk to strangers and send them drinks?" Radha flirted back.

"Only when my unconscious mind tells my conscious mind to."

"Ah, you studied psychology too?"

"Used to at college; thankfully, I am in the real world now."

"And what do we owe this kindness to?" She glanced at the shot glasses and salt-soaked lemon wedges.

He looked at his watch. "It is almost eight; time for a real drink, don't you think?"

That night Sonia slipped away, and the two of them sat and talked till late. They spoke of Jung and Maslow and Nietzsche. They discussed the rift between India and Pakistan and whether the government's stand was firm enough. They deliberated the future of the Indian rupee. They talked about their families and their hobbies. She told him she was adopted, which surprised her, because she had never willingly volunteered this information to anyone before. Those who knew knew, but there wasn't ever any need for emphasis; it was an unnecessary fact, an irrelevant truth. To this day she doesn't know why she mentioned it.

She learned he was between jobs. He had resigned from his role as urban planner in a government-linked company and was waiting to start work with a regional property and development multinational. He said he'd had had enough of red tape and cronyism and he wanted to see if the ethos in the private sector was any better.

The defining factor in her decision to meet with him again over the course of the following months was the intellectual stimulation he provided her. She could talk about things with him that no other nineteen-year-old would understand. He was a voracious reader, a keen learner, a hungry traveller. When she finished college, they took a trip around Asia together. Her parents thought she was away on a shoot but she was backpacking with him across the rain forests of Indonesia, the temple ruins of Cambodia, the isolated islands of Thailand.

She picks up the box of truffles and smiles at herself. Sid is a good man. He is dependable and loyal. There is a knock at the door of her dressing room. "Come in," she calls, and the spot boy appears in the doorway.

"Your shot is ready, madam." He stays, standing with eyes glued on her cleavage.

She is a beautiful woman, and thus men (being men) gawk at her. Her body is tall and lean, elastic from the fifty sun salutations she performs before sunrise every day. The curls in her hair, duly oiled every week, fall over her shapely back like shifting waves of a black river. Her eyes are of terrible depth, her fingers dainty, her skin supple and taut.

Vrinda the makeup artist shoves the spot boy aside, slaps his head, and forces her way through the door. "*Chalo chalo*, get lost, what you are staring at? This is not a free show." He scampers away like a dirty street cat.

Vrinda plumps Radha's lips, pats her makeup, and fidgets with her hair. "Now is your crying shot. Around here the cameramen and crew say they can tell how talented an actress is by how badly her make up is smudged after a crying scene. I have laid it on thick, they will be impressed."

Radha smiles with uncomfortable gratitude, she slips on

her turquoise low heels and stands up to leave the room. She exhales. This is not going to be easy.

The studio is set up like a hospital room. A curtained cubicle, a makeshift low polystyrene ceiling, fluorescent lights and the beeping monitors that mean nothing. She is Amisha, the sister of Pratosh who is clinging to life only to see his sister one last time. His final breaths linger and tremble ephemerally like dew drops.

She has come to bid him farewell and to tell him that she wished he hadn't gone out that evening, that he hadn't driven away after a fight with their father and hadn't been so angry that he slammed his car into the curb which then spun like the devil. She has come to cry her goodbyes.

His bandages are drenched in blood, tubes are taped to his arms, his nose, his throat. A mask is over his mouth. He lays still, eyes closed, waiting for her to deliver her lines.

"ACTION!"

She grips the cold metal grill of the bed with one hand, trying to balance her distraught body, brings the back of her other hand to her mouth and begins to shake. She waits for the emotions to wash over her, for the make-believe sorrow to become real and miserable. She claws into the depths of her being to find Amisha, to raise her from nothingness, to summon her grief-stricken soul.

The well is dry, the tears don't come.

She calls to mind the image of Sid and of walking into a room and seeing him atop another woman. Sonia. She sees her friend Sonia moan in pleasure as Sid's muscular body pounds above. She sees him turn and find her at the door. And he does not jump out of the bed, he does not fall at her feet and beg forgiveness. He looks her in the eyes and tells her he doesn't love her, he never did.

But she doesn't believe herself. Her heart knows her mind is only playing.

"CUT."

The director, a young man with only one film to his name, approaches her. "You need more time Radha? We can break. Maybe you take five minutes to get into it. These kind of shots are the hardest."

"It's alright, let's try again."

"ACTION!"

Radha reaches into her mind, draws out the blurred memories of her childhood before the adoption. There is not much she can find. Has she forgotten? She sees herself clutching her doll Roma in the dark of night all alone on a hard bed. Something stirs inside her. But wait, who is that foggy image of? An old woman, slightly bent but healthy, sitting on Radha's bed across from her, touching her face with her wrinkly hands, playing with her hair, pulling her tightly into her arms and whispering, "It's magic my dear. Love is magic."

Radha holds back her smile. She needs something else, something big and unthinkable like the death of a lover, a parent or a sibling. She had been taught this technique but never used it. She is not comfortable picturing the death of her parents. What if thinking it made it come true? No. She would not do that.

So instead she sees herself an old woman, withered and wrinkled, with unsteady fingers struggling to scoop a rattling spoonful of food and bring it to her mouth. She sees her ribs poke out of her chest, her scalp shows through her scanty silver hair.

And she sees the vast abyss of emptiness still there, this void that she has been running her fingers through every single day, this ignorance. This thing that she feels in every limb in her body and every inch of her flesh. This not knowing the only thing there is to know and not knowing what it is she has to know; what is her purpose, everyone's purpose, the reason she exists, the meaning of life, the goal of being here and now. Where is it she is meant to go and how will she get there? Where is there? Who is she? What is the missing piece?

And so she cries. She cries as she watches the last of her breaths come and go, as she watches her own cremation, she cries because she is at the door of the death and still does not know. She cries like the rain, loud and strong and from the deepest hollows of her unfulfilled heart.

She cries long after the crew fall silent in disbelief, long after the director has called CUT and long after the standing ovation subsides.

Radha glances at her watch for the fourth time in five minutes. Sid gave it to her, a Timex with switchable straps. She wears the denim one today to match her jeans. Actually she pretty much wears the denim strap most of the time, she's always in jeans when not shooting. There is a mugginess in her head, a heaviness behind her eyes from the scene just now. But she feels accomplished; she delivered a performance so extraordinary that the director, ordinarily a hard man to please, called pack up in two takes.

She leans against the gates of Kamal Studios; Sid was supposed to pick her up half an hour ago. It is already becoming dark. Usually when he is this late she hails a rickshaw or a taxi and his apologies follow in the form of flowers or chocolates or a nice dinner out. But today she will wait. She needs Sid. She needs him both for his car and his shoulder.

She hopes he will agree and not try to talk her out of it. She will tell him how important this is, how badly she needs to do it, how many times she has thought about it. That today after the episode with the shooting she knows more than ever that these loose strings that dangle restlessly out of her life need to be tied once and for all, that this is the only thing she thinks will help, that perhaps this is what is missing.

Sid's wine-coloured Hyundai screeches to a halt in front of her. Radha throws her bag in the backseat and rides shotgun.

"What took you so long?"

"Traffic on Brant Road. Accident. How was your day, the shoot?"

She doesn't reply.

"I said I am sorry."

"Actually you didn't."

"Look, I am sorry. Please don't go all nuclear on me now." Sid places a hand on hers. "Let's go to Prego for dinner. Pasta and wine. We'll order your favourite, Pinot Noir. What say?"

She reaches her arm into the back and gets her bag. "I need you to come with me somewhere else first."

"Sure. Where are we going?" he says eagerly.

"Pull up, please." She has taken something out of her handbag and is holding it in her hand. Her voice has dropped and is gravelly with anguish.

He switches on the hazard lights, slows down and stops the car by the curb. "What's up, baby?" His eyes are fixed at the envelope she holds. "What is that?"

"I want to go find her."

"Find who?"

"My mother."

His eyes widen. An irritated driver honks as he passes, almost grazing their car. Sid swears under his breath, "*Saala* is blind, can't see the flashing tail lights."

"I need to do this," Radha pleads.

Sid nods in vigorous agreement, "I know how it must feel, I get it. But why now? Have you thought this through? This could change everything in your life. Are you sure?"

"Yes, I've never been more sure of anything."

Sid takes the envelope from her and examines it. "This is so sudden. Where did you get this?"

"I rummaged through Papa's cupboard. I knew he had it. It didn't take long to find. Papa keeps his things very organised."

"How long have you had it?"

"A few months."

"What? You never told me." His voice is bruised. He runs his hands through his hair.

They both sit in silence.

"Have you seen it?" he says finally.

"No."

The flap is not glued, he pulls it open and unfolds the paper, it once belonged to a lined spiral notebook.

He slowly slips it back inside, blows out his cheeks and faces her. "I think we better not do this."

"What does it say? What is her name?"

"Payal." He breathes.

"She is in Bombay right? I know she is in Bombay. She came back for me a few days after leaving me; she lives here somewhere."

He rubs his forehead and takes a deep breath. He holds her hand. "Radha, lets just go for a drink, ok? Let's go get sloshed."

Radha stares at him in disbelief. "Can't you see how much this means to me? How can you offer me a night of pizza and alcohol instead of finding my mother? I thought you cared." Tears start to roll down her cheeks.

"I do care. I care immensely. But I don't think it is a good idea. Look, what does it matter now? You have your parents, you love them, they love you..."

She grabs the envelope from his hand, opens the car door and storms out. Cars whiz past, the street is dark, there is no footpath. She walks on the open road and a motorcyclist almost drives into her. Sid follows her and grabs her from behind.

"What are you doing?" he shouts. "You are going to kill yourself. Come on get in the car, lets talk."

"I don't want to talk!" she screams over the sound of blaring horns and speeding cars. "I can't believe you of all people would try to stop me from doing this."

They stand face to face. She can feel his hot breath on hers. "Radha, the paper says Falkland Road. Happy? That's the address, Radha. Falkland Road! I was only trying to protect you from more pain. Falkland Road is the red-light area for truckers and day wagers, the poor man's heaven. That is where you will have to go find your mother."

He has not slapped her; so then why does she feel the

sting on her face? Why do her eyes slam shut? Why does her body go limp? Why does her mind die? Why can she not feel her own presence?

She stands still for what feels like forever and then finally looks at him with the eyes of a helpless child in need. "Will you take me?"

He places an arm around her shoulder and takes her back to the car.

The car hums along the lit up streets, past the shine and glamour of the high-rise buildings until all of this starts to recede and fade. They enter an alternate Bombay, an underbelly where the roads are narrower, dimly lit, lined with short squalid buildings that totter. The streets are dingy and filthy, paint peels from the walls. As they drive further in, Radha and Sid start to see them.

The women stand in lit up doorways, sit on the curb in groups of three or four. There are hundreds on the ground and a multitude look down from caged balconies above in their garishly shiny blouses with glittering sequins and colourful stones. Their lips are ridiculously red. There are young girls, too young to wear makeup, eleven or twelve. There are women in their twenties, thirties; overdressed, over-ornamented, overexposed. Some men are dressed as women, their masculine features badly hidden beneath thickly caked foundation and rose pink blusher, they have breasts that are showing beneath plunging necklines. Cigarettes dangle from their mouths, they bite their lips, they rub their legs.

Radha's stomach twists, her heart is sinking fast, she

wants to vomit.

Sid slows down and stops the car amid this hell. "You okay? Shall we leave?"

Radha rolls the window down; she needs fresh air. They hear loud Bollywood music, songs from scenes of lust and sex, provocative lyrics, throaty sexy songs drowning each other out, different tunes coming from different speakers in different whorehouses.

A man in a fraying baseball cap and a tight shirt peers through their window. His breath stinks of liquor. "Something different you want tonight?" He looks at Radha. "Higher price if Madam joins. More work for them." He tilts his head gesturing to the three girls fidgeting with themselves behind him.

Radha turns away. The pimp's drilling gaze has left her feeling naked.

"Payal," Sid asks. "We are looking for Payal."

The man laughs like the evil demigods Papa used to imitate when telling Radha the story of Krishna defeating the demons. "Saahib, here they can have any name you want, Meena, Reena, Tina, Sabina, everything is changeable." He pulls one of the girls forward. "Eh, tell Saahib your name," he barks.

Her smile is meant to be inviting but sends a shudder through Radha. "Payal." She giggles and the other two girls laugh too. "My name is also Payal," another says and then they all start to snigger.

The pimp clears his throat and spits on the ground. "Tell me Saahib, shall I get the bed ready? What a night you will have, I swear you will leave a new man."

Sid gives the peddler a hundred rupee note. "Listen here, I am not a customer, so stop wasting your time. I am looking for Payal. The address says Falkland Road." The man pockets the bill and scratches his neck. "Saahib, you have a better chance of finding the divine goddess among these bitches. None of these sluts use their real name, and Falkland Road has one Payal in every ten."

Radha is not listening anymore. Her eyes travel to the faces of the dozens of women loitering in wait for their customers. There are so many. Tall, short, old, young. Her mother would be how old now? Could she be any of these? She studies their features, face after face, looking for herself in the whores.

She thinks about what would have come to be of her had she not been deserted and left out in the street. Did her mother think death was a better option than living in these brothels? Did her mother do the only thing she thought she could? Did she come back to check on her because she hoped against hope that someone had picked up her daughter from the trash and saved her life, that someone had changed her fate?

She turns to Sid. "Take me home."

As they drive out of Falkland Road, they pass a group of young teenage girls teasing some middle-aged men. A pimp is negotiating. Radha rolls down the window again and throws up.

CHAPTER SEVEN

13th May, 2001

To : Babaji

The flat with the red donation box outside,

Near the ghats,

In the lane of Aashiana Guest House,

Between Punjab Lassiwalla

and Saraswati secondhand bookshop, Varanasi

Dear Babaji,

The odds that this letter has actually reached the hands of its intended recipient are incredibly low. Low is better than none, so I am going to finish writing it anyway. I can only hope the postman in Varanasi will be able to decipher my pathetic attempt at the address.

If indeed it is you who is holding this letter, then I am pleasantly surprised. I don't think you will have forgotten me. It is not every day that a girl faints at the banks of the river and you burden yourself with the task of taking her unconscious body home, having her medically attended to and feeding her. I can just imagine your surprise right now. You are probably wondering why I am writing to you. There are a few purposes actually.

One is to thank you for your kindness, two years have passed and I know it is overdue, but better late than never, yes?

The second reason is that I have been thinking of you often. I don't know why really. Very bizarre.

The most pressing reason though, is that I would like to ask you three questions. There are a lot of holy men that loiter around here but I chose to ask you because you were nice and you don't seem like the kind of person who would pretend to know something he doesn't. Also, people like you tend to know the answers to these sorts of things.

What is the purpose of life?

What is happiness?

Who am I?

I really do hope you are indeed in possession of this letter and look forward to your reply.

Warm Regards

Radha

PS—please find enclosed a stamped, self-addressed envelope.

22nd June, 2001

Dear Radha,

Our postman is a likable man of jovial disposition and a generous paunch that wobbles when he laughs at his own jokes. He is a good friend, and we spend many evenings sharing food and laughter. He eats well and if the meal has been particularly satisfying, he even breaks into song. I have never seen a man so happy to be fed. Perhaps he likes my cooking.

Considering my close relationship with this carrier of correspondence, I am not surprised your letter reached me in stellar condition. The universe has a way of getting things where they need to go. There are no coincidences, a true desire finds its fulfilment.

And yes, you are right. I do remember you, as do the kind gentlemen who helped carry you to my house. After you left, they asked after your well-being. I told them you were fairly well. We are all pleased there have been no further instances of fainting visitors. This does not mean you were an inconvenience at all. It just means that it is nicer when people stay conscious and vertical in public places.

The questions you have asked are indeed very profound. Most people at sometime in their life will encounter at least one of these questions. For some these questions and curiosities come and go like seasons. Speaking of seasons, it is dreadfully warm in Varanasi. I do hope you are having nicer weather in Bombay.

Yes, your questions. I do not know very much about you and thus cannot know how deeply you crave answers. Of course, different people will give you different answers, and all of them may be correct. In an enquiry like yours, there are no wrong answers. It is all subjective. However, since you have posed these questions to me, I will be happy to share my own version. They may not appeal to you, and you may not agree with them. Also, they are not simple answers, they are discoveries gleaned from my own journey.

But first, perhaps we should get to know each other better? I would describe myself as a nameless yogi on a journey to truth. What about you?

With Love and Om,

Babaji

30th June, 2001

Dear Babaji,

I was very happy to hear from you. I would very much like to hear your answers and will tell you a bit about myself.

I am an actress and am currently working on my first film. I can say that I enjoy acting and am told I have great potential. The film is about a girl (me) who loses her brother in a car accident and spends a year in search of the hit-and-run driver, then falls in love with the policeman who is helping her. It is a love story. The shooting for my film ends in a few weeks and I had decided that after this I would take a break but another script that has recently been offered to me is very tempting.

The problem however, is that although I enjoy my work, something is amiss and I am not happy. This is why I wrote to you. In the depths of my own heart, there is an emptiness, which nothing seems to fill.

I wondered for a long time whether it had anything to do with the fact that I was adopted and that I do not know the identity of my biological parents, but I really don't think that is it. I did go in search of my mother. The funny thing is, I was quite relieved that I didn't find her, because I don't know that I could look at another woman as my mother. I think I was chasing the wrong thing. My adoptive parents are the best human beings in this world, and they have loved me more than life itself. I really don't care very much who was physically responsible for my human existence.

I have a boyfriend, Sid. I think I love him, but I don't know for sure. I know that he loves me. He proposed to me a month ago, said that he wants to spend the rest of his life with me. I didn't reply because I cannot picture my life with him. Not that there is anything wrong with him, not that I don't care for him. In fact, it is because I care for him that I didn't accept. How can I commit to something when I know that even after having it, I will be empty? It is not fair to him. He doesn't think that way. He says I am all he needs. Unfortunately, I can't say the same. But he doesn't know this. Yet.

The only thing that I have going for me is my career and

of late, I get a sense that although I love what I do, this is not it either. There has to be something more, something deeper, something richer.

I don't talk to people about these feelings. I don't know that anyone would understand. On the outside, everything is fine you see. I live in a comfortable house with loving parents, I have a good professional life, I have a man who wants to make me his wife. But sometimes I feel like I want none of these, none of it is adequate.

Have you ever felt that way? Is that why you became a yogi? What is a yogi anyway? What does it mean that you are on a "journey to truth"? What truth? And by the way, you mentioned we must get to know each other. I have told you a lot about myself. Shouldn't you do the same? Let's start with your name. And perhaps the recipe of that daal I ate in your house—it was very tasty. Though unlike your jovial postman, I didn't break into song. Speaking of which, please thank him on my behalf. I owe him.

Love

Radha

17th July, 2001

Dear Radha,

Yesterday when Gajendran the postman, inquisitive fellow that he is, brought your letter, he asked why I was suddenly receiving mail from Bombay and who is this strange person that writes my address in such a peculiar fashion? I told him it is an actress, no less, from Bombay. He was thoroughly impressed that a Bollywood actress was writing to me. I asked him to consider that aren't we all actors?

All the world's a stage,

And all the men and women merely players;

They have their exits and their entrances,

And one man in his time plays many parts,

I love that play by Shakespeare. I have only written one verse of the piece, but it is much longer. Have you read it?

Your letter was interesting, and I learned many things about you. In it, you have asked me some more questions.

Let's see. What is my journey to truth? I cannot think of a way to describe it, but I can tell you a story and I hope it will convey an answer.

One night, an old lady was alone on a dimly lit street. She was frail and bent, her aged eyes searching the wet ground under a streetlamp. A man happened to pass and felt sympathy for the woman because she reminded him of his grandmother. "What are you looking for?" he asked kindly.

"I've lost my needle," said she.

He offered to help and she was grateful. Another passerby noticed and enquired what these two had lost. A needle, he was told. "Oh that will be hard to find; here, let me help." And so he joined them too. More people passed and joined and soon there were no less than fifty bent heads scanning the floor for the lost needle.

Finally, a young passerby saw this unusual gathering and begun asking the people what was going on. He tapped many shoulders, but all he got was a shrug. Nobody knew. Finally, he reached the little old lady who quite irritably informed him she had lost her needle. "Did you drop it here?" he asked.

She all but strikes the poor fellow with her umbrella. "You can either help us or ask questions and be a nuisance. No. I did not drop it here. I dropped it there." She pointed to a little door nearby. "I dropped it inside my house."

"Then why are you looking for it here?" he asked.

"You are a silly young lad, aren't you? Can't you see? I have no lights in my house. How am supposed to find it in the dark?"

I hope you understand the gist. I journey inward, where in the cave of my heart I hope to meet myself, my true self, the self that is one with all of creation. That essence is Truth. It is this quest that makes me a yogi; one who unites with his own self, one who discovers the fountain of peace within, one who is detached from the transience of the world, one who relies on none for his happiness, one whose only goal is liberation.

Now, we are rather stubborn regarding this name business. I have already answered that I do not have one. But I suspect what you are trying to know is what most people are curious about but never ask me upfront. They almost always start with a question like yours. What is my name or which city I am from, or where my family is.

Since you have told me many things about yourself, I suppose it is reasonable for you to expect the same of me. I will tell you the story. But please know that I will speak of the man I was in the third person, for he is other than me. He died a glorious death, he died a saviour, and it is from ashes of his personality that a new man, Babaji, was born.

Brij hailed from Bombay, your city. He lived a modest life in a small house with his mother, father, and sister. He sold second-hand cars and he traded scraps and engines. He had some good friends, and one of them in particular went on to marry a very rich young lady. This friend became a millionaire overnight. He needed loyal advisors, friends he could trust. He called Brij and offered him a job, and soon Brij found himself in a nice corner office with a breathtaking view of the Bombay Stock Exchange. Because he was a crafty fellow, Brij didn't have to work very hard at all. He played golf and drank imported whiskey and went on business trips with his friend. They travelled the world, signed deals, lived in five-star suites, ate like kings. Life was good. Brij believed he had found the key to happiness, and the world would now and forever be a source of joy and contentment.

Then it happened. One birthday, when he was on a train from Kyoto to Osaka, his mother in Bombay begun feeling a strange numbness in her left shoulder. She must have thought nothing of it, because she proceeded to drape her simple sari and brush her silver hair in preparation for her trip to the temple. She was going to distribute food to the poor, you see. After all, it was her only son's birthday, and she wanted to make sure she did enough to secure God's blessings for his long and healthy life. And even though her son had moved out to a plush apartment and never called her anymore, mothers are mothers.

As she opened the door to leave, she clenched her left breast and fell to the floor. Brij didn't know this at the time of course; he received a phone call when he reached his hotel. "She fell and the maid called. By the time I came home she was gasping, struggling to speak. Then she stopped breathing," his father said. "Just like that."

His father also told him that her last words were few, and it was Brij's name she uttered before she died.

That night, as his friend and employer Gaurav consoled him, he thought about the fragility of life, about the things he should have said and done, about how he had failed her. Then, while waiting for his booking to come through for a flight back to Bombay, Brij spotted a lump in his upper thigh. He knew just by the way it looked and felt that he should worry about it.

Brij came to the river to immerse the ashes of his mother. He sat at the banks and held all of her in an urn. He had to cover it because otherwise she would fly away, she would escape into the air and float into the trees or kiss the clouds. She was dust. That was all she was now. Dust. And he would be too if the cancer spread. Dust, sooner or later. That day, for the first time Brij prayed, not that his cancer go away, not that he be saved from death. Brij prayed for his mother and he prayed for all the mothers before her. He prayed for every man that had turned to dust and all that were waiting their turn.

When his cancer was cured, he came back to Varanasi, because he missed the river. He sat at the feet of the Ganges for days, he didn't know how many. He hardly ate, hardly slept. One day, as he sat and looked out into the horizon, he felt a tap on his shoulder.

"What do you seek?" the old man asked Brij.

"Truth."

And that is how Brij met his Guru, it is how Brij died, it is how Babaji was born.

Well, this has been a long letter. Now that the matter of introductions has been thoroughly addressed, I ask that you read the attached papers. These are some writings from earlier days when this path was new and my questions were many, strikingly similar to yours actually. My teacher answered them all patiently. I hope you find these notes and papers insightful. Please write to me only after you have read everything.

Love and Om,

Babaji

⁓ↄᴄ⌒

25th July, 2001

Dear Babaji,

Thank you for sharing your life story with me.

It is difficult, perhaps impossible, to express what I felt when reading your journals. As my eyes drank your words, the world begun to melt away. I laughed, I cried, I stopped breathing. I was hopelessly tormented and yet immensely rejuvenated by your every syllable, your every thought. When the last page was read, I no longer recognised myself.

Compassion, love, free will, destiny, karma, meditation, solitude, renunciation, self-discipline, oneness. Your words roll around in my mind.

Something has happened. I cannot explain it. Sugar has lost its sweetness, sleep eludes me, I cannot hear when people speak. The world spins but I stand still. So very still. In this stillness I know I will find myself.

But I have so many more questions. Where do I start?

What is the path to happiness? What is love? What is intelligent living? What is meditation? How can I cultivate compassion? What is destiny? What must one renounce to find truth? How must one learn to meditate?

Please, Babaji, do reply my letter. I want to learn more. I want to understand. I am tired of looking for the needle outside. Take me inside.

Love,

Radha

2nd October 2001

Dear Radha,

I am sorry it took this long to reply your letter.

I smiled when reading it, because you have even more questions then when we started out. I seem to be doing the opposite of helping.

Oh yes, I had forgotten to give you the recipe of the daal. Here it is:

4 tsps ginger, grated

1 cup yellow lentils, boiled till soft and ground

4 green chillis, chopped

1/3 cup coriander, chopped

2 large tomatoes, chopped

1 tsp turmeric powder

Salt, and chilli powders to taste

2 tbsps oil

The method is very simple. Heat the oil in a pot, cook the ginger for a minute. Add in all other ingredients with 2-3 cups of water and cover. Let it cook for about 20-30 minutes. Enjoy with rice and remember me.

My dear, indeed you ask very important questions. Try to spend a few minutes every day in silence; the quieter you become, the more you will hear. Listen to the wind, it speaks. When people speak, listen to them too. Silently hear everyone. Accept what is good. Reject and forget what is not. That is intelligent living.

There is no path to happiness. Happiness is the path. And happiness depends on what you can give not what you can get.

Grow your love. Love is to the human heart what the sun is to a flower. Conquer your mind. Mind can make a hell of heaven or a heaven of hell. Forgive, forget. Flood your mind with love. Look into the eyes of those you have quarrelled with and embrace them.

And have faith. Faith is to believe what you do not see so that you may come to see what you believe.

It is difficult to continue writing and to answer all of your questions. This body is unwell again. The doctor says it will take a few months more than the last time to get rid of the cancer.

I have enjoyed reading and writing these letters. But I am afraid I may not be in the best of health for some time to come. I wish you the best.

Blessings.

Love and Om,

Babaji

22nd October 2001

Dear Babaji,

Your letter arrived late. By the time you receive mine, I will already be with you.

Love,

Radha

PART II
MIRA

CHAPTER ONE

20th June, 1964, Daripur

Mira is to marry today. She is to marry a man she has never met. She is sixteen.

The pairing has been arranged by the elders of the family and she will comply with their wishes.

The groom fulfills all the prerequisites nicely. He has skin the colour of milk coffee rather than black tea. This means he will produce well-complexioned children, more so because Mira's skin is also a warm toffee. The combination is perfect. He is of good lineage, and neither him nor any members of his family have had any altercations with the law.

Mira's parents are a little disappointed with the fact that he is no doctor or engineer. He is, however, self-employed and owns some properties in the city. He will be able to offer Mira a comfortable life and provide her with all the necessities. This is acceptable to them.

It is mid-afternoon, and she sits alone in the large room. Like the bodies of thousands brides-to-be before her, her body has been rubbed with turmeric paste by women relatives earlier this morning. This ritual is said to soften and beautify the skin and prepare it for the touch of a man.

The ceremony took place in the courtyard in the presence of the holy Tulsi plant, the same plant she's circled every day since she learned to walk. It is believed three circumambulations daily around the Tulsi while chanting the lord's name brings great blessings.

Her mother followed her while she did this, mumbling prayers with feverish enthusiasm for a good husband for her only child and daughter. He must be a noble, wealthy, handsome, and wise man who will sweep her little princess off her feet, she prayed.

Mira never understood how a plant could bestow such wishes, but she never questioned it either. And she didn't know that in other parts of the world, Goddess Tulsi had a botanical name; basil.

She grew up believing her mother to be a very a wise woman. She had seen proof of it many times by the countless fascinating things her mother could do, like gazing up at a clear sky in the morning and being able to tell whether or not the rains would fall at night. Like knowing if the crops will be sweet by looking at the colour of the leaves even before the mango season started. Like being able to make stuffed potato bread soft as clouds by kneading the dough just so.

And so Mira obeyed, she chanted Krishna's name and circled the holy Tulsi daily. She didn't complain like her irreverent cousin sisters. Now, true to her mother's promise and the benevolence of Goddess Tulsi, her husband has arrived.

But he is the wrong man.

༺✦༻

He waits for her outside at the dais in front of a fire lit by pious vedic-mantra chanting Brahmins. Their voices unify in pitch and intonation, high then low. Elongated syllables and abrupt pauses, a systematic rhythm summoning the seven levels of heaven, invoking the five elements and the nine planets to prepare to bless this union of two strangers.

Mira will have to circle the fire with him seven times. She will be asked to promise loyalty and chastity. Like brides before her, she will have to keep her head low and not meet his gaze. Being demure and coy on the wedding day is a sign of good upbringing. But there is one bigger virtue.

Virginity.

She is devoid of that.

She has already given herself to Neel.

During the morning ceremony, Shama Didi and Radhika Chachi, both in their sixties, giggled while spreading the yellow paste on her arms. They joked that that is where her husband would touch her first. They said he would play with her fingers and then slowly run his hands up her arm, and then he would come closer, and inhale her body—therefore it was important to scrub well. The other ladies joked that if he was too inexperienced, he may not bother with any of that.

Shama Didi told Radhika Chachi, "I still remember your wedding day. Your old rascal must have had many failed attempts before he finally threaded the needle, the both of you were in there well into the next afternoon. And my lord, I have never seen that much blood."

Radhika Chachi turned beet and grinned, exposing her missing teeth. "*Arrey*, he is a city boy! Like the heroes in the movies. Maybe he will sing also to her," someone said.

"No time to sing. He must be counting the minutes." Shama Didi laughed though reddish teeth stained by tobacco. "Our Mira is so beautiful, just look how her skin glows. Why Mira, he is so handsome, you are going to be very busy tonight."

Mira had looked away, allowing the elderly women to mistake it for shyness. All she could think about was Neel and how he had touched her face first, with the tips of his fingers, trailing them down to her neck. Her body had flickered like a candle. Currents rushed through every vein. His hands, those hands . . . even now she recalled how his hands had felt against her skin.

A shiny new Fiat is parked just below her bedroom. It is part of the dowry that has been agreed on, and it will be the car in which she will be taken to the city. She will also take with her other items promised as dowry, mainly cash and jewelry.

She turns her head every few minutes to take a quick look at it, as though it will magically disappear and she will wake up from this terrible dream. Ice blue. That is the colour of the car and it reminds her of the irises Neel once brought her. They were beautiful and sky-kissed. She has heard that her husband-to-be is in the business of flowers. He has a flower shop.

The prestigious lineage of Zamindars can well afford to splurge on their only child. They are wealthy; their house—the largest in the village—is built on more than forty acres of land. Inside the shed are the fattest cows of the village and in the barn there are healthy goats, chickens and horses with eight farmhands to look after them. Five houseboys and three maidservants cook and clean the house and the grounds.

Mira's parents were able to afford to have someone come from the city twice a week to teach her English. Neel. Her tutor. It was with him she slipped deep into the recesses of her own body and soul, he floating alongside.

She often waited for him at the doorway, her hungry eyes transfixed at the dusty distance of the village road. He would arrive bearing presents hidden from view: colourful sweets from the city vendors, notebooks with pretty red roses on them, magazines and cassette tapes with all the famous movie songs. She was thirteen when Neel had turned her blood to honey. He was twenty-one.

Lately, he had started calling her a complete woman, because of her full breasts and rounded hips.

They did not have the luxury of being alone often, and she would sneak away from the house after he'd "left". He would wait by the farmlands under the Peepal trees, and there they would spend precious stolen moments.

When a proposal for her hand in marriage had come from the neighbouring village last April, her heart sank. Her parents' soared. The groom was the nephew of an all respected elder and lived in Bombay. What a blessing, a lottery they had said over and over.

They thanked Lord Krishna for showering upon their daughter the good fortune of such a rare opportunity. It had been the only topic of discussion within the family and they'd sent a photo of Mira through the middleman. In it, she stood in the garden, among purple marigolds, with her waist length hair in a loose braid.

All of her family prayed again and again that the city sahib accept her. But she begged the blue God for a rejection.

And when that didn't happen, she started to think of ways to end her life. That seemed to be the only solution. The other option was to run away with Neel. But how would her mother cope with the shame that followed? Her daughter, her Mira, the one that made her eyes glisten with pride and made her heart soar with joy. Her Mira eloping with a tuition teacher? That would surely kill the woman.

She examines her reflection in the mirror at the dressing table, turning her head this way and that. Her hair is pulled up in a neat bun, her lips are plumped with rubied gloss, her jawline is accentuated with bronze powder in the right places, her cheeks are blushed and her skin looks flawless with the thick layer of foundation and pressed powder.

Looking at herself dressed like this, she starts to feel a thickness grow in her throat. Her insides are churning. She dashes to the basin and throws up nothing. She has not eaten in days. She wipes the yellowish white, bitter bile from the corner of her mouth and drops of sweat break through the make-up. She cleans the smears and smudges, takes a deep breath, and runs her hand over her left thigh, feeling for the knife. It is there. It is strapped securely in place beneath her sari.

She is ready.

Accompanied by her cousin sisters, Mira steps out into the living area of their home, where everyone including her future husband waits.

A hush falls over the room full of wedding guests because they have seen the beautiful bride appear in the doorway. Her sari is draped over her head and falls halfway over her face. She can see only a little. Some faces in the crowd she recognises, but many are strangers.

Strings of marigolds dangle over the walls, lanterns made of silk hang above and the *shehenai* starts to play as she is guided into the draped *baldachin*. She tries to peek at him, out of curiosity more than interest, but she cannot make anything out because as is custom, his face is covered with a veil of white jasmine flowers that hang from a string tied around his forehead.

Mira catches sight of her mother standing alongside Radhika Chachi and other womenfolk.

"As beautiful as the full moon," her mother mouths as tears of joy start to flow. The kohl in her eyes travel down her cheeks, leaving tracks of black ink.

Mira is led by the arm toward her destiny. Her heart sinks further with every measured step. She lifts her gaze ever so slightly toward the room of spirited relatives. She cannot spot her Neel. He hasn't come. She realises that she hasn't expected him to—and yet she has. Part of her had wanted him to whisk her away from the wedding hall, to declare his love in front of the world, to be ready to fight anyone for her hand; even though she had forbidden him from coming at all. She had told him she would not be able to bear seeing him anymore than she could bear seeing her mother hang herself from shame.

She had had the misfortune of falling in love with a beggarly tutor man, one that would not do at all in the eyes of her family. There is only one option now.

Her heart all but stops as she brushes her hand lightly against her thigh, feeling for the knife beneath her heavily embroidered sari. Nine yards of deep and rich silk, the colour of blood. Gold thread and crystals cover almost every inch of fabric. It is draped and pleated around her waist. Its weight, like a burden, bears heavily on her. She is led to her place on the left side of her husband-to-be. Here she is, this is it.

"Don't be nervous," her groom's voice is thick but gentle. "You are so beautiful, the photograph did not do any justice."

Her lips tremble and her hands turn cold.

"I must tell your father it would be criminal to take a dowry from him. I hope that big motor car is not yet paid for, and can be returned," he whispers. The curtain of flowers hangs over his face, separating them. But from the corner of her eye she catches the tiniest glimpse of only a portion of his face.

"Please stand," the priest announces loudly.

She cannot move even the smallest of muscles. Her body has frozen; her limbs exist but they are separate from her. She has no command over them. Her mother smiles proudly at her hesitating daughter. This is the way brides should be; modest, shy, elegant.

She steps forward, helping Mira up by the arm. The room is silent. The head priest begins his devout chanting of mantras. He sprinkles ghee and raw rice into the pyre at the end of every stanza. The smoke from the fire stings her eyes and tears flow like a river let loose.

"Please start the *pheras*," the priest orders.

Her groom leads her around the fire. She follows him, counting the rounds. One, two, three, four, five, six.

Seven.

She is married.

The sweet scent of ginger lilies hangs in the air. The room is cozy and warm, the four poster bed decorated with strings of flowers on all four sides. Mira sits waiting on rose petals and cream silk sheets. Karan will want to consummate this marriage tonight.

Now is the right time to do it. She can end it all before he walks through the door.

Neel drifts at the banks of her mind like the debris of the many unfortunate fishermen's wooden boats that sink and crumble after being defeated by a storm. She reaches to her ankles to lift her sari and takes out the knife, gripping it tightly against the flesh just beneath her left breast. One stab is all she needs.

But her thoughts are churning madly, and her mind feels like it is going to explode. She does not know that Death is his own master and not a servant she can summon at her whim. She does not know that to take one's own life is the strangest of paradoxes; one must excel at both bravery and cowardice.

So she frets with fear. What will happen in the hereafter? Will she be free of this pain of separation? Will she be able to see Neel from the other side? Will she writhe for very long, like the fish that her father pulls out of the river? Will everything go dark forever?

The door creaks open, and she stuffs the knife under the mattress. Her pulse races and fear wrenches her insides. Her body shivers as Karan comes near her and sits down.

Please don't touch me.

"This is an awkward arrangement," his smile bleeds through his words.

She does not reply. Not because she doesn't want to, but because she is afraid that if she opens her mouth to speak, her voice will betray her. She starts to pray with all her heart that he leaves, that he goes away. That she can be alone, even if only for a minute, enough time to wedge this knife straight into her chest, and break her already broken heart.

"Maybe all those old grannies told you to say little to your husband on the first night. But I would rather like to hear your voice," he speaks with kindness.

She looks up only slightly, just enough to see his face. He places his finger on her chin and lifts her head, allowing her a full view. They are now eye to eye.

"You must be exhausted. This sari looks heavier than you."

He has strong features; a pointed nose, a wide jawline, and dark brown eyes. His hair is jet black and shiny, like the onyx charm bracelet Neel gifted her two years ago.

"I know we don't know each other. And it is ridiculous to spend the rest of your life with a stranger. My parents changed after we lost my brother. It broke their heart and I became the only child. And this was their wish. I don't like it any more than you. But we are where we are."

Tears escape, rendering her insides naked in front of this stranger.

"Hey." His voice drips with sympathy. "What's the matter?"

"I don't know," she lies softly.

"I don't mind a good cry myself." He laughs a little. "Why don't we eat something? I am starved. I wish our families expressed their love by feeding us rather than dressing us up. And some of my relatives didn't smell too good."

Through the sniffs and sobs, she hears herself giggle.

"Samosas? There were plenty left over. They're in the kitchen." He gets up and opens the door. "And let me see if I can find some of that sweet rice. I did see some pudgy cousins of yours hovering around it through the ceremony." He leaves the room.

She chuckles at the realisation that he was referring to Radhika Chachi's grandchildren, the twins. They looked so like baby elephants, and they ate like horses.

She is finally alone again. The tears have stopped. She pulls out the knife. The blade glistens in the light from the chandelier as she examines it closely. Its pointed edge is sharp and long enough to cut more than halfway through her. She imagines its passage through her flesh and shudders. Her shoulders tighten and her breathing halts with the fear of pain and a painful death, of leaving this world that she knows and understands to go where no man has ever returned from.

The door handle clicks, and she hides the knife quickly.

"Guess what. They really did finish the rice." Karan places a plate full of stuffed potato bread in front of her.

"You don't mind crumbs on the bed, do you?"

CHAPTER TWO

18th August, 1970, Bombay

Mira nestles twenty-four red roses within a generous bunch of fine broad leaves. She then takes a clear plastic sheet with glittery gold specks and wraps it around the arrangement, securing the bouquet in place with a twinkling emerald ribbon.

This morning's batch of flowers is exceptional. The lilies are whiter than milk, the chrysanthemums are in every imaginable shade of pink, and the roses are the healthiest she's ever seen. What she would love to see, though, are the faces of the recipients of the hundreds of fragrant bouquets she's arranged over the last few years. But she has never been tasked with any of the deliveries. Karan and their errand boy, Moorty take care of that part of business.

She examines the roses and adjusts a few just so that they are caressed evenly by the greens. She finishes the bouquet with a spray of sugared water to make them last long and healthily. But as she arises from the plastic chair to hand the arrangement over to Karan, she is jolted, her knees threatening to buckle. Then there is an unmistakable warmth between her legs. Her heart lurches as she recognises the familiar sensation. She squeezes her thighs shut just as thick hot liquid, what she knows from experience to be blood, starts trickling down her thighs.

Her body trembles and freezes as Karan turns around to take the flowers from her. She wills, commands, begs her body to obey and for the love of Krishna to stop shaking. For her heart to stop racing and her eyes to not slam shut. But terror is a competent adversary. Shamelessly, the tears stream down her cheeks.

His hands reach out for the flowers and his eyes flit across her face as if in passing. But he raises his gaze back upwards from the bouquet. He is lingering on the horror in her face. His eyes slither down her torso, down her waist and settle at her thighs. She starts sobbing. Choking. Whimpering.

It is an unfortunate morning. It brings the total to three lives that have blossomed and withered in Mira's womb. In her mind they are all beautiful. Perfect. Shining. Two boys and a girl. She sees them when she shuts her eyes, all of them, even this one that has shrivelled quicker that the very same roses she handles every day at this little shop off Anvarally Road.

A fragile belly is a convenient place for Death to reach. He's claimed them at two, four, and now three months respectively. Of course they haven't died. Nothing truly dies. They have left. Rather, their souls have left the limbless masses of flesh, like fragrance leaves the lilies.

When Mira first miscarried, she put it down to punishment for her dishonourable sin of giving her body to Neel. When it happened the second time, she deemed her wretchedness unforgivable. She had hidden her truth from Karan. The knife had been used and more than enough blood was shed to turn her dishonour to chastity. The blooded sheets brought much joy to the womenfolk. She still bears a small scar, a souvenir of her deceit, on her right calf.

Like Mira, Karan is an only child, and his dream had always been to have many children. At least five, he often said when they were newly married. The first mischance had chipped away at Karan's kindness. When the second one happened, he didn't even console her.

And now he stands frozen with his blazing eyes boring into her. He used to be handsome and gentle but lately his features have distorted. Especially now. His face has taken on a severity that speaks of his utter disgust with her.

"Follow me." He spits at her, as though commanding a pet who has soiled his master's prized furniture. He storms out of the shop and she follows with an obedience that can only come with fear. He waves down an auto rickshaw and orders her to enter.

"Take her to the general hospital," he instructs the driver and pushes a twenty into his hand.

The driver, a skinny but mean-looking fellow, is distracted by a young shapely woman in a tight navy *kurta* crossing the road ahead. He waits to finish surveying her and till she is out of sight before shoving the note in his pocket. He then pulls at the lever by his side. The three-wheeler clamors to life and they bump and jolt out of the narrow, potholed lane.

The thick liquid starts to seep through her sari. She can feel the fabric go warm and heavy. It will stain the beige cotton, dyeing it into the colour of the roses she lovingly arranged only minutes ago.

Fresh currents of terror run through her as she eyes the upholstery. Angry scars of ripped tattered leather expose discoloured yellowish foam. She eyes the driver, searching for a compassionate face. He chews on a toothpick, devouring the end as though it is coated in sugar. She is not sure whether the blood has started to stain the seat through and decides he will not forgive her if it does. And she has no money.

She holds on to the side bar of the rickshaw and raises her buttocks a few inches above the seat, balancing her body mid-air. And this is how she rides, squatting and legs shaking, for fifteen jagged minutes that go on for all of eternity.

~*~

The ward stinks of urine and disinfectant and her head pounds from the putrid smell. There are twelve beds in total, all occupied. Other people here are unlike her. Their diseases are either visible or audible. The old shrunken woman beside Mira wheezes as she breathes, a low pitched eerie whistle. Mira hears the phlegm rattle and crackle in her lungs.

Mira's bed creaks when she turns to the other side. The pillow smells of mothballs and vinegar. The woman to her left looks about her age. Her torso is bare and her breasts are tightly wrapped in stained bandages. She is asleep but she still mourns.

That could have been me years ago, she thinks, *had I wedged that knife into my heart like I'd planned.* If she'd really had the courage to go through with that first stab, she knows she would have kept going till her arms failed her. She has reached within herself many times, desperately looking for bitterness. For some kind of hatred towards her mother and father. It was they who had pulled her out of the familiar and the comforting, into this city of strangers. Into bed with a stranger.

But there was never any resentment when she searched for it. There was only longing. And love. A lot of love; for her mother, her father, her village, her community and their punishing values. This angers her and yet, in some strange way, it is comforting.

Because that is what love does, love connects, love comforts.

She had cried the entire night before leaving her maternal home. It feels like ages ago now. Every member of the village had come to say goodbye to the Zamindar's daughter who'd landed herself a city boy and was going to live a fancy city life. They envied her, she could tell from the way their smiles reached their eyes. From the way they showered her with hugs and blessings. They did not mind being left behind, they did not resent her good fortune. They wished her well.

If only wishes were horses.

Neel hadn't come to say goodbye that morning. Neither had he never tried to contact her afterward. Somewhere between today and the last time she saw Neel, she isn't sure exactly when or how, the realisation that he never really cared for her crept in slowly. It slithered and settled in a dark squalid forgotten corner of her mind. She buried it, covering its stench with the fragrance of the flowers she handled every day.

But every now and then, in desperate moments like this, it broke free and sliced every old wound open.

Neel was hungry. Nothing more.

She was young and stupid. Nothing more.

It was sex. Nothing more.

She feels so foolish now that she thinks about him. Not because he put her out of his mind so easily, but because she couldn't do the same.

The morning she and Karan left for the city, she sat in the car with misty eyes as Karan steered the brand new Fiat out onto the dusty road. She watched all the people she had known and loved become smaller and smaller, till they disappeared altogether. The outskirts of Bombay were a hundred-and-thirty-four kilometers away. She counted each one, keeping track with the painted and numbered stones by the roadside.

Karan had tried to make conversation, he talked about how big and beautiful the city was, how the lights sparkled so bright at night that you couldn't see the stars, about the streets where each new building grew taller than the last. But her answers were monosyllabic and he eventually gave up. She was thinking about her mother. About how she had painstakingly taught her to roll chapatis in perfect rounds, how she had coiled her hair in immaculate braids and sung her sweet songs till she surrendered to sleep.

They drove for hours; evening came before she could see the twinkling lights of the city in the distance. As they slowed down and entered busier roads, Karan pointed out landmarks and monuments. The shop he bought his meals from, the street where the post office was, where his first job was, where the *dhobiwallas* stall was, and dozens of other names of places she didn't care to pay attention to.

She had never before seen so many cars and people in her life. Her heart raced and a sinking dread overcame her. This was going to be her new home, this crazy place with all these strange looking people in their strange clothes. That night, in their two-bedroom apartment, he made love to her.

And although he was so close that their breaths mingled and their bodies merged, she had never before felt so alone.

No birds sung the next morning or any mornings after; instead, crows cawed in the hazy city sky.

Gone were the trees, gone were the smells of wet earth and corn fields. Gone was the old toothless cobbler that cared for her shoes from the time she was three, the uncle who gave her candy each time he saw her outside by the town centre, the washerwoman—aka village gossip—who knocked for laundry the same time every day and sat right there on the porch for hours speaking ill of one or another.

Gone were Uma and Kanchan, the best friends she'd shared a pact of lifelong friendship with. Gone. Just like that. Like this baby she just lost, and like the two before it.

Her heart flutters like a bird trapped in a cage as evening comes. Karan will arrive at any moment and she will have to face him. With her head hung low and her shame bare to see. Her failure a sickness as dire as any patient in this hospital, her gashes as exposed as the wounds of the woman across her.

What can her justification be for robbing him of the very thing he so deeply desires? What will be her apology? What will be her redemption?

The rackety sound of clattering plates draws near. A nurse wheels in a trolley with supper. A serving of bread, rice, lentils, and spiced cauliflower is placed by Mira's bedside. The sight of food brings on nausea no different from the morning sickness she had been suffering till just yesterday.

She turns away. The thought of food is revolting.

Karan arrives. He stands by her bedside. The rigidity has left his body, his eyes have softened. The storm has passed.

"What did the doctor say?" He fondles his stubble.

"I want to go home," she says softly.

"How do you feel?" he asks with deliberate indifference.

She is running a fever; she can feel it burn through her body. She imagines him placing his hand on her forehead. She wants him to know how her body has been ravaged by these repeated attempts at giving him his child. She wants his sympathy.

He does not touch her.

"I want to go home," she says again.

He nods sagely and mutters that he will go and pay the bill.

On the way home he stops at a restaurant and orders generous portions of meat and rice. They sit in silence till the food arrives. She plays with the edge of the tablecloth, fiddling with the holes in the embroidered cutwork. There are phantom sensations in her belly. Sensations of scraping from within, of scooping out, of hollowness.

The food arrives and neither eat very much.

At night they are awakened from their slumber by the sound of the doorbell at some minutes after three. Karan utters an expletive, rubs his eyes and leaves the bed to see who it is. Mira creeps out and follows close behind. In her parental home, it was said guests that arrive without warning either bring news of birth or death. The hairs at the back of her neck stand on end.

At the door Raju the watchman shuffles with a colourless face. He is a narrow man, young and short, but has always been oblivious to his physical limitations. He wears his Gurkha uniform, probably the smallest size available, like a coat hanger. Mira has always felt safe in her house because Raju guards the compound with his life and his rifle.

She glances at his sides; just as she expects, he is not carrying it now. His eyes speak of trouble, and his words confirm it. He has come to inform Karan of an important phone call. The caller, he says, is still on the line on hold. Karan throws on his shirt and rushes downstairs to the management office to attend it.

Mira has already guessed from the darkness that covers Raju's face, from the ever so slight quiver in his voice and his hurried tone, that he knows what has happened but has chosen for Karan to hear it from the caller rather than from him.

Minutes pass and Karan returns with hunched shoulders and watery eyes. They pack in silence. They will leave by the morning train for Poona.

CHAPTER THREE

19th August, 1970, Poona

Have you ever noticed how still I become in sadness? A melancholy heart is the most painful place to be. I rather prefer my natural state of happiness when I can soar light as a feather.

So there you have it. Time, indeed can fly.

I stand still and stretch till eternity for Karan. Minutes pass with the likeness of decades and the day runs for a thousand ages.

My condolences for the loss of his dear father. It is never easy to part with a loved one. Harder still when one has recognised their value until they're gone.

⁓ჯ⁓

Thoughts of the fragility of life occupy Karan's mind as he and Mira ride the six o'clock Deccan Express to his parental home. They arrive in time for the formalities to begin. Karan's father was an honest and noble old man. He is honourably mourned by many. The home is filled with cousins and friends at hand to provide comfort to the aggrieved.

"I never understood," Karan says to Mira in bed that night after cremating the man he has idolised and revered all his life. He is solemn and contemplative. Death does that to people. It strips away the density of the ego, it exposes the delicateness of life and the helplessness of man. "Maybe this is what they call karma. I never realised that it was not your fault that we couldn't have children. You cannot help it, just like I can't help what's happened to father."

His words squeeze the air out of her lungs. She lets them ring in her ears, watches them blur the boundaries between them. For so many years she has craved to feel close to him. He had grown hard on the outside, like the melons she helped her father harvest in the peak of the summers.

Now he is open again. He sees her again. In this moment she is not subservient, he is not superior. They are equal in their vulnerability, equal in their sorrow, equal in their loneliness.

A woman's heart is soft and porous, efficient in forgiveness.

She moves closer, close enough so their bodies touch. His is warm and spent, drained.

She wraps her arm around him and nestles her head in his shoulder, allowing his drumming heart to beat through her so she can absorb some of his grief and lighten his load. They fall asleep like this, bodies touching in soothing communion.

Karan leaves the next day at an hour of the morning when the colour of the sky is the same as that of the ashes. He holds his father in his hands, all of him, in a clay urn. He will be gone for six days to fulfill his filial duty of immersing the ashes in the holy Ganges. Three days will be spent in travel and another three in the company of priests conducting prayers for the onward journey of the departed soul.

Mira will stay and tend to her mother-in-law, a woman she has never spent enough time with to either love or hate. These last years, Karan visited his parents alone while she stayed in Bombay to keep an eye on the flower shop.

Now she is apprehensive. What if the woman has tendencies that most mothers-in-law are known for? Name-calling, criticizing, nagging and belittling ... she knows she does not have it in her to back answer. She does not wish to be disrespectful. She resolves to conduct herself with utmost care and do her duties as a daughter-in-law with diligence. This, she deduces, will ensure all undesirable situations are avoided.

The day is spent with a steady stream of well-meaning relatives in and out of the house. They come bearing home-cooked food, packets of milk, fruits and flowers. There are solemn hugs and consoling whispers. Mira stands over the kitchen stove for most of the day brewing one hot cup of masala tea after another. As evening descends upon them, the visitors wane and Mira is left alone with the widow in the austere white sari.

Mira, as the daughter-in-law, is also required to wear white as a symbol of mourning. But her sari is georgette and bordered with light pink paisleys. Some colour and appeal is warranted because unlike her mother- in-law, she is a *suhaagan*, a woman with a living husband.

It is just the two of them in the house, and she starts to overthink in a disorderly fashion. Should she ask Amma if she is ready for dinner, how close should she sit, should she offer some words of consolation, what is the appropriate time to retire to her bedroom, will she have to wait to be dismissed?

Upon over-analysing the matter of dinner, she concludes that she shouldn't wait to be asked to serve it because that will lead to her appearing lazy and lacking initiative.

Thus, she kneads the dough for the chapatis in fifty perfect strokes, just like she has been taught to, and allows it to rest under a damp cloth. The neighbors have brought some steamed beans and curried squash, she heats these and serves up a modest meal.

Even sugar loses its sweetness on the tongue of an unhappy man, and so it is that Amma struggles to eat.

But Mira does not understand this. She worries that perhaps the food lacks salt, moisture or flavor, or that she's rolled the rotis too thick and they have turned rubbery. After a long wait, driven by the unquestioning respect that is fitting of a dutiful daughter-in-law, Mira forces herself to enquire, "Shall I get you something else?"

In response, Amma lightly pushes the plate away from herself and arises from her chair. "I shall sleep now." Her tone is indifferent but inoffensive.

Mira eats very little herself, clears the dishes and puts a glass of milk to boil with two slit cardamoms. She does not want the woman to become unwell from lack of food, or there will be hell to pay when Karan returns.

Amma's bedroom door is open. The curtains are drawn and the room is bathed in darkness. Mira peers inside but does not see the faint silhouette of her mother-in-law sitting at the corner of the bed, head in hands. She assumes Amma is in the bathroom getting ready for bed.

She also does not see the frayed rug with the uneven corner slightly rolled up and jutting out on her path to the night stand. She enters, glass and saucer in shaking hands and proceeds, quite expectedly, to trip over the ill-placed carpet.

The glass escapes her hands and she lunges forward as all balance is lost. Her ankle throbs as she tries to prevent herself from falling on her face. But this isn't what halts her breath. Amma is shrieking in pain and Mira has realised that the glass of hot milk has landed on Amma's lap. She has successfully scorched her mother-in-law.

She pulls herself up to her feet and fumbles in the darkness for the table lamp. She locates the switch and flips it on to find Amma clenching her teeth and wincing in pain. Her breaths are coming in loud shudders and her eyes are shut tight as she rocks back and forth.

"Oh no, sorry Amma," Mira repeats profuse apologies over and over as she dashes with a hobble into the bathroom for a pail of cold water and the tube of Burnol from the medicine cabinet.

She is now petrified and the tears are streaming down her cheeks like rain. What blasphemy, she thinks, burning her grieving mother in law like this.

She kneels at Amma's side, "Please let me rub this in."

Amma squirms and lifts her sari to expose the offended blotch of skin on her left thigh. It turns from a light pink to an angry red in front of their very eyes.

Mira cowers in shame, bracing herself for scoldings, some curses about what a useless barren woman she is, about how she cannot do anything right, about how she should have been left in the village like the cattle.

But instead she feels cold bony hands on her cheeks. Amma lifts up her face so their eyes meet. Hers are watery from pain but soft.

"Rub it in gently please."

Mira mouths more apologies as she applies the ointment on the affected area. Little bubbles are starting to appear.

She touches Amma's feet, hangs her head in shame, and gets up to leave. When she is almost out the door, Amma calls out to her.

"Child, I haven't slept alone in years, this bed feels so empty."

Mira turns around and fills out the other half of the bed.

CHAPTER FOUR

3rd December, 1973, Bombay

Do you believe in love at first sight?

There is a love that that exists without reason or condition, one that flows without restraint or measurement. It is a love that holds the universe together. It is in the heart of a mother. Her heart, so pure that it turns love to food.

༺༻

"You are a brave one," Mira whispers to her firstborn.

He is cloaked in cloth the colour of the sky and Mira holds him with the care one must when they are caressing the heavens in their arms. His little fingers rest on her naked breast as his tiny mouth draws milk from her body. He suckles gently, making the softest gurgling sounds, squealing, falling in and out of sleep. She can feel his warm and alive breath against her and can smell the powdery sweetness of his skin.

"You stayed inside like a good boy, because you are the

special one, as precious as the sun and as beautiful as the moon," she whispers. "I waited so long for you, and you came so perfect and flawless." She watches him without blinking, for fear that she will miss a flutter, a twitch or a smile.

She thought she was having a baby to appease Karan, she would have never imagined it would alter her heart so extraordinarily. In this moment, as his cheek rests against her bosom and his skin melds into hers, she knows this child to be the purpose of her life. She knows him to be the reason she married Karan. She knows the answers to all the whys and why me, why nows. She knows that this one joy is enough to shadow all her sorrows, it is enough to neutralise all the sacrifice, it is enough. It is more than enough.

For now.

Karan arrives the hospital at lunch time with a stock of cloth diapers and some clothes. He reaches over to the baby and runs his fingers through its soft hair. "Thank you," he breathes to Mira and kisses her lips lightly.

She smiles. "I am a mother." Her eyes well up.

"Yes, and he is exquisite." He kisses his son's forehead. "Doctor said we can take him home today; I bought some things from the market on the way here. How are you feeling?"

His concern for her is not something she is used to. His words flood her heart with joy, filling its nooks and corners. She silently thanks Lord Krishna in her mind for finally making her worthy of Karan's unconditional love and enabling her to prove her worth and her value.

"I am alright, still a little sore but not even conscious of it. This one makes it all go away. He smiles in his sleep and makes funny faces. I think he dreams."

Karan pulls the suitcase out from under the bed and begins packing her belongings. "They say babies dream of their past lives," he muses.

"Then he must be dreaming of me, he was mine in all his lives and will be mine every life hereafter."

They name him Jeevan; Life.

CHAPTER FIVE

12th May, 1977, Bombay

She has been gone sixteen days with Jeevan. It was supposed to be ten, but Karan had sent word that she could and should stay on. The fresh air was good for the boy, he'd said.

Jeevan enjoyed the wilderness of the village, he was in no hurry to head home. Every night, Nani told him fascinating tales about demons and gods, princes and maharajahs, fables and superstitions. She told him how once, years ago, one of their cows had run away and how their pet dog, Pooji, had found her and brought her home. Nani also made for him *gulab jamuns* steeped in sugar syrup, and round *ladoos* with pure butter and honey from the bees in their very own garden.

Nana took him on rides in the tractor. He allowed him to sit between his legs and hold the steering wheel while he drove around the lush farmlands. He gave him one rupee every day for massaging fresh coconut oil into his hair, and if Jeevan did it with exceptional vigor, he received a handsome three rupees for the job.

The day Mira returns to Bombay, it rains. She gets off the train and hails a rickshaw outside the station. She knows Karan would have come—if not for her, then at least for Jeevan. But it is seven o'clock and he is in the shop. Business has picked up lately. Karan has said over and over that his son is his good luck charm and that ever since he was born, the flowers may as well fly off the orchards into the customers' hands.

She arrives at the compound of the building and pays twelve rupees to the rickshaw driver. Jeevan rubs his eyes; they are red and sticky from exhaustion. She coaxes him out of the rickshaw and pulls him up along the two flights of stairs. Her suitcase is heavy with gifts; clusters of green grapes from the vines in their gardens, tins of sweet fudge made from the milk of their own cows, and there is also a hand crafted wooden horse for Jeevan.

She sweats and pants as she arrives at the doorstep and fumbles with the knot in her sari for the latchkey.

She places the suitcase at the door and carries Jeevan into his bed, tucking him in. She is relieved for having forced him to finish the slice of bread and two cooked eggs on the train, because it would be impossible for her to be at peace had he slept hungry.

She surveys the house. It looks like it has not been cleaned since she left. Newspapers are strewn everywhere, dirty dishes and soiled utensils sit in the sink, grime has collected around the stove, the containers for sugar, tea, biscuits, rice, and pretty much everything else are not in their rightful place in the cupboards.

Two buckets of unwashed laundry, piled high, await her outside the bathroom. She washes her face and tucks the hanging *pallu* of her sari around her waist and starts to clean, first the dishes and all that stinking mold. Then she sweeps and mops the floor. She picks up the first of the laundry buckets to stow it away behind the kitchen in the washing area.

As she lifts it up, she catches the whiff of an unfamiliar scent from Karan's shirt that is on top of the pile. It is a sweet and fruity smell, what she knows city women wear. It is perfume.

Karan had bought her a bottle once which she hardly ever used.

She places the bucket on the ground and lifts the shirt closer to her, inhaling deeply. The earthy smell of her husband has mingled with this mysterious sweetness. Her body goes cold. She dashes to the bedroom and stares blankly at the bed, letting her gaze linger at the pillows. She lays down on the bed. With all the effort she can gather, she breathes in the scent of a woman other than her, a woman whose hair smells musky.

Tears don't come but neither does surprise. There is just a sense of free fall. No bottom, no end, only falling.

Her body has known for a long time what her mind has refused to acknowledge.

Now she allows herself to pay attention to the signs she has been ignoring. They were subtle and nondescript but unmistakable. They started to appear after she had failed him the privilege of fatherhood for the very first time.

His gaze hovering at the chest of the *machiwaali* in the Sunday market whose sari blouse was always cut a little too low, revealing a jet black mole just where her breasts began. When the wretched woman handed over the fish, it was he who took the package and made the payment, his hands never failed to touch hers.

Then there was the way in which he interacted with the younger of the women customers who visited the flower shop, sometimes giving the "modern" ones a generous discount, taking a keen interest in conversing with the shy ones.

Incidents such as these never escaped her notice. They pinched her even if for the briefest of moments, and she'd entomb them in some inaccessible part of her psyche. Her mind chose, as the minds of most people do, to be comfortable rather than precise. Why not live contentedly in a castle of inaccuracies rather than pound on the hefty doors of painful truths?

What she has never been able to bring herself to ignore though, and what has been perhaps the most hurtful, is that whenever their bodies are hooked into each other, instead of looking at her and enjoying her face immersed in pleasure, Karan always looks away or keeps his eyes closed tight.

When they made love after that first miscarriage, he wasn't consumed by her anymore. He was consumed by himself.

Some days while in the shower, she'd catch the reflection of her own tanned naked body in the mirror. She'd examine herself with the eye of a critic. Was the colour of her skin too dark? Her shoulders were broad, too broad for a woman.

Now as she lays on this bed, her brain conjures images that suffocate her. What does she look like, this woman who has occupied her place in her absence? Is she more beautiful? Is her flesh not scarred by childbirth, is her skin taut with youth? What is it that this stranger gives Karan that Mira hadn't given?

With these nameless faces and faceless names floating through her mind, the knife of betrayal twists inside her, deeper and deeper.

She has given him a child, has given him what he wanted. There is no justification for his disloyalty. She curls up in the corner of the bed and waits for him to return home. Two hours pass before she hears the key turn. Her lips crease into a thin line and her eyes narrow as the door clicks open. She marches into the living room.

"How are you?" Karan throws his keys on the side table. He smiles at her, a sincere smile it is. How could he lie like this; how could he act like he had done nothing wrong; what kind of fool did he think her to be?

Mira glares at him and his face grows dark. "What is wrong? Why are you looking at me with devil's eyes? Where is he?" Karan drifts into the corridor, opens Jeevan's bedroom door, peeps inside and returns to the living room. "How come he fell asleep so early? Didn't he sleep on the train?" He unbuttons his shirt and rubs his eyes with his thumb and forefinger. "Very tired, what is there to eat?" He settles into the sofa and puts his legs up on the coffee table.

Mira stands in defiance, not even her breath moves. She does not reply, but her hands hold his shirt so tightly that her fingers are turning white.

"What is it? Why you look like you've eaten sour mangoes? What happened? Your parents said something?"

Mira throws the shirt at him.

"What are you doing? Left your mind in the village?!"

"Smell it," she demands.

"You've become crazy or what? Asking me to smell my own dirty laundry. You are supposed to wash this." He flings it back at her. His eyes blaze like fire and his hand rises, rigid and ready to deliver a slap.

"Who has been here?" she shrieks.

"What the hell is wrong with you? Little I am nice to you and you climb on my head. What shit is in your brain now?" He moves to strike, but she ducks and he misses.

"It smells of your bitch." She charges at him like a bull, hitting his chest with clenched fists, screaming and sobbing. "Who? Why?" She wails, again and again.

He grabs her arms and delivers a thundering slap that

flings her across the room. She hits her head on the corner of the cabinet and falls to the floor.

"Come to your senses. You have just come back and this is how you treat your husband? Don't you dare pull that shit with me ever again. Few days you have gone to your parents' house and your brains have turned to rot. Don't forget this is not your mother's house. Behave yourself!"

She crumples to the ground now, so afraid that her body rattles.

Karan has never hit her before. Almost. Once. But he never really went through with it.

"Who is she? Who has been in my bed?" Mira whimpers, weakened and defeated. She crouches in the corner like a caged animal.

"Don't ask me stupid questions," he comes closer, so close that she can feel his hot heavy breaths hit her face like gusts of putrid wind. She turns her head, digging her face into her shoulder.

"Here, look at me." He grabs her by the chin so hard that she hears her jaw pop.

"Don't I give you everything you want? I pay all your bills, I send you to your parents, I never stop you, I keep you like a queen." He lets go of her face and stands up straight. "Ungrateful woman." He spits in her direction. "Maybe your place is in the village. If you are not happy, you can go back there, leave my son here and get lost."

Mira sobs in silence.

"Papa." Jeevan stands in the hallway, his eyes heavy with sleep. "Who are you angry at?" he mumbles drowsily.

"You woke up?" Karan runs to him, scoops him up and smothers him with kisses. "I came to your room but you were fast asleep. Do you know what Papa bought you when you were away? Remember that black jeep you wanted?" Karan hugs him and kisses his face. "This little boy has come home. Oh ho ho, see how big and heavy my boy has become! Come, Papa will tuck you in and tell all about how the mechanic fixed Papa's motor car." Karan hurries to the bedroom with Jeevan in his arms. Jeevan does not see his mother crouched on the floor.

And they both disappear into the dark corridor. The man she was never sure she loved and the boy she was sure she loved more than her own life.

And in this moment there are two choices. But Mira only sees one.

CHAPTER SIX

1ˢᵗ October, 1985, Bombay

Change is inevitable and gloriously whimsical. The most virginal of ironies, it is fluid, yet is the only constant.

It is at the heart and soul of every phenomena in nature, requiring neither consent nor provocation.

Change is wonderful really. If there were no Change, there would be no butterflies.

It is my staunch ally. Separate us and we cease to exist. We intertwine and weave through nature, ever in motion, spinning madly like two drunken lovers, making leaves go brown, turning night to day and back, transforming seed to tree and tree to fruit.

From the moment of birth till the eventuality of death, and everything in between, it is to us that each being is linked as closely as a dancer to his dance.

Years passed and change danced with disease. And what

a wretched, unstoppable rhythm it was.

Children with distended bellies and sunken faces perished by the thousands. Entire villages vanished, whole families succumbed to the famine. The rest of humanity was appalled. It "changed" their hearts. Now, that is an achievement. People rallied together, they gathered to raise funds, they sang songs in aid, they delivered supplies and sustenance. It helped, but only a little.

I was not disheartened, because I knew from experience that Change would Change for the better. Crops would grow again. Rains would fall. Health would return.

There were also puzzling signs of a mysterious ailment that claimed a multitude of lives. Upon painful and meticulous examination, men of science learned that it sprung from man's instinctive act of copulation. It seemed to arise with frequency between same-gendered mating. Death had found a creative new excuse to arrive.

This too did not sadden me much for I know man to be a resilient creature. His instinct to stay alive is as strong as any force in the cosmos. Either a prevention or a cure would emerge from him.

Aside from these mournful happenings, Change was also in another, bigger place. Men spotted an enormous hole in the earth's protective layer. This bruise was a result of man's ignorant, thoroughly irresponsible abuse of nature. Pitiful really, leaving all life forms vulnerable to aggressions of wind and weather like that.

If only men had realised that this Change was irreversible.

Thank goodness not all Change was bad. There was progress, too. New means of communication that would make entire encyclopedias and libraries available at man's fingertips were being conceived by brilliant minds. A click here and a click there, and people were becoming connected.

These were exciting times, and I was thrilled to see what else was to come. This "future" that was to flow through and into me looked promising.

⁓ஐ⁓

"I am only saying this for our future," Mira says softly as she stands in the doorway of the bathroom.

A white towel wrapped around his waist, Karan bends over the washbasin. When exactly the slight padding had accumulated around his previously flat belly, or the isolated strands of silver had stealthily crept onto his temples she wasn't sure, but she has never quite got used to the elder Karan.

As a couple, they are still intact after that night years ago, which proved to be the first of many corruptions in their marriage. One could surmise she has stayed to keep her family name unblemished. Or for the well-being of her child, to spare him the stigma. Perhaps out of fear of being ostracised by society. These are all true.

Most appropriate though, would be to say that she has stayed because a life other than the one she has grown to know and accept is inconceivable. For who can stand up and claim they do not fear the utter despair of being alone? Of giving up all they have known themselves to be—of walking away from every shred, every slice of identity that has come to define them?

Labels are sticky things. Mother, wife, daughter-in-law, daughter. Before one realises, the label is mistaken for the content. Even if the container has gone empty.

Shaver in hand, Karan tilts his head up and examines his chin for any defiant bristles that have escaped his recently ebbing eyesight. "What future? We have Jeevan. And yesterday was such an auspicious event. I am so uplifted and happy—why must you ruin my perfectly good mood?"

The thread ceremony for Jeevan had taken place the previous day. It had been scheduled at the behest of her mother-in-law, Amma, after two attacks to the heart of Mira's father in a short span of a year. She insisted they fulfill this essential ritual for Jeevan urgently. It was auspicious, she had said, that as many grandparents as possible bless the boy on the sacred day he embarked on his rite of passage into his faith.

Together, Mira, Karan, Amma, and Mira's parents had stood over Jeevan as the priest sung his hymns and conducted a modest ceremony.

"Please," she pleads with him, "it has been twelve years. If not now, when? Today is the perfect opportunity. If only for my sake, will you think about it?"

He wipes the remnants of shaving foam and turns to

face her finally. "I am a complete man. It is not my fault that you are not a complete woman."

With that, he shuts the bathroom door and leaves her standing outside.

"It will bring you a bright Future," Amma says, handling the sacred cotton cord Jeevan wears across his twelve-year-old torso. "One strand represents the Past, one for the Present, one for your Future,"

"Do I have to wear this forever?" Jeevan rolls his eyes and twists his face, "It feels strange wearing a thread under my shirt. What about when I shower?"

Mira shoves a towel in his hand. "I am glad you asked, because it is seven-thirty and you are still running around. Nana and Nani's train is at noon."

"But Mummy this thread? Shall I remove it or not?"

"You wear it today, then after we finish doing the *daan* you can take it off and I will keep it at the altar till you need to wear it again." Amma smiles, mischief dancing between the wrinkles in her face.

"When is that?" He draws his head back and peers over a frown.

"When you have your wedding, after I am gone," Amma teases.

Mira slaps his bum and that sets him moving, "First shower, then think of marriage."

"I'm not the one thinking of marriage!" He huffs and storms into his bedroom.

Amma looks most pleased with the reaction she has managed to elicit from the boy. "Look at his height, as tall as his father," she muses aloud, as though she's never mentioned it before.

He has the same wide jawline and symmetrical features as Karan. It is easy to tell who his father is, even with his back turned. He moves with more of a strut than a stride. To Mira's delight, and she never fails to point it out, he has also inherited the best of her assets. Her thick, healthy hair. And the way he smiles, how he tilts his head to one side. She loves this smile, loves seeing herself in him.

Mira sits beside Amma, puts on her oval-shaped reading glasses. They give her the appearance of a stern schoolteacher. She flips open her spiral notebook, "Can I go through this with you? Tell me if I have missed out anything for the *daan*."

"It is an act of charity, it doesn't matter what we give, as long as we give from the heart. If you have purchased the rice, milk, flour and ghee, then that is more than enough," Amma says.

Mira reads her list aloud anyway, "There are also tea leaves and I bought some notebooks, pencils and other stationary. They all go to school and they will appreciate this. Who will buy all this for them? And I asked the ice-cream*walla* to come there by nine o'clock. The children don't know. They are going to be so happy."

Amma runs her hand over Mira's head, pride evident in her eyes. "Bless you child, you are kind. God knows when was the last time they had ice cream. *Daan* is so important, especially after an auspicious blessing like our Jeevan has received. If everyone in the world shared a little of what they had with the underprivileged, there would be no poverty. Karan's father was very generous that way. Every month he went to the slums, and all the children would come running out of their huts the moment they spotted him. I sometimes feel it is his good karma that is bearing fruit."

Mira has always believed in this theory and she now nods in agreement. It was no small miracle that Karan's fortunes had multiplied copiously in recent years. Surely it was the unseen hand of fate years ago that led the director of the Bombay General Hospital down Anvarally Road that Friday evening in search of a florist.

> *"I am sorry my darling, I know our love is stronger than my stupid schedule. Happy Anniversary.*
>
> *Forever Yours,*
>
> *Minesh"*

This was the note the middle-aged, tormented, and luxuriantly mustachioed man had requested be written on the card. He then waited by the roadside while Mira brought to life one of her finest works of art: sun-kissed posies, pink chrysanthemums, and milky white lilies.

It became apparent not too long after that, "Forever Yours, Minesh" was also "forever apologising" Minesh, in addition to "forever coming back for more flowers" Minesh. Clearly, he wasn't a man deft at keeping his promises to his dear wife. He returned requesting special arrangements with the most exquisite blooms available and always waited while they were being prepared.

So it was that a friendship developed between Karan and him. Some months later, when the florist at the hospital was asked to shut shop due to persistent challenges with sobriety leading to some rather unforgivable behaviour, Forever Yours Minesh proposed to Karan that he take up the prized opportunity.

Karan did not need time to decide or evaluate. Any florist worth his salt knew the kind of volume of business a hospital was capable of generating. He jumped at it.

Now here they are. From a two-bedroom apartment in an old rickety building by the wet market, to a four-bedroom house with a garden in a middle-class suburb. From one little cubicle of a flower shop, to a chain of stores (Blooms & Blossoms), in all of the seven major hospitals in Bombay. Amma was right: certainly this was the result of good karma, perhaps by ancestors long gone having sown the seeds for prosperity that were now bearing fruit.

Karan no longer spends his days shuffling stems in a tiny shop, he spends them shuffling paper in a three-hundred-square-foot office.

"Mira," he calls out to her. She jumps out of her skin at

the sound of his demanding voice. She drops her notebook, springs out of her seat, and leaves Amma mid-conversation.

Perhaps he has had a change of heart, perhaps her ancestors too have done the groundwork for her deepest desires to be fulfilled. She rushes into the bedroom.

"Where is my blue shirt? The striped one?"

She feels foolish to have hoped for more. There is no way he is ever going to agree to adopting a child. What was the point, he always argues, to bring home someone else's trash? What if the child is the result of the union of two immoral, criminal or vile beings? Why can't she be happy, he says, with what providence has decided for her?

She retrieves the shirt from the bulky *Godrej almirah* that is more of a locker than a cupboard. The garment is where it is supposed to be, third blue shirt from the left of the rest of the blue shirts.

He slips on his socks, "Where was it? Put things where I can find them. I have told you a hundred times. Blues with the blues. Some corner you will go and hang it in, and then I have to waste so much time,"

She sets it on the bed.

"Wait," he says just as she is leaving, "see if you can find a white packet at the night stand."

She does and inside are eight identical small transparent bottles filled with tiny white pellets, homeopathic medicine from Doctor Mishra, whom Karan has great faith in. She inspects the labels. "Heart" where the condition is stated.

The name of the patient is left blank.

She becomes confused and worries. Karan is only forty-four years old.

"Give them to your father," he says.

She breathes a sigh of relief and no longer knows what to feel about him. Here is this man that at once demands, orders, decides everything that happens in this house. A man that clearly expects the status of lord and master. But he can be so kind and thoughtful, he can suddenly say or do something that she can't but love him for. This is why she has chosen all these years to do the only thing she knows how to do. She has accepted him. He is what he is and this is how she must think of it.

"Something came for you at the office after you left on Friday." He reaches into his briefcase and pulls out an envelope, "here, looks like it is from Delhi."

Her heart skips a beat. Could it be? The stamp on the corner bears the smiling face of India's controversial late prime minster Indira Gandhi, whose ill-fated assassination occurred at the hands of her own bodyguard the previous year. The letter is addressed to her with her maiden surname. She turns over the envelope and sees the name of the sender. A thousand suns rise in her heart.

"Who is it from?" Karan asks.

"Uma."

"Who?"

"We were like sisters," she whispers to herself and steps out of the bedroom. She dashes into the kitchen where she knows she can be alone and undisturbed. She opens the envelope, taking care not to damage it in any way.

She has thought about Uma often. In the earlier years during her visits to Daripur, she never failed to enquire about Uma's well-being with members of her family. At first, the answer was always that she was well. Her father would proudly announce that she was studying in Delhi, that she would be the first woman in his family to graduate from college. Mira had even written to her the odd letter or two.

And then suddenly, Uma's name could no longer be brought up with her parents. Letters came back with the "return to sender" chop. She unfolds the flimsy, single-lined foolscap sheet.

"My Dear Mira,

How do I start this letter? To ask you how you are would make me feel as though you are far away. In truth, you have never left me. That said, I pray you are well and happy, along with Karan.

I think of you often.

I am sorry for this gap in time between us, I had many problems, as you may have already heard from my family.

You will be happy to know that I am in contact with them again. They have forgiven me for all that transpired in those confusing years, water under the bridge as they say. I have made good all their dreams and wishes for me.

They gave me your current address. I did send you a letter some five or six years ago. It returned unopened. The postal services people informed me that the recipient no longer resided at that address, and that there were no forwarding details registered.

I am still in Delhi. I now have a stable job and fend for myself. Romesh is history. I should have never given up my education for that man. What happened between us is a long story, but a common one. I will tell you when we meet in person. Luckily, I had the good sense to go back to college after the madness with Romesh was over.

You will not believe what I do for a living now. Not only did I graduate with my BA, I went on to get an MBA and then a PhD. Yes, I know it is hard to believe. But something inside me woke up from deep slumber. Disappointment does that. There was nothing I wanted more than to immerse myself in knowledge.

I now am a teacher and I could not be happier. The children I teach are not really children, they are teenagers and their energy is amazing.

The memories I have of our beautiful times together in Daripur are what I turn to when I miss you. I hope you will forgive me for my absence the last few years.

I wonder if you are still in love with flowers. I hope you are; you used to write about them to me so fondly. I do remember you had a miscarriage, I hope and pray God has blessed you with children.

My telephone number is stated below, you will be able to reach me quite easily on Sundays. Weekdays I work and weeknights I retire early. Saturday nights are reserved for socialisation with friends, although none of them come close to the friendship I have with you.

I hope this letter has reached you and wait with all my heart to hear your voice again.

Lots of love,

Your friend forever,

Uma

~⁂~

The white van marked BLOOMS & BLOSSOMS will move smoothly along the roads of Bombay today because it is a Sunday. On weekdays one can see nothing but the clogged traffic ahead, but on Sunday the city becomes beautiful and clear, the road wide and welcoming, the skyline visible and grand.

The company van serves as a fitting mode of transport for the family. Green leaves and rose petals painted in pink, blue and red rain over the bold, earth-coulored logo on either side of the vehicle.

Karan utters some words that are inappropriate in the presence of the elders as well as his child as he steps onto the gritty floor. There are remnants of mud, delinquent petals and still-wet grainy shoe prints. He's told the delivery boys a hundred times to clean out the van before the weekend.

"Good-for-nothings," he mutters as he vigorously scrapes the bottom of his shoe against the floor, trying to release a slippery leaf from its sole.

Mira takes her seat next to Karan. Behind them are Jeevan and his three grandparents. They travel along the main artery of the city on the same highway that on a weekday would have imprisoned them for two hours, no less. It is quiet in the van except for Jeevan, who enquires with great interest about exactly what is being handed out to the home.

Mira answers him absently. She explains why they are going to the orphanage and the importance of such actions. She also answers all questions thereafter about how long they will take, where they will have breakfast, why Nana and Nani have to return to the village so soon, and other such details children insist on knowing.

There are many other questions that follow. Fortunately for Mira, these are directed to his three grandparents, who are supremely happy to be pestered by him. Mira's mind meanwhile, becomes available to mull over the letter she has received from Uma. She travels back in time, page by page and chapter by chapter, flipping past memories of the shop and Amma, Jeevan, her wedding, the early days of marriage. Until she reaches the village.

She, Uma and Kanchan, friends since as far back as she can remember. When they were little girls they played on the terrace. They flew kites and invented games with sunflower seeds. They would pile a handful of seeds in a heap and see who can scatter them farthest with one blow. They would sneak into the neighbors' yards, climb the trees and steal bananas, mangoes, and sapodillas. One time they got caught red-handed stealing from Radhika Chachi's tree and oh! how she spanked them.

So much havoc they created in the village. Their mothers complained that they were worse than the boys. Then there was that one afternoon they walked past the corn fields through the shrubbery and swam the river all the way to the other side. It was forbidden to cross the river, but they did and there they discovered a house they had never seen before. It was shrouded in the trees and bushes, rickety and decrepit, made of rotten wood and creaking windows. They poked around from the outside and waited for ghosts to come out.

So consumed were they circling and scrabbling through this old deserted house that they completely lost track of time. When the sky begun to grow dark, their bellies growled and it occurred to them they had left their houses just after lunch; they must have been gone hours. When they crossed the river to go home, at the banks they were greeted with village folk straddling lanterns and bearing sticks ready to beat the beast or human who was responsible for their disappearance.

What a scolding Mira got that night! Kanchan was beaten to pulp, and Uma wasn't allowed to go out for a whole month. It was the saddest month of Mira's childhood.

Uma was the one that had come up with the idea of

crossing the river. She was the one that came up with most of the fun ideas. She was just one of those people that made Mira laugh a little louder, smile a little wider, and feel a little happier.

Even now, Mira smiles at the thought of the mischievous twinkle in Uma's eyes. Funny how some people can be apart for years and still be strung together by some unseen force. Yet others can sleep in one's very own bed, bear children together, and be utterly disconnected.

She had wanted to dial Uma the very moment she finished reading the letter, but there was much else in the way. She will call her this very night. And this thought alone is enough to please her heart.

"What is your hurry to leave? I still don't understand; I will be alone again," Amma says to Mira's parents.

"Mataji, it is said even a drop of water from the daughter's house is a debt on her parents. When my husband was unwell, you all were already too kind. Karan coming all the way to pick us up and bringing us to the city, putting us up at home and arranging appointments with all the doctors. *Baba rey baba*, how many lifetimes it will take us to repay!" In a typical gesture to demonstrate the sheer gravity of the blasphemy, Mira's mother uses her hand to lightly slap her own cheeks, first left then right then left again.

"Don't say that Mama—it is our duty," Karan intervenes.

"Please don't burden us further, *beta*," Mira's mother addresses Karan.

Her father adds, "And you won't be alone Mataji, you have Jeevan, Karan, Mira. I hope Mira is doing a good job of looking after you."

"Your daughter is a diamond," Amma reaches over to Mira's shoulder and rubs it, "you have raised her well. The very day he passed away she insisted I cannot be left alone, and every year she tried to convince me to move in with her. Finally, when Jeevan turned six, she made him come and ask me for his birthday present."

"Yes, and I asked Amma to come back with us," Jeevan chimed in.

"Yes yes. I know she put you up to it. *Arrey* they came and packed my bags and took me with them."

Mira glances at the front mirror and sees the faces of her parents. Their smiles are wide and proud. A smile spreads over her lips too, because she knows she is the reason behind theirs.

Ever since Amma had moved in, life had become inspirited, more manageable. There is something soft and reassuring about having an elderly parent at home. To know that there is someone to turn to, someone wiser, selfless, who has seen more and lived longer. Like the shade of an old sturdy tree, ever dependable to give one protection and relief from the piercing rays of the sun.

She filled all the gaping holes, all the awkward silences in Mira's marriage. Her presence softened Karan; there seemed to be more order, less aggression, some discretion.

A mother has a way of making her son behave, even if he is grown to double her size.

The van arrives at a corroded metal gate, beyond which stands a dilapidated three-storied structure that must have been built decades before the British left India. The spluttering of the boisterous engine alerts the occupants. Their benefactors have arrived. Children of all shapes and sizes spill out of the main door like bees from their nest.

They come to the gate, assorted heights and builds, dressed in hand-me-downs either a size too big or too small. The girls are in ill-fitting frocks, tattered in places, with ribbons in their not very well-combed hair. Boys wear their shorts or pants too high at the waist with mismatched t-shirts. Dozens of pairs of twinkling bright eyes stare unblinkingly, skinny legs poking out of the gate, while little hands clutch at the bars. Some dangle and swing, others giggle and shuffle and curiously wait for the visitors to alight.

Mira bites her lip so hard that she tastes blood. A colossal injustice; so many children, all beautiful, all unique with no home and no one to call their own. And here she is, thirsty for another, but helpless.

A man and woman step out from a side door of the building into the cluttered foyer and negotiate their way through the unusable muddled assortment of dolls with missing limbs, broken car seats, handicapped bicycles and a dusty sofa with naked wounds to its padding.

The tall and lanky host is sufficiently grey to look rather distinguished. He approaches the gate. His pasted-down,

Brylcreemed hair glistens like the silver plates Mira had received in her dowry, the ones she only served from when guests came, for they scratched easily when scrubbed. They also tended to go dull and required frequent polishing if used too often, unlike her regular steel plates.

"Eh *chalo chalo*, move back. How are they supposed to enter? Come on, out of the way." He is not unkind, but he speaks with the firmness that is necessary to get the attention of the overexcited children. Mira herself has spoken this way numerous times to make Jeevan listen.

The man shoots a look at the tallest three boys. They are around Jeevan's age; one of them has a patch over an eye and another one has a slight limp. They spring forward and shoo away the eager crowd, like the farmhands in Mira's village clearing cattle.

There is a woman tailing the man. Mira assumes she is his wife, for the pair murmur with each other, not with the distant disposition of mere colleagues but with the comfortable ease of a married couple grown old together. The old woman efficiently, despite her dwarf-like frame, gathers the children and settles them under the shade of the porch.

The children sit cross-legged in a group, fidgeting, playful, pointing at the visitors, craning their necks left and right to see what is being offloaded from the van by the chain of older orphans. The sacks come down one by one while Mira and the others alight the vehicle and enter the premises.

Sadness drapes over Mira like a cloud. It is a cruel sight. She recalls all the pregnancies and the losses. Everything comes alive again. The days and hours of fervent prayer, the scores of visits to various temples beseeching every deity for mercy, the numerous ayurvedic homeopathic and allopathic medications to awaken her indolent womb.

Of course, she has seen beggars on the street, scores of them, little boys and girls wearing barely anything and roaming every nook and corner of Bombay. But although she longed to put her arms around them and take them home to a hot meal, she knew them to be different. Those children had parents, albeit loathsome wretched ones, who dragged them into a profession of knocking car windows on traffic stops and pestering pedestrians on footpaths.

This. This is heartbreaking.

How could mothers ungratefully squander away their best blessings? Did they not understand how rare this gift of motherhood is?

She observes each one intently. The boy with his front four teeth missing, he looks comical when he laughs, which is the entire time. Another one with a mole the size of a ten paisa coin on his cheek. An albino girl with eyes blue as the ocean. Such blue blue eyes. She had never seen anything like them. There are a few toddlers, all in the laps of older children.

Karan shakes hands with the warden, they say something to each other; both smile and Karan follows him into the building. The elders stay on the porch and speak to the children. Mira's father entertains them with tricks that Mira still remembers from her own childhood: the disappearing coin, the cut off and then magically rejoining thumb, the "guess-which-hand the candy is in" game.

Jeevan stays by Mira's side.

After a few minutes of interacting with the children and encouraging Jeevan to do the same, she points to the pile of amenities they have brought with them. "Go and touch that."

"Why?" Jeevan asks.

"Because *beta*, all this charity is being done in your name for your well-being, your hands must touch it."

Jeevan runs his hand over the top of the pile and quickly returns, "I am hungry; can we go now?"

A blaring chime, the same tune as the music box Mira owned as a child, with the red velvet lining and the rotating carousel inside, grows louder and louder. The children jump up from their places and run toward the colourful ice cream van.

Older boys promptly bring order to the chaos and make the children line up single file. *Everybody gets one turn only, and if you don't line up properly you wont get even a bite. And no dropping.*

Mira watches them fondly as they wait at the window for their cones of pink or brown or white heaven. That is when she sees her, half-hidden, head peeking out from behind a pillar. Curious, Mira approaches the beautiful little girl, whose eyes are so innocent they pierce right through her heart. She is no older than four or five. She wears a faded pink dress with washed-out blue and yellow posies embroidered onto the hem.

"What is your name?"

The little girl twirls a strand of her shoulder length hair and shuffles from one foot to the other.

"Radha."

"What a beautiful name. Don't you want ice cream, Radha?"

"But my dowwy is sleeping,"

Radha squats and pets the tangled blonde hair of the impaired doll.

Mira feels guilt rush through her. Jeevan has always enjoyed the best toys and has outgrown them nonchalantly.

"Would you like me to watch her while you go get some ice cream?"

The little girl catches Mira unawares. She throws her arms around Mira, hugs her tightly, and digs her head in the nook of Mira's neck.

At first Mira does not know how to react. Part of her wants to hug the child back but she is wary because what if she falls in love and cannot let go? She will have to let go, she knows this. Mira wraps the little girl in her embrace. The child's body fits hers as perfectly as a daughter's should.

If only she can convince Karan.

The girl releases her hold on Mira. "My dowwy's name is Roma."

"What a lovely name."

"I am her Mama."

"*Radha, chalo* come." An older boy arrives and takes her by the hand. "Don't you want ice cream?"

Mira watches the little girl float away, an angel without wings, a thing of tremendous innocence. She will never forget that hug. Ever.

CHAPTER SEVEN

17th March, 1990, Delhi

It is the tender thread that binds one man to another, a gratifying affair that can alleviate discomfort and sorrow, good as any medicine.

True friendship is beyond me, in the sense that it cannot be bound by Time or distance. Oh, friends are welded together by forces mightier than yours truly. They are tangled at the roots, forever in and of each other.

Where does it come from? Who is to say? Who is to say exactly when the drop that started the river fell? Perhaps it is the result of brushing past each other as strangers for lifetimes before finally recognising them as familiar, before hearing one's own laughter in the voice of the other and saying, "There you are, my friend. How long I have waited, incomplete."

It is love, nothing less: the frenzied kind of love that has its hand outstretched, its shoulder ready. The kind of love that is blind to fault, and bleeds with compassion, that loyally accompanies whether tears fall or joy overwhelms.

To come upon a true friend is kismet; to keep them as such is wisdom.

※

Mira loiters outside the heavy wooden door, her hesitant finger hovers over the doorbell.

"Just ring it Mama, Amma is getting tired standing." Jeevan presses her finger down, and an unpleasant clang reverberates in their ears. Uma opens the door. Here she is, in flesh and bone. She looks different from the blurring shadow of Mira's memory. But she is as real as Mira's own body that now stands paralyzed.

A smile breaks out on Mira's lips and arrives in her eyes as a flood of tears.

They hug, holding one another in victory over time. "It's been so long," Uma chokes as she releases herself and considers Mira's face.

They stand there at the door, taking each other in as though moving is too big a risk, an opening for the distance of decades to creep back between them. They take in the concreteness, the physicality of each other, swivelling madly between disbelief and gratitude.

Uma snaps out of the spell first. She looks at Mira's mother-in-law, then at Jeevan and apologises, "Come on inside already everyone, look at us shameless girls, leaving you all standing out here like that."

She calls for the houseboy, Ramu. He promptly appears out of some secret chamber of the corridor, and somehow with two hands is able to manage both suitcases and a duffel bag.

Uma escorts them into the modestly furnished living space with just enough seating capacity for four. A boxy television, one that hasn't shrunk in bulk along with technology like the others, sits on a console. It looks like it has seen better days. Striped lime green curtains hang over a double window. There is a round dining table in wood and four chairs around it. One chair is missing an arm. The furniture of the house reminds Mira of her earlier days in Bombay, when all she and Karan could afford were the basic necessities.

As Mira sits down, she sees the antique coffee table that is so beautiful it seems out of place. It is studded with what looks like blue opal and lapis lazuli at the corners. The base is a carved elephant with jeweled eyes.

Uma clicks a switch by the side of the wall and a clattery ceiling fan whizzes to life. Ramu emerges again magically from a hole in the wall, with four condensing glasses filled with iced water.

"How was the journey?" Uma asks.

This horrid tone of formality from Uma now. So foreign to Mira, like someone else's skin on her body. But these are the superficial necessities, the gap bridgers, the social norms that demand their dues.

"It was comfortable, we left early in the morning. The flight was delayed some," Mira replies, her own voice seeming foreign.

"How old are you, son? You are taller than your mother."

"Seventeen," Jeevan replies, sipping from the wet glass.

"And what a voice you have," she marvels. "Mira, this right here is no boy, he is a young man. I can't imagine that the boys in my class will start sounding like that in a couple of years."

Jeevan laughs awkwardly the way teenagers do when adults discuss them in their presence.

"Mataji, would you like to put your legs up? Please, think me as your daughter, as Mira. Anything you need just say. Perhaps a light snack?"

"I think I would like to lay down. You girls also have a lot of catching up. I am not the least hungry. I will wash up and take a short nap if that is okay with you."

Uma shows Amma to the bedroom. Mira follows. It is a basic dwelling, clean, with a window and a view of some lush shrubbery. But a terribly small attached bath, just enough for the bare tasks for which bathrooms are built.

"Mataji, there are towels in the cupboard and a bar of soap. A jug of water is by your bedside. If there is anything else you need, please just let me know," Uma says before leaving the room.

In the living room, Ramu brings out some biscuits and tea.

"This is too much trouble, you should have let me stay in the hotel," Mira says, the casualness between them returning as quickly as it had vanished.

"I cannot believe you would say that. It is so lovely to meet your family. If you had flown in on a weekend I would have come to the airport even, or at least if you had taken a later flight. Never mind, you are here now and I could not be happier."

"I have to drop Jeevan off early in the morning."

"Yes, you mentioned. Law, that is quite something." She turns to Jeevan. "You must be a very intelligent young man."

"He is top of his class," Mira announces with pride.

"Mama, I am going to go outside for a bit. Is that okay?" Jeevan drains his glass. "I just want to get a feel for the place."

"Delhi is so much nicer than Bombay, you will see." Uma then proceeds to give him a series of directions, tips, and recommendations.

"*Arrey*, he is not going for a week! Down only he is going," Mira laughs as she dips a biscuit in her tea.

The boy leaves, promising his mother he will return before dusk.

"I can't believe you are here," Uma says now that they are finally alone.

"Me neither." Mira shakes her head in wonder. "How

time has flown. You look so ... so ... different."

Uma bursts out in self-conscious laughter, "You say it like it's a bad thing. Remember now, I have spent more years of my life here than in Daripur." She plays with her cropped cut hair.

Mira giggles. "I'm not saying it is bad, you look better like this anyway. You carry off these jeans better than all those long flare tents they called skirts, and God knows you would rather be dead than in a sari."

"You are so mean. It never looked that bad also on me." And they both laugh. And it is sweet and familiar. And they are little girls again.

Until Uma stops abruptly. Her gaze drops to her feet. She is silent for a long moment, pensive. Then she speaks so softly that Mira can barely hear her, "It is not easy to see you in white."

"I am used to it now; I have come to terms with it," Mira speaks loftily, but something in her voice lacks conviction.

"You are too young Mira, to wear this ... this ... it is not even a colour. You have your whole life in front of you. You are only forty-one. Society has changed. Look around you, it is a different world. No one will judge you."

Mira forces a smile, bitter though it is. "Firstly, white is a colour, it has all the seven colours within it. Secondly, I am not unhappy wearing it; I am doing it for Karan."

Uma gets up and sits beside Mira, she whispers with the concern of a sister, a mother, "Karan is gone, he would not have wanted this for you. He would not have wanted for you to be unhappy. He would have never wished that you live the rest of your life wrapped in a white sari like his mother."

You did not know Karan. Mira is surprised at the coldness of her own thought.

~~~

Evening falls and Uma declares that she would like to take them out for a meal. "You haven't seen Delhi till you've enjoyed the wonderful restaurants," she says. And the new thing is pubs. They seem to be sprouting everywhere. They decide on Chinese, because that is Jeevan's favourite cuisine.

After dinner, they return home and Jeevan takes the sofa in the living room, Amma the guest room, and Mira shares the room with Uma.

Uma sits at the dresser screwing open a plastic bottle, soaking its contents onto a square of cotton wool, dabbing it over her face. She does the same with another. And another.

"What are you doing?" Mira stifles a giggle.

Uma turns around. Her face is moist and shining. "Cleanser, toner, moisturiser." She gestures at Mira to come closer. Mira kneels in front of her and Uma starts with the cleanser.

"You never told me what happened with you and Romesh," Mira says as she feels the cold liquid against her skin.

"Do we have to talk about that sick man now?" Uma

crinkles her nose as she examines the swab of cotton. "You really need to cleanse often."

Meera takes the cotton from Uma's one hand and the bottle from the other. She places them on the dresser and looks directly at Uma, questioning her intently, "You never explained what exactly happened, why you disappeared like that, and no one in your family would even so much as entertain any questions about you."

Uma breathes in and sighs aloud. "You remember how my parents always dreamed I would be the first girl in the family to graduate with a degree?"

"How can anyone forget? It is all they talked about since you read your first word at school. We must have been five or six when they started talking about how they would distribute *mithai* and *laddoos* to every single person in the entire village when you graduated."

"When you married, it was just Kanchan and me. And Kanchan left a month after you. I was so lonely. But I knew I would be leaving soon. I was afraid to go live in Delhi in a hostel and all of that."

"We were still in touch then."

"Yes, I still wrote to you. Even when I fell in love with Romesh, I was still in touch with you. But then..." here Uma hesitated, "I married him without telling my family or anyone."

"You what?"

"Yes, I did. One fine day my parents showed up at the

hostel. The warden told them I had moved out months before, and she gave them my address. You can imagine how shocked and livid they were. They showed up at my doorstep at eleven at night. Romesh opened the door. He was completely boozed up and incoherent. I came clean. Told them I dropped out and was working as a receptionist. They tried to talk sense into me, told me of the sacrifices they had to make to pay for my education and the stay in Delhi and all of that. I told them squarely that it wasn't my dream but theirs, and my dreams were all fulfilled with Romesh. They left that very same night. Walked out into the deserted street and took a train home after telling me I was dead to them. I let them go. Didn't stop them. I was in love."

Mira stares in disbelief.

"They were heartbroken, I was angry and we cut ties. Only to be face to face with a man who woke up one morning and decided that he didn't love me anymore. He said he couldn't stand to be in the same room with me, couldn't stand me. It was his house that we lived in; I had to pack up and leave."

"Where did you go?"

"I certainly couldn't go home, how would I face them? So I just stayed with a friend for a while, till I found a sales job and made some commission and moved to my own rented apartment. Then I signed myself back into college, worked days and studied nights."

"You are so brave, so very brave," Mira breathed.

"Nothing compared to you. Look at you. I don't know how many women would look after their mothers-in-law like this, bringing them on a trip."

"Amma is sick. Sclerosis of the liver. She is already weaker. Karan's death has broken her; she is shutting down slowly."

"He was so young." Uma takes Mira's hand in hers. "You are so young. What happened to him?"

Mira tells Uma everything. The miscarriages, the flowers, the change in fate, the visits back to Daripur. The human heart is efficient in forgiveness. It is respectful of the deceased. It tends to retain with clarity the good memories, and does away with the vile. Thus when telling Uma—who had only seen Karan briefly at the wedding—what Karan was like, Mira skips over the parts about the adultery, the short temper, the apathy. Instead she talks about his open-mindedness in allowing her involvement in the shops, about how he was not a fussy eater, how he worked so hard that some nights he never came home.

And she tells her of his death.

How she had slept to the sound of the water running in the bathroom. Karan had been in the shower. How she awoke when the sky was just beginning to turn colour. How his side of the bed was untouched, and the water was still running.

Her horror at the puddle seeping out through the crack of the bathroom door, the splashing sounds her feet made as she made her way in on wobbly knees, how the sight she was met with is one no woman should see. How Karan lay there, splayed like an eagle on the floor, cold and blue. Like he was made of ice.

She does not tell Uma how beautiful he looked, at peace.

Cardiac arrest, they said. Rare for a man his age. But he was bound by blood to it. His father had succumbed just as suddenly. Just like Karan, Mira adds, to leave like that. He was a man who valued his autonomy above all else. He left when he pleased, abruptly with neither warning nor permission.

"I cannot even imagine how hard all of this must have been. I wish I was there for you."

"Time is a great healer. I could not have imagined my life like this, solo. It is fortunate that I had the business to keep me busy. But I knew very little about it. I was only involved in overseeing the purchases of the flowers and the arrangements. I did not know much about how the business was run. I threw myself in the office affairs, started to learn the nuts and bolts of things. It is still all very alien to me. All the banking and the paperwork, I don't understand most of it. But we have some good people who work for us. Bit by bit, I am learning."

"Hats off to you. You are so different now, so mature. Not the same Mira I ran around trees and played marbles with,"

"Yes, I got old."

"Come off it *yaar*. For the hundredth time, you are not that old. You've just entered the forties, and forty is the new thirty."

"Where do you even learn these things?" Mira quips. She gets up from the floor and lays down on the bed. "I am so sleepy. Jeevan has to be dropped off at the boarding house before eight. Then we can spend two days just talking,"

Uma switches off the lights and lays beside her. They hear each other breathe and it is a soothing sound. It feels like home, like they are little girls again, chuckling, playing, holding hands, biting one small boiled candy into two, sharing it and promising a friendship that will last forever.

CHAPTER EIGHT

19th January, 2008, Bombay

There are stories other than the ones that occur in me. They are told, not lived, happening in quite the same way as now; with a zealous narrator and an enthusiastic listener. Fables, legends, anecdotes, parables; they come in every shape and form, carried from one generation to the next.

I lean closer and listen, enraptured when mothers whisper such stories to their young in bed at night. Who among us can resist a good bedtime tale?

I would like to narrate one of my favourites. I have heard it in so many varied forms. Each time the character, the name, the place changing—but the essence staying the same. I do hope you will like reading it as much as I enjoy telling it.

There once lived a man who possessed in his heart a great desire. He dreamed of a beautiful house set in timber, held together with stone, surrounded by trees in a vast expanse of green.

Many would be the windows and much would be the sunlight that came through them. Many would be the bedrooms with linens that were lush and mattresses soft as clouds. Many would be the friends that would visit this marvelous mansion and make merry. This imaginary house never left his mind even when he ate, drank, worked or slept.

One day our dreamer decided the time for procrastination had passed. He could no longer tolerate his desire. He set about building this wonderful mansion of his dreams. He worked faithfully for many springs and summers clearing, digging, gathering, building. After much sweat and toil, he stood before the majestic structure, more beautiful than anything his mind had ever conceived.

Many were its windows and much was the sunshine that came through them. Many were the friends that were invited to a grand party that the man planned for this wonderful house that had finally come to be.

Comrades dressed in their finest arrived at dusk for the stately feast. They were ushered into the grandiose dining room where cups of wine in silver goblets floated about like twinkling stars. Grand chandeliers dangled from ornate ceilings and long tables were lined with food worthy of kings.

The healthiest lambs had been slaughtered, their sweet young meat roasted and generously spiced. The highest grade of rice was procured from nearby townships and luxuriously buttered. Sun ripened pumpkins were baked to perfection and scooped for delicious pies.

The visitors were spellbound, they congratulated the man on this greatest of achievements. There was no other place like it, they said again and again.

Late at night, when the last of the guests had left well fed and sufficiently intoxicated, the man lay in his opulent bed. He could not remember a time he had been happier. What a thing of joy his house was and how fortunate was he to be the master of it. How lovely it would be to grow old in the comfort of this splendid place. He fell into deep, peaceful slumber with a grin on his face and a song in his heart.

Unbeknown to him an event was unfolding beyond the parlor and the three guest bedrooms. Inside the kitchen, a candle that had missed the not-so-keen eye of the town's prized, albeit geriatric cook, burned too close to the wicker basket that held the wine soiled linen.

As is expected, our new and proud homeowner awoke at an unearthly hour when the sun was still at rest. The devil itself had entered his lungs. He coughed and spluttered violently before arriving at the dreadful realisation that his beautiful new dwelling was aflame. Wasted were the years of hard work and dedication, the aches from sheer labour, and the heady pride.

But it was not a time to hold onto any of that. The house had turned on him. It was time to run. And so he did. Coatless, shoeless and penniless, he watched the house burn like a gigantic furnace, the flow of his tears proportionate to the breadth of his smile only hours ago.

The poor man walked away dejected and devastated,

but wiser. He now knew that the very things that bestow unbridled joy have within them the capability of delivering as much sorrow. This is a universal rule, it is part of being human. Where there is the potential to love, there is the danger of pain.

Mira has lived for fifty-nine seasons of Dahlias but witnessed their different hues for only forty-three.

In this time, the city's landscape has transformed. Everything has got bigger and faster. Aged and tottering double- or triple-storey buildings have all been bulldozed out of existence, and skyscrapers soar in their place. Mira's favourite sundry shop around the corner has not disappeared, but a large grocery chain has sprouted next door. Its floors sparkle seductively, its racks are stocked generously, its products are priced competitively. The entire neighborhood has slowly but surely been converting. Letters have become extinct, but mailboxes choke with flyers promoting cleaning services, tuition teachers, and mattresses that promise to cure cancer. Cars have morphed into noisy, speedy machines.

Mira has been forced to change the way the flower business is run. She has learned to use the internet, and Blooms & Blossoms has a website. Bouquets are bigger, fancier, complicated. Balloons, candy, wine, teddy bears, crystal vases, are offered to customers along with flowers.

People have changed. It is harder to make them smile. Flowers just aren't enough anymore.

The sixty-year milestone hovers dangerously near. This does not trouble Mira even a little. She has hardly noticed it, for she has never before been happier. She is in love with a small girl of four going on five, with the child of her child: a girl with dark waterfall hair and little hands that grip Mira's fingers like roots grip the earth. The girl who says, "I wuv you Dadima" before she goes to sleep every night.

It is said that the interest earned on an investment is always sweeter than the capital. Indeed, Mira enjoys Isha much more than she remembers ever enjoying Jeevan. When she wrests memories of Jeevan's childhood from her stubborn mind, Karan always appears and claims centre stage.

With Isha, it is so different, so free. She enjoys her without a care in the world, without the trappings of responsibility, without the careful measure a parent must adhere to so that delicate levels of obedience and discipline are maintained.

Jeevan had Isha soon after marrying his college sweetheart, a rather long-legged and high-cheekboned young lady with a love for all things linked to the law. All three of these things played a part in Jeevan falling head over heels in love.

He, Maya, and Isha live with Mira for a few reasons. Firstly, Jeevan never moved out other than the time he was in college. When he returned from his studies, he found that he was most uncomfortable with even the thought of his mother living alone. Secondly, the two young lawyers were neither well-known nor well-accomplished. Moving out wasn't even a viable option. Thirdly, a four-bedroom house complete with a houseboy who did all things domestic like washing and cleaning was not a luxury to be renounced.

Not only do they reside with Mira, they also operate their modest practice out of the Blooms & Blossoms offices. Jeevan specialises in corporate and securities law, while Maya's interest lays in cases concerning intellectual property.

A perfect arrangement, anyone looking from the outside would say. However, we must know that one must never mistake the glitter for the gold.

And gold, as it happens, is the colour the flowers on the dress Isha demands to wear for her fifth birthday. Mira is to buy it for her on this fine afternoon in January. The family dines at Isha's favourite restaurant, Papa's Pizzas, and sets about the shops. Isha has high expectations for this yet undiscovered present. It has to have "woses" like her Dadima's flower shops do. She says she will be willing to make do with "hydwangeas" but flowers in gold are a must.

Mira, Jeevan, and Isha comb the bulging racks at the children's floor of WadiaSons while Maya spends some precious time at the women's department.

"How about if we find you a dress that has flowers, but not in gold?" Mira appeals with her precious grandchild. "That is all that's available my doll."

"We could try at the Emporium, it not so far. It is Sunday, no traffic. We'll get there in twenty, tops," Jeevan suggests.

"Can I help you?" An eager salesgirl appears. Her tag

reads INTERN.

"Our princess wants a dress with gold flowers but you don't seem to have anything of the sort."

The intern tilts her head up and drums a finger on her lips. "Just one moment, ma'am, I may have something, I will be right back," she says and hurries away.

Maya returns from her spree. "Sorry sorry, I needed shoes and the zipper in my black slacks keeps getting stuck. And then you know *na*, I hardly get time to shop, so I picked up few blouses and all."

Jeevan relieves her of the swollen shopping bags. "Ya good good, but now let's go from here. They don't have what Isha wants, let's try Emporium."

The intern returns carrying plastic packets of iron-on gold flowers. "This will do? We have some plain dresses over there," she points to the far end.

"Isha, *beti*, is this okay?" Mira hands her the packets for inspection.

She beams, "It is posies, Dadima!"

"Wow you are so clever." She kisses Isha on the cheek. "Yes they are posies. Aren't they pretty?"

Isha gives a fervent nod of approval before adding sadly. "But I want it on my dress."

"It is magic posies, we can stick them on. Come, Dadima will show you." Mira pulls out a lace-collared white cotton dress and places the packet over the skirt. "It will look like this, see?"

It has been years since Mira has thought of little Radha from the orphanage. She tries to recall the colour of the flowers on her dress. Yellow? Blue? She had wanted that little girl so badly. And now years later she is seeing her own grandchild's eyes twinkling, just the way Radha's had.

"So is it ok or no?" Jeevan asks impatiently. "I am getting bored of all this. Decide and let's go; we will play Snakes and Ladders at home."

"It is nice, Isha, look how pretty the flowers are. Let me get you a nicer dress though." Maya shuffles through the hangers and picks one in lime green. "This is your colour. And Mama is also wearing the same colour for your party. We can both be matching and we can take loads of photos," she places the green dress it over Isha's body.

Isha glances at herself in the wall mirror. She looks far from convinced. She swivels her gaze between the white dress her grandmother is now holding with great discomfort and the green one her mother is encouraging her to choose.

Mira holds her breath and silently wishes that the child goes with the preference of her mother. She even replaces the white dress in the rack and takes the green one from Maya, "This is so much nicer. Come, let's go pay for it."

"But I don't like it," Isha objects. "I want white. I want to match with Dadima."

The drive home is quiet as far as the adults go. But Isha is talking. She is excited about her new dress, and she wants Daddy to drive home faster so Mama can show her the magic that will transfer the flowers from paper to cloth.

Mira has been through incidents like these before. New mothers can be possessive; this much has become clear to her in the years prior. Although she can't remember feeling this way with Amma when Jeevan was born. Perhaps, it is because Amma was all she had and when Amma came to visit, it was only for short periods of time. Although Mira always wished Amma moved in earlier, when Jeevan was a baby because she had no one to share the first step, the first word, the first tooth with. Karan was never a part of that sacredness. He was never home at such times, and if he happened to be, his reactions were tame.

It does give Mira much joy to see the wholesomeness in Jeevan's marriage that she never saw in her own. Jeevan was so different from his father, even in the little things. When he entered the room, it was always Maya he acknowledged first. His hand would find its way into hers when they walked. The light kiss on the cheek when he said goodbye, the laughter, so much lovely laughter between them. And Mira was careful to fade into the background, to stay in her room often, to not be in the way, to not tip the miraculousness of that laughter. She had learned the subtleties of timing and deliberate absence from many a family meal.

When Maya had just had Isha, Mira would often find that whenever she suggested anything, she was met with an unwelcoming formal smile. This was acceptable to Mira. After all, Maya was an educated, intelligent, modern woman. During her pregnancy, she read more books about having a baby than Mira had read on all subjects combined in her whole life.

So she quickly readjusted her boundaries, stepped aside and let Maya lead. She let her decide when the child must sleep or feed, be introduced to solids and playgrounds, potty train and start school.

But the bond they had, Mira and Isha, was not something defined by silly things like these. It was made of stardust and twilights, of moonbeams and silver linings, of inexplicable elements unseen and unbounded. Elements that rendered any human powerless. And Isha always chose her grandmother. The only way Maya could win was if she let go.

At night, Mira hastens her departure from the dinner table. Space. Everything gets better with space. She knows this. She knows the timing. They need their space.

"Dadima, story?"

"Not today child, I went roaming in the sun with you all day *na*. Now my head is angry with me," Mira rubs her temples. "Dadima is old. Tomorrow I will be better and then we can do a new story."

"You ok, Ma?" Jeevan knits his brows with concern. "Your b.p. is ok? Have you been checking?"

"I'm fine *beta*, just tired. Age is catching up." She smiles. "Goodnight."

Jeevan wishes her. Isha kisses her. Maya ignores them all and continues to eat.

⁓

It is around eleven o'clock when Mira is awoken by the boiling in her chest. She pours herself a glass of water from the jug by her bedside and paces her bedroom till the discomfort grows unbearable. She should have expected this. The greasy lunch with ingredients like cheese and dense breads, which her body is still unaccustomed to, is not going to be digested without a fight.

She ventures outside, walks through the corridor to the cabinet where there are cures for fever, cold, flu, mosquito bites, muscle aches, nausea, cuts, burns and many other conditions common to a running household. She locates the strip of large white chewable antacids and places two tablets on her tongue, crinkling her nose at their dry chalkiness.

When she was younger her body accepted anything her palate craved. Deep fried spicy *pakoras*, tart chutneys, creamy desserts, she could eat them all in one day. But she is no longer the master anymore. Her body decides what can and cannot be consumed. She tells herself now like she has a hundred times before that she needs to remember this.

"What do want me to say?" Jeevan's raised voice carries from inside his bedroom.

She slides the drawer shut softly and inches closer to the bedroom door toward the muffled sobs. She knows this is wrong, she must not eavesdrop on her son and his wife. But she also knows with a mother's instinct that this conversation is likely about her. She agrees with herself that she will listen only for a moment, only till she is sure she is not the cause of their disagreement.

"Come on darling, leave it *na*. It is only a dress."

"It is not about the dress. It is everything,"

"I know. I know. Shhhh now, please stop crying."

"She is hell-bent on making my child hate me."

"Don't think that way, you are overreacting."

"It is always me overreacting, everything she says and does is ok, is that it?"

"Ok you tell me what did she do? Maybe if you hear yourself say it you will also realise she didn't intend it."

"Isha is my child! She came out of my womb, not hers."

"Yes I know but it is only a dress. And besides, Isha made the choice, not her. It is a dress, darling, a dress. It is not a big matter."

"It is not just a dress, it is her birthday dress. And my daughter would rather dress like her than me. Where have I fallen short? What is she telling my girl behind my back? Why can't we just be by ourselves? Why do we have to put up with this? I just don't want her in my life. I hate her."

Silence.

"What can we do, darling? Everything is in her name. If only my father had made a will. Why she won't just write it off to us now is beyond me. She is sixty, she is not going to live forever, she should know that. We can't walk away from it all. We have to think of Isha. We have to think of the child you are carrying."

There is neither thunder nor lightning. Strangely, the stars stay suspended in their rightful places. The ground does not crumble beneath Mira's feet. The earth continues its orbit. Everything looks deceivingly as though it is where it is supposed to be.

How was this possible when the universe has just keeled over and collapsed?

Mira's head hangs like the lowliest of beggars being declined even so much as a dirty old coin. She drags her feet to her room where she retreats to a corner in her bed. The room takes on the tenor of a prison. It is deafeningly silent and the stinging words she has just heard ring in her ears with the fury of a thousand drums. Why is she suffocating, where has all the air gone? Are the walls really closing in? She shivers, she is cold. But there are warm drops of sweat dripping, trickling, running away from beneath her sari blouse, crawling over her belly like insects making their way down to the earth.

She can see the wall of her life in front of her. Photographs framed over the years now hanging in her room. Everything in her life collaborated and displayed on that one slab of concrete. Moments that actually happened. Precious ones that now seem to have slipped from her hands. Just like the many vases she dropped while arranging flowers when her fingers were young and not yet deft.

They had shattered to pieces too, those vases. Just like her heart has now.

Her wedding photo hangs, the blurred reminder of a woman she no longer is. The girl from the village, who circled plants for a good husband, who thought love was a thing easily gained, who wore shoes only on occasion, who thought long and hard for names for her cows and chickens, who laughed so easily so often. Next to her stands Karan, the veil of flowers parted to reveal his face, so gentle and unassuming. So handsome he was. Even till the day he died.

A portrait of Amma. Dear lovely Amma. How she misses her. She has prayed for her soul every day. Assorted photographs of Jeevan as a little boy, one on their trip to Lonavla, another where he is gripping the steering wheel in Karan's car, one on his first day of school. But where her gaze lingers longest is on the photo of Isha in a bright red dress, her hair pinned with glittery white clips. It is from her first birthday, around the time she learned to say Dadima.

There will be another who'd call her by that name soon. Why hadn't they told her? What did they think? That sharing their joy with her would reduce it in some way? Did they keep it from her to spite her? When did they plan on telling her? Why? What was there to hide?

She named him Jeevan; Life. He had come to change her life. And he had. And now he changed it again.

Her house, too, feels as though it is burning. She too,

now knows that the very things that bestow unbridled joy have within them the capability of delivering as much sorrow.

She gets up from the bed and opens the *almirah*. A large suitcase sits on the top shelf, dusty but good for use. It is too high. She won't be able to reach it. The houseboy will have to help her when he comes in the morning. There wouldn't be much to pack, this suitcase would suffice.

PART III
GAURAV

CHAPTER ONE

5th July 1984, Bombay

People run for all kinds of reasons. Some run for health, some for leisure, some run away from something, yet others toward something else.

~·~

Gaurav runs as though his life depends on it. He runs fast enough for his brain to be forced into silence by the screams of his throbbing heart and he no longer exists as man, but only as a pair of pounding limbs.

He has done this every morning for four years now, ever since he discovered the joys of the sport quite by accident.

It happened on an evening like any other when he was still in college. After his classes, he got off bus 92A at the stop nearest to his house. He proceeded as usual on foot past Amba Road and then through the small back lane out to Hamsa Street. Just when he turned the corner from the laundry shop he heard a low-pitched whining that was coming from behind him. He could tell it was at a distance but then a few paces later the hum grew to a growl and it started getting nearer and nearer.

Instinctively, Gaurav turned and took in the sight of a set of wild red rounded eyes, a wrinkling muzzle and canine teeth. Man and dog made eye contact and then the beast leaped for Gaurav's calf. Oh boy, did Gaurav run for his life.

The crazed dog chased him relentlessly past the crossing and then two subsequent ones. Finally after his legs could no longer move as fast and his breaths had turned into gasps, he came upon an abandoned shop secured shut by iron grills. He stuck one foot in one of the grooves of the grills and pulled himself up with his arms. Up he climbed, higher and higher till he reached the top of the shop and where the rusted signboard dangled alongside him. He lost a shoe to the dog that day but the rest of him was intact.

He has never trusted a dog again. But something good did come out of the entire sordid ordeal, he learned that a good run can save a man's life as well as keep his spirits aloft.

Gaurav likes it out here in the mornings when the sky is blanketed in black and the world is still unconscious. Unlike the rest of his hours, this is the one time in the day when he is ahead of everyone else. For this hour at least, he is king. He owns the whole of Bombay, the cracked roads and the uneven footpaths, the putrid garbage piles and the shuttered shops, the deserted alleys and the slumbering street sleepers. He also owns all of Marine Drive where the salty sprays of the sea cool his pulsating body as he sprints from one end of the boulevard to the other and back.

He feels the burn in his legs. He is tired today because he lay awake most of last night disturbed by the thick drops of rain pattering on the roof above his room. The air is thick and sticky and his shins are specked with black droplets from the slush puddles he's pounded through. He hurries up the steep stairs of his tottering building and enters his home. It is located in the thick of Bombay city, a stone's throw from Gateway of India, right where Marine Drive stretches at the shores of the Arabian sea.

And yet his house is unlovable because the doors hang feebly from their hinges, the floorboards creak wearily from the weight of their despondent occupants, the walls slice mercilessly through its small area to create the illusion of personal space.

His bedroom is just about big enough for the furniture it houses; a battered table wedged between a creaky bed and the single-door wardrobe. The walls are infested with moss. He sits down at his study table pushes the little window open. From here he has a direct view of the Palace Hotel across the road, Bombay's oldest and most prestigious five star choice from the days of the British Raj. It is home to affluent sahibs and wealthy foreigners. In the evenings, he can hear the sounds of peddlers calling out to tourists and trying to sell their miniature statues of the Gateway or the Taj Mahal or Gandhi or other such national phenomena that Indians themselves never think much of. He can hear the trotting of decorated horses as they pull lighted chariots cramped with fascinated white passengers, the blaring horns of cabs and cars, the trings of bicycles, the zooming of motorbikes.

But now, at the crack of dawn, the city is silent and only just beginning to stir to life. He pulls down his shorts and sits at his desk as is routine. He waits. His eyes search the arched balconies. Only a few of the rooms have their curtains drawn open and inside are visible the silhouettes of just-awakened guests pottering about. An old man sits alone in a balcony mindfully sips from an elegant cup.

His eyes flit toward his wall clock, he will give it a few more minutes and if nothing of interest surfaces, he will make do with just his imagination. A couple more curtains are drawn, sleepy faces appear, cigarettes are lit, newspapers are opened. There is nothing for him here. He almost gets up when he sees her.

She is in a room on the second floor of the hotel and is stark naked as she unpacks her suitcase. Her rounded breasts bob like the water balloons he played with as a child. So smooth is her body, milky and supple, inviting. He begins to touch his own. He's only ever seen a white woman with no clothes through this window, he has never touched one. He imagines running his hands over the curve of her spine, his brown fingers leaving their trail of cinnamon over her translucent flesh.

Guilt flutters through his heart. Every time he does

this, every single time, Asha appears in the eye of his mind. Usually he is able to resist her, to tuck her away just for these few minutes of the day and indulge in this one guilty pleasure. But today she smiles and beckons him, slips her white blouse off her shoulders. He sees the arc of her tanned waist, he feels the warm sensation of his lips against her body.

The bare-bodied stranger disappears into the bathroom. He pushes his chair back, pulls up his shorts and leaves to take his bath. The water is warm and welcoming against his moist body. Today is his lucky day. He can feel it in his bones. He has not one, but two job interviews and, come hell or high water, he will find employment. He takes his bath, dries himself and slips on his only pair of dress trousers. That stupid hole in the left pocket, he will have to keep it in mind all day. Thirty precious rupees had escaped the day before, and he'd returned home starving.

He dresses, knots his tie and steps out into the pungent smells and sharp sounds of sputtering cumin, sizzling curry leaves and crackling red chilies in the living room.

"Eat before you go," his mother says. She stands at the stove, dressed in a pastel green sari, back turned to him. As always, she senses his presence. She throws a handful of finely chopped tomatoes into the pan and they make a loud searing sound as they dissolve with the oil and spices. His mouth waters. He walks over to her and kisses her forehead. "Amma, I am going to be late; I will go."

"Please don't leave without breakfast. Two minutes more and it will be ready. God knows how long it will take you to reach your interview. So much you run, stomach must be grumbling. Sit, eat and go, hot hot."

He knows better than to upset her. Something like this would leave her feeling rejected and in a sour mood all day. It is sure to bear rotten fruit and if today he fails again at his pursuit for employment, it will only be because he broke her heart. So he sits down patiently at the table, waiting for her to finish her cooking. He will let her feed him, ensure she is satisfied and she gives him her blessings.

The door of the only other bedroom clicks open. A lump forms in Gaurav's throat. His father pokes his head out of the crack of the door, peeps to find Gaurav and steps out into the hall. Gaurav can see the surliness in his face even through the thick blobs of shaving foam.

"How many today?" the old man taunts, his voice still gruff from sleep.

"Two." Gaurav readjusts his tie even though it sits perfectly.

"Where?"

"One in Parel and the other in Bandra."

He gazes distastefully at his wife. *Nothing ever comes out of it.* He mumbles to himself but he does so loud enough for Gaurav to hear.

The door rattles long after he has returned into his bedroom and slammed it shut.

Gaurav grits his teeth. "It is a wonder that fucking door

has not fallen off yet," he mutters under his breath. His mother touches his shoulder reassuringly. "He is not well. You know, *na*. Don't be angry. He is just stressed it is taking so long. He is also waiting to retire. Try to understand son, when he was your age, he had already taken over the expenses of the house. Come on now sit, see how good breakfast is looking today."

She plates his food and places it at the table. He can feel the moisture from the fragrant steam settle over his face but Gaurav is not hungry anymore, he wants to pick up the plate along with its contents and smash it against a wall.

"Come *beta*, please eat." His mother's face has shrunk, her eyes threaten to tear.

But he does not have it in him anymore to please her. Not today. He pushes his chair back, gets up from the table and leaves the house without another word.

The sorry excuse for transport awaits him outside. It looks even rustier and dirtier than when he left it there the previous night. The motorcycle has changed hands many times over and done much time on the road. He bought it cheap two years ago using the three months' pay he earned at a summer job. It is an embarrassment, but it gets him from one place to another. He kicks the foot clutch, and the bike sputters to life with the reluctance of a dead old man being forced to breathe again.

He drives straight down the narrow lane into Mara Road and then takes the hidden left leading into the housing area where his best friend Brij lives. Gaurav knows these cramped streets well, Brij and him have played together on them from as far back as he can remember. Twenty-five long minutes it would take him to get to Brij's house on foot. When there was a match scheduled between the neighborhood boys, those minutes stretched till forever. Growing up, the two went to the same school, shared the same lunch, picked on the same kids, copied the same homework (usually Gaurav's) and complained about the same things.

In the last term of the first year of college, Brij's father developed a cough that lasted through term break into the second year. It got progressively worse and one morning the man coughed up blood. Doctors said something sinister was going on inside him and a few tests later they dropped the big C word. Brij dropped out. It fell upon Brij to manage the expenses of the household. The cost of the medicines to manage his father's weakening body was more than rent and grocery bills combined. To top it all off, there were school fees to be paid for his younger sister. Fortunately, Brij was not academically inclined and so dropping out of college for him was the silver lining in the dark cloud that had descended upon his family.

I'm telling you, all the world is moving in the wrong direction, school is for slaves, he used to say.

Right now Gaurav could not agree more. Even with his degree from one of the finest colleges, Gaurav is roaming amidst stunted old buildings and filthy streets, half-naked children and heaps of waste at every corner. He prays he will not fall prey to the same fate as his underachieving father.

He does not want to spend his days serving a potbellied sahib, standing at the threshold of a miniscule shop in Zaveri Market calling out to passersby like a whore seducing unwilling clients.

Madam, discount discount.

Very nice cutlery, first class design.

Come inside, see the shine on the plates.

Please madam, see new item, special item.

Brij's building stands like a frail old man with brittle bones barely holding on to life. It is some eighty years old and when viewed from certain angles, Gaurav can swear its spine is bent. He pulls up by the side of the building a few minutes ahead of time. He kills the engine, gets off his bike and reaches into the pit of his briefcase for his pack of Gold Flakes. There is only one left, bent and disfigured. He straightens the stick with the tips of his fingers, lights it with a match and inhales deeply.

He thinks of the woman from the morning. She was something else. He could write poetry about her skin. She was so young though. She must either be the wife or the daughter of a rich man. Else how could she afford to stay at the Palace Hotel? He had heard women in foreign lands earn as much as men do, perhaps she was successful in her own right. In any case, he knows the cost of one night's stay at the hotel and it is equivalent to a month's rent in a building like his own. How is that fair? But it is a beautiful hotel, he has been inside and he has memories of it.

When he and Brij were no older than twelve or thirteen, they used to sneak in through the back doors often just for the fun of it. They would crouch behind the industrial-sized cabinets and freezers as cooks in their white uniforms rolled unending balls of dough into *naans* or *parathas,* roasted skewers of chunks of juicy lamb or chicken in the tandoor, garnished plates with drizzles and drops of this and that. The boys watched them hurl abuses at each other and scream instructions over the counters.

The smell of that kitchen has never left him. It makes his mouth water even now. Never again has he seen bread that fluffy or meat in such abundance. He would watch as blobs of butter and spoonfuls of ghee were generously slapped on to everything; brushed over the kebabs, doused onto the breads, sprinkled over long grain rice, rubbed into mutton chops. Many a time they were tempted to swipe a piece of hot grilled chicken breast or a fluffy garlic paratha, but there were just too many people in there and if they got caught, their backsides would be roasting in that very same tandoor.

This one time, they scampered through the kitchens, evading the chefs and kitchen hands that were too busy with a particularly demanding catering assignment. They crept out the side door into a quiet service corridor of the hotel. Once there, they waited, crouched behind the room service trolleys covered under the white tablecloth until the coast was clear and the service elevator was empty.

The goal was to make it through to any of the guest floors and see if they were lucky enough to spot an unattended housekeeping trolley in the corridor. They had been up the elevator before and knew that beds were turned down between six and seven o'clock. They also knew the trolleys carried shampoos and shower caps, bottled water and chocolate mints. If their timing was right, they would be able to have a go at it while the staff were in the room tidying up.

They made it out of the elevator on the third floor and stood tall. They could be anyone, the son of any hotel guest from a faraway land, completely deserving of roaming place like this. They walked the soft carpeted passage, eyes searching. As they turned the corner, they spotted an unattended trolley parked against the wall. Used towels hung out from a bin attached. The large oakwood door of room 3212 was ajar and when they peeped inside, they saw a uniformed staff straightening out the grand double bed. Brij snickered as he dug his hands into the box of chocolate mint squares on the trolley.

"Take for me also," Gaurav whispered.

"Why are you so scared? Come, come, take it yourself. Be a man," his friend snickered.

Gaurav's heart beat so hard he thought it would pop right out of his chest and into the box of chocolates. He dug a hand and clumsily stuffed the loot into his pockets. Some chocolates fell to the ground, Gaurav hastily gathered them and shoved them into his underpants. Brij took a few bars of soap for good measure and both boys turned around to run.

That was when it happened. A loud sound and stinging pain in Gaurav's cheek. He had been delivered a thundering slap he was never to forget for the rest of his life.

Beggars! The man in the crisp black suit and the gold name badge screamed. *Bastards.*

"We are guests!" Brij shouted back.

The man slid his finger through a hole in the breast pocket of Brij's t-shirt and tugged, ripping it down to the hem. He then glared at the both of them and burst out laughing.

Guests alright, guests in the lock-up once I hand you over to the police.

The boys bolted like thunder, tears streaking down Gaurav's face, heart pumping madly.

From behind them, the man shouted more insults.

This is not a place for beggars like you.

Keep your ugly faces in the gutters where they belong.

If I see you anywhere around here again, I will skin you alive.

Son of a bitch.

Gaurav can hear the words even now. *Beggars. Son of a Bitch.*

"Still hiding from mama and papa?" Brij whacks Gaurav's back, almost tipping the cigarette out of his fingers.

"*Saala chutiya,*" Gaurav curses, "let me have one in peace. I've had a shit morning."

"Why? You didn't do your running this morning?" Brij

pants like a dog.

Gaurav sucks hard and throws the smoldering stub in the drain. "Lets go, come on. I won't make it on time."

The motorbike splutters through the lanes and out onto the main road.

Brij adjusts his sunglasses. "Where to today?"

"Parel."

"One hour at the least it will take you. In this heat you will become chutney by the time you reach—"

"What else to do? As if I have uncles who are sitting near my house to offer me a job."

"I have been telling you for the longest time but you don't listen. Every day you go roaming in the sun looking for a job like the million other graduates. Leave it all. Do what I do. Selling used cars is good money. I switch one or two parts inside the car and the buggers don't even come to know. You see me in five years, I will have my very own car. My colleagues are lazy, they should just keep going the way they are; keep on making their stupid excuses and miss work. Whole day they are killing one family member or the other. One can't come because the father is in hospital, the other's kid has a fever, someone else has to visit relatives in the village. No drive, no motivation these scoundrels have. I will keep closing all the sales and raking in the commissions. I swear that Pradeep's mother has died five times, and the bastard is an orphan."

"You know what? If I don't get something soon I will

have to take you up on it. I am sick of running around on this toaster."

"That it is. Every time I get off my butt is burnt. Change the cushioning."

"*Saala,* every day you get a free ride and then you complain about cushioning."

"You are the one that started the complaining. I was sitting here enjoying the putrid dusty Bombay wind hit my face. So what happened today anyway? He said something again?"

"He doesn't need to say anything. The way he looks at me is enough. I can't wait to get a job and get lost from his shitty house."

"Arrey stop stop, you're driving right past my place." Brij jumps off the bike before Gaurav can bring it to a stand still. He grips his friend's shoulder reassuringly. "Don't worry *yaar,* today it will happen."

Gaurav waits at a red light on the junction of Grayor Road. He squints into the distance to see the bold lettering atop the tall green building; ATUL TOWERS. He glances at his watch. It is a quarter past nine, thirty minutes before his interview. Plenty of time.

He twists his torso and stretches out his arms trying to relieve the soreness in his back. *About time these useless government people paid attention to the roads. They need to fill the potholes instead of their pockets. Promises after promises. Bloody rogues.* He decides he will vote for the opposition in the next elections.

He checks his reflection in the side view mirror and runs his hands through his hair. He will have to find a bathroom to wash his face before he goes in for the interview because it is covered in grime from the hour of travel in the clogged Bombay highways. He can see the streaks of sweat that have sliced through the layer of dust on his cheek and the side of his face.

An elderly man negotiates his way in careful measured steps along the footpath. His skin is leathery and wrinkled; he is stick thin with a head of scanty silver.

The light turns yellow. Gaurav clamps his foot on the clutch. There is a loud shriek, and the bustling pavement comes to a halt. Everyone turns in the direction of the scream.

"*Chor! Chor! Mera* bag!"

It is the old man. A young boy races away with the man's cloth bag clenched tightly in his fist. Because Gaurav has himself been a victim of snatch theft, it does not take any hesitation before he jumps from the seat of his bike and gives chase. Bystanders are doing what they do best: they are by-standing with the impotence of stunned statues.

Gaurav pins the teenager down to the ground. He had lost three hundred rupees to a thief like this and now having this boy in his grasp feels as though he is getting even. Gaurav sits on top of the thief and more curious pedestrians gather. They have finally found some shreds of bravery, just enough to hurl abuse from a safe distance.

"You bloody dog, you should be put on a leash!"

"Jail the rascal!"

"Go back to your house so your mother can change your diaper!"

Gaurav pulls the boy to his feet by his collar. The thief bolts, tripping over once, recovering quickly and then scurrying off into an alley. Gaurav watches him go, dusts the earth from his clothes and staggers over to the old man to hand the bag back to him. More noise from the crowd ensues. They begin to praise the vanquisher.

"*Arrey*, what a hero."

"Full Amitabh style—height is also same."

" ... what to do? Police are all sleeping, we have to look after ourselves."

The old man's voice quivers, "Thank you son, it would have posed a big problem for me if this bag were lost."

"It's nothing. Come, let me drop you to the end of the road." Gaurav starts his bike and gestures the man to sit behind him.

"Thank you. Just drop me off at Atul Towers up ahead. I have to deliver some urgent papers to my daughter in that building."

Gaurav is squashed in the elevator with six men and three women. He sweats at the brow. He may look like all these people in the tie and shirt and belt but inside he feels like an impostor. They are the chosen ones, they have jobs, they are the employed middle class of India. This interview had better go well. He can't take another day of roaming the streets. If he only got his foot in the door, he thinks, he would outperform them all.

He shuffles to adjust his shoulders and prepares to alight on the fourth floor. The doors open directly into the posh reception of Zinmac Industries Private Company Limited. He steps out into the cool blast of the air-conditioning. He can't believe his luck that he even heard back from this company. The reception area is modern unlike all the other obscure hole in the wall offices he's been to. This place is posh with leather sofas and a coffee table, a curved grey reception desk, a floor that shines so bright he can see a bit of his own reflection in it.

"Excuse me," he says to the petite, glassy-eyed receptionist. Her head is shaped like a rat, the front of her face protruding as a snout would. He finds her unsettling because he is terrified of rats.

He'd developed the phobia the night his sleep was interrupted by a clammy, uncomfortable sensation in his big toe. In his half awake half asleep state, he jerked his foot but a weight clung to it and there was a tugging pinch in his toe. He forced his frozen body up and found himself staring into the beady insidious eyes of a fat furry rat. In its mouth, it held a sizable chunk of his flesh. Of course he shrieked in terror and grabbed his pillow, shooing it away. It did scamper off through the windowsill but not with any urgency. Shameless.

He had to see a doctor and get a few injections, take an infinite number of pills and have a bandaged toe for a long time. After that, every night for weeks he lay awake listening to the scratching that came from the pipes in the walls, from behind his building where they scavenged in the garbage dump, and many times from within his own head.

And when he did manage to sleep, nightmares haunted him. He dreamed of droves of them infesting his room, his house, the alleys and roads, the whole district. They always ended with him being buried in thousands of them, every inch of his flesh gnawed and chewed to the bone. Many nights he awoke with phantom nibbling sensations in all parts of his body.

"Can I help you?" The woman's voice is squeaky and shrill.

"I am here for an interview."

She hands him a clipboard and he starts to fill out a form.

"You can sit over there." She waves him to the plush red sofa.

He sits down and starts to fill it out, the usual questions that he's answered dozens of times on forms like this. Senseless really, they have his CV, they know his gender.

When he is finished he hands it over to that rat lady

and waits to be called. The phones ring without respite and her manicured hands shuffle between the three sets with efficiency.

No, I told you already Mr Bahri is not in today.

Yes, please hold.

We are on the third floor.

She is in a meeting, can I take a message?

He surmises she must have been working here long and tries to make a rough estimation of her salary. Two thousand rupees? Three? More?

He waits with veiled impatience. It would be a dream come true to get a job here. A few minutes pass, the elevator doors open again and he is surprised to see the old man he had dropped off in the lobby only a few minutes ago before he'd gone off to park his bike. And now here the man is, hobbling out toward the reception. Gaurav is about to get up and greet him but the man proceeds single-pointed toward the reception desk and speaks with Rat Lady. They whisper and they chat and he hands her some files from the very same bag Gaurav helped him recover.

Now that Gaurav really looks at them, he sees that there is a similarity in their features. Similar chin beneath the silver stubble the old man has. And yes, his head too is a egg-like. Could they be related? Had he done a favour to an insider? Was there something here to leverage on?

The implications of this could change everything. A rush of excitement runs through him as he approaches them both.

"*Beta*, you are here?" The old man is overjoyed to see Gaurav. "This is the brave boy I was just telling you about," he says to the Rat Lady.

Her beady eyes soften.

"Thank you so much for helping my father. I really needed these." She blushes and it only makes her look uglier. "I'm so sorry it has been a busy morning. Let me get you a glass of water while you wait. I will try to speed things up."

By the time he has drained the glass she has brought him, Gaurav knows that Brij was right. Today it will happen.

⁓ↄ⁓

The shiny silver plaque on the walnut-coloured door reads, "Executive Director."

Gaurav draws in a long hard breath, clears his throat, and knocks.

"Come in," a severe voice replies from inside the room.

A grand mahogany desk graces the centre of the room. Behind it on an oversized leather chair sits a man that Gaurav is certain is the lost twin brother of his math teacher from the ninth standard. The bald shiny head, the pointed beak-like nose, and the ears that stick out awkwardly. The resemblance is strangely comforting, and Gaurav is less nervous because of it.

When Mr Bindra moves to pick up his cup and sips it, Gaurav sees that although they are uncannily alike, there is no similarity in demeanour. Professor Kamble was a clumsy man of inexplicable uneasiness. Things were always slipping out of his hands or from under his feet. Either he was dropping his textbook, or searching for the pen stuck in his ear, or tripping over himself.

This man here moves with delicate deliberation and admirable confidence. He is the kind of man people open the car door for, the kind one expects to see lunching elegantly at the Palace Hotel, the kind that knows something others don't and the kind that can change Gaurav's life. He is the kind of man Gaurav wants to be.

Mr. Bindra does not look up from his stack of papers. The silver fountain pen in his hand moves deftly over the bottom of a page. He sets it aside. And signs another. And another.

"Please." Pause. "Take a seat."

Gaurav does as he is told. This is the first time in his life he is seated in front of a man of such importance and affluence. Butterflies flutter in his chest, not a result of anxiety but of impending possibility. He takes in the opulence of the spacious and well-decorated room. Potted plants on the windowsill, a marble top coffee table with carved wooden legs, a finely tufted leather sofa set (much nicer than the one he sat on in the waiting area), filing cabinets crafted in oak.

The director finally places his pen down on his desk and looks up. Gaurav shifts and swallows the odd ball in his throat. A cough escapes.

"Are you sick?" Bindra cocks his head back as though afraid to catch the flu.

"No, sir. Not at all."

Bindra inhales thoughtfully and leans back. The large chair makes a squeaky sound as it dutifully bends to accommodate it's occupant. "I have seen your resume,"

Gaurav does not know if this statement warrants a reply and so he chooses to remain silent. Bindra waits, his eyes boring into Gaurav's face.

"Yes, sir," Gaurav finally blurts to ease the tension.

"This does not happen often." Mr. Bindra shrugs. "I don't usually do the interviewing for these kinds of roles."

Again, Gaurav thinks of something to say. What comes to mind is, *I know*. But he bites his tongue. Rat Lady has already told him that because his application is for a position in Finance, he is supposed to be interviewed by the CFO. And if the CFO is unavailable for some reason, he would have been interviewed by the Human Resources Director. Both of these great men have chosen today of all days to go on "emergency leave." If the norms of the common Indian employee apply, then emergency leave is most likely a visit to the in-laws or a hangover from last night's drinking.

Rat Lady has also told him not to worry, "You will be in there for five minutes max. He is not going to ask you about your education or your experience. Your resume is on his table. He will ask you the same questions he asks all the people he interviews."

She then proceeded to divulge unsolicited information on the standard interviewing questions Mr. Bindra is known to ask a candidate. Gaurav has already formulated the answers. He feels like he has entered an examination having seen the question papers already.

Mr. Bindra declares with authority, "I am not going to ask you about your education, I have read your resume. I am more interested to learn your thoughts and your aspirations."

I know.

"If today was the last day of your life, what is the one thing you would make sure you do?"

Bingo.

Gaurav's muscles relax and he tries to swallow his triumphant smile. "I would fix the problem of the study table in my bedroom, sir."

Mr. Bindra furrows his brows and leans a little closer. "That is a rather unexpected answer."

"I don't like leaving things unfinished, sir."

"What is wrong with your study table, Mr Gaurav?"

"It has a shaky leg, sir."

"Oh so you're a procrastinator, you've been waiting till the day you die to fix it," Mr. Bindra says with a faint tremor of amusement in his voice.

Gaurav uncrosses his legs, sits up straighter, leans forward and looks Bindra directly in the eye. "No Sir, I have been waiting for a job like this so I can buy a new one."

CHAPTER TWO

25th April, 1985, Bombay

Asha.

A calmness settles in his spirit each time he utters her name. It is the most beautiful arrangement of syllables he has ever encountered. He mouths every single one with deep affection. The *aah* is released in a breath that is the sweetest of sighs. The *shh* and *aah* quieten his mind as his senses take her in. His soul rests in its sound as his lips taste sunshine and honey.

Asha—how fitting is the meaning of her Sanskrit name. Her parents must have known the moment they held her in their arms and sensed it the second they laid eyes on her, from her very first delicate breath, that she was someone's Wish, Desire and Hope.

There are so many things about her that he loves. When

people walk past her casually, and not note her, not stop to take in her beauty, it always surprises him. Can they not see what he sees? Do they not grasp the enormity of her being? Perhaps they are blind, and he alone is lucky enough to see.

He is lucky, very lucky that he has her. Having a lover who makes a man want to be his best is a powerful thing, for he acquires strange new gems that were previously absent from his personality. Like a bud kissed by sunlight, he blossoms. Humor, wisdom, courage, loyalty, strength all come as boons from the Gods, bestowed as tokens of appreciation, as encouragement to love more and more.

Gaurav needs no encouragement though. Loving Asha comes as easily as breathing. When she smiles, he can taste it. When she sighs, his own breath slows. When she looks into his eyes, his soul undresses for her.

They meet every day. In the months when the madness of the Bombay monsoons isn't upon them like a deranged mistress, they walk along Marine Drive taking in the steady rhythm of waves crashing against rock.

"She does this on purpose," Asha says.

"Who does what?"

"She's sprinkling blessings."

"Oh, the sea. Pray tell why."

"She approves. She wants us to stay like this forever."

He squeezes her hand tight. A part of him believes her. They fit so perfectly after all. The sea may very well have noticed.

"This smell is making me hungry," she says as they pass the hawkers and the fragrance of peanuts roasting in spices fills the air.

Gaurav stops and takes out a ten-rupee note, offering it to the toothless vendor. The old man rolls up a newspaper cone and pours two scoopfuls of nuts into it.

"Do that thing, *na*," she says.

"You never tire of it?" He places a peanut on his palm, claps his fingers with the other hand and sends the peanut flying into his open mouth. She laughs as though she's never seen it before. And he gets his reward in the dimples that appear in her cheeks.

"You know what will be good with this? Tea. Let's go get some." She waves a taxi even before he can reply. He follows her the way he would like to for the rest of his life.

They arrive at Babulnath Road in minutes and settle in a cozy corner of the teashop which really is more of a dump and hardly a romantic place. But it serves the best milk tea in town and it is where they first met. Well, perhaps "meet" is the wrong word. It is where he first laid eyes on her and when his universe first shifted. A thatched roof, rusty wrought iron tables and rickety wooden chairs, clay stoves and wood fires surround them. Not exactly a place one would expect to come face to face with one's destiny.

"*Sahib*, you are looking." Chotu had chuckled at Gaurav that day. "Chai is getting cold and Sahib is getting warm."

Gaurav had playfully slapped the boy's back, "You should be in school, rascal, not serving tea and samosas and harassing customers."

"What to do *Sahib*, this is only being my transit stop job. When I become a hero, nobody is asking for degree, only autograph." Chotu flicked his hair and pulled his non-existent collar up. "But you are finding heroine already." Chotu raised his eyebrows and smiled cheekily, gesturing at the stranger. "She is coming first time."

Gaurav clucked his tongue and hissed, "Softly." He slipped the boy five rupees. "Who is she?" he whispered.

He had noticed her not because she was beautiful, not because of the way she tilted her head back when she laughed, or how a giggle left her lips effortlessly. Not even because of the way her eyes shone like black diamonds in a pearly sea or that ever so faint dimple in her left cheek that made her look like a girl child in the body of a woman. He noticed her because his heart recognised her from somewhere. Like some missing part that he had been born without had finally been found in this most mediocre of places.

She sat with another girl, but that face didn't register. He only saw the perfectness of her presence and the hankering in his heart.

"I don't know *Sahib*. I told you *na*, first time coming. *Sahib*, I can be your connection." Chotu grinned naughtily and extended out his hand. Gaurav blushed, but slipped him another fiver. He then scribbled on a piece of paper, *Me breathing the same air as you is a cause for celebration. Dinner or lunch?*

Chotu delivered the note with a smile and a wink, gesturing at Gaurav's table. Asha—of course he hadn't known her name then—had glared at him angrily. He thought she looked adorable, so he smiled in return. She thumped the table, paid the bill and stormed off.

But Chotu had already overheard the girls' conversation earlier and it only took a pair of sunglasses from Chor Bazaar for him to share the valuable information that the girls were from Rapson College three bus stops away.

Thus began Gaurav's part-time career as a watchman. He skipped his own classes and waited for hours outside her college, watching for her. Days elapsed, then weeks without sight nor sound of her. Then one perfectly ordinary day, as he waited beneath a tree in the scorching sun, he saw the friend who had been at the teashop with Asha. He approached her with the eagerness of a man having found water after a long drought. He requested that she "please, please" formally introduce him to Asha.

She offered him only a crumb of consolation. "I will have to check with her, you know." She then laughed as though he was the most awkward act from the circus. And all the other girls in the group laughed too.

If you asked Gaurav, he would say he thought it went rather well and that the chances were good his love story was about to begin. But Asha on the other hand, laughed at his utter madness when her friends told her of his request.

"He loiters there for hours every day waiting for you."

"I have been wondering who is the good-looking man standing in the sun and the rain."

"I think he is in love with you."

"*Arrey*, he is not bad. If he loses that ugly bike, you should consider."

Her reply was simple. "How ridiculous! He thinks he is in the movies."

He waited and waited. Every time he saw Asha's friends, he would try and enquire as to whether they had helped convey his message. They avoided him like the plague. His prospects for a happy ending were growing grim as there seemed to be no beginning.

Then out of the blue, when he had almost given up, the wheel of fortune turned in his favour. The rain hammered down and the gusts of winds forced the smaller shops shut but Gaurav stood there drenched to the bone and shivering like a leaf. She could see him from inside the college gates. She had actually been seeing him for all the weeks that passed. Of course he didn't know. But on that day, as he shuddered and shook, as the rain fell and as the thunder clapped, she melted away. She could take this no more. She opened her umbrella and went outside to meet him.

"You think you are some hero? Why do you wait like this every day?" She held the umbrella above them both.

"In the hope that you will notice me."

She giggled. "You're insane."

He was. And she loved him for it.

They have barely sipped their chai when the bells from the temple ring. "Can you hear it? It's just starting. Let's go *na*, just for the *aarti*."

They step out into the busy street. The moon hangs like a pearl set in the amethyst sky. All that is unruly roams the streets. People jaywalk, illegal hawkers trade their wares of food and drink, cars honk with abandon, half-naked beggars tap windows and people for a few *paise*.

But this is Bombay, and people know to duck when an errant auto rickshaw appears out of nowhere; they know to swerve out of the way of the old man carting empty glass bottles or watermelons, they know even without looking to step over and not onto despicable things left carelessly on the footpath.

Gaurav grips Asha's hand tightly and they cross through the rowdy traffic. They come to the cluttered shacks at the foot of the temple. It is the oldest place of worship in the city. Vendors peddle prayer beads, coconuts, sandalwood powder, garlands, flowers, and fruit.

She picks out a garland of red roses and white chrysanthemums, and they make their way up the long sets of well-worn stone stairs.

"May he who makes the earth spin without falling, the sun shine without burning away, he who placed the soft sky as a blanket over his children, may he forever keep the young hearts tied together in love," intones a grave old man sitting on the landing at the last flight of steps. His gangly body is bare to the waist and he is seated in lotus position. Awry strands of thin silver hair fall from his sunken cheeks to his chest, his forehead streaked with three lines of ash. He looks much like the sages in the mythological comics Gaurav read as a child.

"He's a fortune teller," Asha exclaims, "and he just blessed us,"

Gaurav does not much believe in the occult or the ritualistic. He has always been of the opinion that engaging with men like these is a form of encouragement to their dubious trade. And he definitely does not like the sight of this man. But Asha is already bubbling with excitement and pulling him towards the old man. He cannot bring himself to disappoint her, so he goes along. Together they sit down on the damp stone floor in front of him.

The psychic smiles, exposing his chipped, reddish, tobacco-stained teeth. He welcomes them by anointing their foreheads with ash. His long fingers reach for Asha's hand; his nails are long and there is dirt, most likely ash beneath them. He examines her palm like a surgeon peering into an open torso, studying the erratic lines for a long time and then knits his eyebrows. His face tilts this way and that. He brings her palm up closer up almost to his nose. The look of confusion in the old man's face makes Gaurav uncomfortable.

The man meets Asha's eyes with sympathy and softness.

He then crumples his forehead in resignation and shakes his head, as though offering his condolences.

"What?" Gaurav finally asks when Asha's eyes start to glisten with tears.

He drops her hand and peers at Gaurav as though he is a guilty man, as though he has committed the worst of sins. "Not meant to be," the man finally mutters.

"What is not meant to be?" Asha exclaims.

Gaurav grabs her arm. "Let's go."

With tears flowing, she follows him up to the doorway of the main temple. There they stand, looking into each others eyes, his tender and hers moist. Gaurav holds her hands in his own. "He doesn't even know us, they are here for money; they know nothing but to prey on the ignorant and superstitious."

She nods and he wipes her tears with his fingers. His broad arms encompass her delicate body. "You wanted to go inside before they finished the hymns."

Lamps that are lit with clarified butter illuminate the temple for the evening prayers. The chorus of classical songs fill the open space and the sunset offering of gratitude for the blessing of another day is about to begin.

They stand among the crowd in front of the sanctum sanatorium. Inside is a brass idol of the three-eyed Shiva. Gaurav reaches out for the vermilion paste at the corner of the altar. He takes a pinch between his thumb and forefinger.

"No," she quivers. "This means . . ."

"I know what it means," he says with the confidence of a man who has made his decision.

She smiles now and she trembles. "Gaurav," she whispers, "there is nothing else I want more."

"I know. There is nothing I have been surer of in my life. It is a matter of time anyway; in a year or two this will happen in front of the world. Why not prove the old scoundrel wrong here and now?"

"But my parents, your parents . . ."

"Shh . . . don't think so much. No announcements. Just you and me for now. We will work the rest out later."

With a smile on his lips, and Shiva as his witness, he does what only a husband can do for his wife. Using his forefinger, he rubs a line through the parting of her hair with the red paste. He then anoints her forehead with a red dot.

"I love you," he whispers. "If there is anything that is meant to be, it is us. Forever."

CHAPTER THREE

7th October, 1987, Bombay

If one desires to know a man's character, one must give him power.

There are two choices available to men. There is the good, and there is the pleasant. The good is an arduous choice, paved with hardship. It is the road less travelled, but one where the end is most certainly worth the journey. The pleasant is usually the preferred choice, the road of instant gratification, lined with little parcels of happiness and comfort. But this path ends with wretched sorrow.

∽◡∾

GAURAV DUBEY

Supervisor, Purchasing

Zinmac Ind. Pvt. Co. Ltd.

His name has never before been a thing of value to anyone but him. He has written it hundreds of times on his exercise books, his school lunch box, test papers, forms, his resume and countless other insignificant places. But now it stares back at him printed in bold and capitalised letters holding a dazzling new promise.

Somewhat powerful and somewhat valuable.

The space above it is bare and beckoning. He looks at it, into it, through it till the print blurs and his eyes water. *Go on, one little scribble,* he tells himself.

He picks up his fountain pen; its smooth thick surface between his fingers is familiar and comfortable. He has used this pen to sign dozens of documents daily. But never has he deliberated this long. He poises its nib on the sheet and his hand almost starts to move. Almost.

Poor Gaurav. One can't but feel a slight tinge of empathy for the man. Undoubtedly, it is difficult and many struggle with decisions like these. Honesty is an immensely delicate virtue. It is easily breached. So very few are able to withstand temptation—even fewer when no one is looking.

This is a big step. And as is common with all first times, there is hesitation, there is angst.

He considers what this will mean for him. If he signs, will he get caught? And if he does get caught, what will the consequences be? But again, how will he ever get caught? Certainly he will be careful. *It is a win-win situation*, he reasons with himself. The more he tosses the man's proposal in his head, the less dishonourable it starts to appear.

A stranger had first called two nights before. Gaurav had finished his dinner and retired to the privacy of his room after the obligatory fifteen minutes of polite conversation with his mother (and in the unpleasant company of his silent, judicious father.)

"Phone call for you," his mother said, knocking his door with urgency. Surely it wasn't Asha. They'd just met that evening.

"He says his name is Parekh. He is from your office." She seemed quite pleased at a call from his workplace late at night. Surely this meant her son was important, indispensable. It was an urgent matter, the man had said, and this delighted her even more.

The man's name didn't ring a bell, but Gaurav took the call anyway.

"Sir, sorry to be disturbing you late at night." The stranger's voice was gruff, but sickeningly enthusiastic as he introduced himself.

Phoenix Dyes and Chemicals. Gaurav vaguely recognised the name. He'd seen the letterhead. It could have been on one of the recent quotations he'd received. His firm was looking to buy resins for one of their manufacturing subsidiaries and many companies had submitted quotes for the lucrative contract. Gaurav, as the head of purchasing, was the man who would eventually decide who clinched the deal.

"We have submitted the tender last month. We would

be the most best choice," the man said, before butchering his second language some more, "we are economical and very pleasure to work with."

"How did you get my home number?" Gaurav asked. He made an effort to sound annoyed although he quite enjoyed being buttered up rather than being the one doing the buttering.

"Please don't be angry Sir, we had to search a great deal. I am sorry to disturb in your family time. But these discussions require a relaxed mood. May I request we can meet you tomorrow at a place of your choice? We can explain in detail why we will be the best choice for you."

Man's first brush with his moral compass is an interesting thing. Gaurav's pulse jolted then thumped as he begun to comprehend the possibilities of such a meeting. At first he thought to politely decline and hang up. But then...

"Palace Hotel," Gaurav said, "we can have breakfast at 7:30. I only have half an hour."

He arrived early on his bike—though the hotel was only across the road—because he would have to go to work straight after. He parked the unsightly vehicle a few hundred meters away, out of sight of the posh building.

A bearded and turbaned doorman greeted him with a *Namaste* and a respectful bow, then waved him through the palatial glass doors of the hotel. The lobby smelled of fresh lilies and tea brewing with cloves. The hotel had been refurbished since his stolen visits years ago. High ceilings, commissioned art on the large walls, opulent chandeliers with glittering crystals hanging above, it was all beyond luxurious. He sank into a love seat in the lobby. And he waited.

The best place for worry is an idle mind. So he began to worry. He began to wonder if he blended in and checked himself against the scattered guests. Sure he looked like them, but they all seemed so comfortable inside themselves and inside this place. They moved with an assuredness that this is where they belong. They weren't worried. He was. What if he was spotted by an employee who for some inexplicable reason knew he was the invasive voyeur from across the road. What if they had seen him spend hours watching the balconies of their hotel? Worse still, what if they recognised him as the boy who got caught stealing chocolates all those years ago?

His eyes searched the area; maybe the man who'd slapped him so mercilessly was here somewhere and would discover him. Security would be called, he would be escorted out.

Beggar. Bastard. People like you don't belong here. Gutter class.

The words tumbled through his brain like the small stones that rattled in his pocket when he was a boy.

Ridiculous, he thought. *Get ahold of yourself.* He shifted in his seat, tried to relax his legs, sat back and focused on breathing evenly.

Parekh arrived with a protruding belly and questionable

taste in ties.

"Mr. Gaurav?"

"Yes, hello."

Clammy handshake. Awkward smiling. Coffee shop for breakfast.

"We are not trying to influence your decision at all," Parekh said as he spooned a heap of scrambled eggs onto Gaurav's crowded plate. They were the yellowest he had ever seen.

A waiter filled his glass with chilled orange juice. Guarav replied evenly, "I recall your price being on the high side."

"Sir, our quality is better."

"How so?"

"We can provide better service." The glint in the man's eye was unmistakable. "We can provide many extra benefits, Sir."

The man went on about the history of his company, the location of their factory and the names of firms he had done business with. None of this interested Gaurav at all. What did interest Gaurav at that moment was the waiter pouring buttermilk into his glass. How they got it so thick and creamy was beyond his understanding. He'd never tasted anything that rich. Come to think of it, he'd never felt this rich either.

Gaurav was sorry when breakfast ended. But he was full and content. Parekh called for the check and pulled out a fat wad of currency. As he flicked through the lump of fortune, Gaurav eyed the bills of larger denominations. He counted, one, two, three, and then one, two. Almost two thousand rupees went in the bill-bearing leather folder. Parekh then pulled out some smaller bills from the middle of the bundle—three hundred rupees to be exact—and placed it over the two thousand.

"Tips," he said with a smile of mock humility.

Gaurav coughed uncomfortably, arose from his seat, folded his napkin and placed it on the empty chair. "I have to get going." He glanced at his watch.

"Oh yes sir, of course, you are an important man. Thank you for joining me today and giving me your precious time."

He shook Parekh's pudgy hand and then with careful discretion wiped his own hands on the back of the finely upholstered dining chair. He began rubbing the back of his neck as he considered the conversation. Parekh was still with him and still speaking of the fine advantages of his company's product. To Gaurav, it was just noise and he couldn't hear any of it. He was too busy thinking about the unwelcome possibility that this man would now offer to chaperone him to his vehicle and god forbid see Gaurav's colossal hunk of rickety scrap. What a highly embarrassing exposure that would be.

"Can I drop you to your office, sir?" asked Parekh, again too politely.

The stone in Gaurav's throat melted and he almost

sighed out loud in relief. "Sure, that is perfect. I came in a taxi," he said, quite willing to tolerate the irritating man for a little longer.

They approached a silvery grey car at the open car park. Parekh beeped the vehicle, and Gaurav entered the passenger door. The car smelled sharp and woody.

Parekh took the wheel and stated the obvious. "New car, sir." He then fiddled with the dials. DJ Akhil's voice boomed through the speakers, cool, clear and crisp with not a shred of static, as though he was in the car with them. Asha's favourite song came on, a slow ballad about lovers meeting like waves in the ocean. Gaurav wished she were here with him to see this car, to see how soft the cushioning was, how wide the seats were, how smooth the ride was.

Parekh was unusually silent through the drive and when they arrived in the vicinity of Gaurav's office, he parked the car away from the main entrance on a side street in the shade of an old oak tree. He alighted from the vehicle and jogged around it in time to open the door for Gaurav.

"Thank you for the breakfast and the ride," Gaurav said politely. He was careful not to extend his hand for another damp handshake. But Parekh offered and Gaurav had no choice but to oblige him. As the two men shook their goodbye, Gaurav felt a hard object in Parekh's palm. When they parted, Gaurav was left holding it.

"It is brand new sir, please do us the honour," Parekh said, looking around nervously. He then began to walk away, turned around once, folded his hands in a Namaste, smiled awkwardly and kept walking, faster and faster till he was out of sight. Gaurav stood there, key in hand and a car that was not his. Not yet.

Gaurav thinks now that perhaps he should have given chase right then. Or called Parekh soon after to inform him that this is an unacceptable behaviour. Two days have passed, and he is still in possession of the key and the man's calling card. He has used neither.

A loud knock at the door brings Gaurav back to the four walls of his office. It is three-thirty and the tea lady wants to know if Gaurav wants a samosa with his chai. He waves her away and picks up his pen yet again. Grit from the polluted roads roll in his fingers as he rubs the back of his neck. It wasn't there yesterday when he was inside a vehicle instead of on top of it. Yesterday he had arrived at work with his shirt fresh and crisp and his body still smelling of soap.

There are far-away places he can take Asha in this car. They will play songs on the radio. He can see this so clearly now, he can even hear the music. He has some cassettes at home that have all her favourite songs on them. She will hum along when they are played in the car, when she is next to him. He can hold her hand with one hand while he drives with the other. The road will be smooth beneath the wheels. They will go for long drives to nowhere. They can drive forever because they will be comfortable in the leather seats and in the air-conditioning. He will lean over and kiss her as they lie on the hood beneath the stars.

She will like the colour of the car, she likes silver. She

will be so happy. She is worthy of it, worthy of the best that life has to offer. He eyes the key again, the calling card, and then the agreement with Phoenix Dyes and Chemicals.

It is hard. Very hard. But some lines, once crossed, disappear altogether.

CHAPTER FOUR

10th May, 1988, Khandala

Gaurav returns, out of breath but refreshed. It is nicer to run in the silence of the valley and the cool mist of the hilly terrains. The weather at the hill station, especially in the early morning hours, is a welcome contrast from the punishing, year-round heat of Bombay. There is none of the crude and unnecessary honking, no human traffic to jostle through, no repulsive stretches of injured footpath and no stench of city garbage. It is just him, the grassy plains, and the slumbering sun.

He clicks his key into the keyhole of room 362 on the third floor of Hotel Metropolitan as silently as he can. He turns the doorknob and pushes the door open. Asha stirs, adjusting her naked shoulders beneath the covers. Splendidly they curve into comfort as she settles onto her stomach. He catches a glimpse of her bare breasts as she turns and he resists the urge to touch her.

Instead he climbs into the shower. Had he been able to afford another couple of hundred rupees, he would not have had to wrestle with the faucet in protest at iced water that spurts out as though it flows down directly from the tip of the Himalayas.

He soaps his hair, thinking of the Palace Hotel. What might the temperature of the water in the showers there be?

He shudders in the cold water before his body acclimatises. He is grateful that the hotel is clean at least. And Asha did not complain even when they had to call in the housekeeping last night to unjam the window. In fact, she never complains about anything. She is good that way, not at all a hard woman to please. It is one of the many reasons he loves her.

After he dries off, he creeps softly under the covers and lays beside her, letting his hands wander over the curve of her back, to the nape of her neck and then to her hair. He plays with her curls, such soft curls. He twirls locks of them around his fingers.

"Aren't you tired?" She turns over and purrs. Her eyes are listless and drowsy, the same way they are when they make love. His hands begin to roam her body.

She meets his eyes, takes his hand away from her thighs and brings it to her lips. "Again? Really? And you've been out this morning too. Where do you get the energy?"

"Hmm, you energise me." He kisses her forehead and

trails his fingertips over her waist. "I could go on forever."

She whimpers, "I'm so tired, enough my sweet, we really need to stop. We shouldn't be doing any of this."

Gaurav gets off his elbow, lays on his back and exhales in frustration. "We are engaged for gods' sake, the wedding is months away, it's all official. Your parents have even made the announcement to family, they approve of me. What is all this guilt about?"

"Yes they do, but they don't approve of us going away on a dirty weekend like this. Do you know how many stories I had to make up? They think my whole office is on this big outstation trip for this grand seminar on applied techniques for vertical farming."

He laughs. "What the heck is vertical farming? It's the eighties. What do they expect? That they will hand me a woman as beautiful as you and I will hold hands and sip from the same straw?" He kisses her lips, gently, tenderly.

"Oh so now it's my fault, isn't it?" She giggles and pulls away. She rises from the bed and covers her bare body with the bed sheet. "I'm going to get dressed, and you, my dear stallion, are going to feed me. This is not humane at all you know, working me all night and then starving me like this; I could report you for abuse."

He tugs at the edge of the crumpled sheet, pulling her back into his arms. "Oh yeah? Who's abusing who? This is deprivation."

She opens her mouth in mock horror. "Deprivation?"

She giggles, "Oh please, you're hardly deprived; you were quite a busy man last night. Come on now, let's go. Don't you have to get home soon, too? Tomorrow's the run, right? Is Brij finally going with you?"

"Yes, he's the only one in our group who's not from Zinmac." Gaurav gives up and gets off the bed. He carries her effortlessly into the shower, "Let us feed you now and get you home safe to your old-fashioned father."

"Yes, let's get me home early so your future father-in-law doesn't get wind of what you've been up to."

CHAPTER FIVE

11th May 1988

The athletes gather before dawn like a flock of kingfishers. The only difference between the two is that the humans stand beneath the Gothic domes of Victoria Terminus Station, and the birds are perched high above. Both sets of creatures flutter with enthusiasm for their voyage, for the day will soon begin.

The runners will cover twenty-odd kilometres of the city's crowded pavements, starting at the Terminus, sprinting past the Mahalaxmi Temple, and then through Flora Fountain. The concrete route is anything but scenic.

Participants for today number at more than a hundred divided into five teams from five different companies. Young and nimble men and women, dressed in their breathable sports shirts and track pants in different colours for different companies, with logos of the Chamber of Commerce and the National Leprosy Foundation embroidered on their lapels.

Gaurav had introduced the concept of running to a wary group at Zinmac. One bought in, then another and another. Now he has an eager herd of followers. Even Brij has become a believer after having buckled under the years of Gaurav's tenacious persuasion. The sport enhanced his performance in a variety of aspects, both decent and otherwise. Gaurav's devoted mentees love the sport now; their paunches and hunches, thyroids and haemorrhoids have started to behave.

Thus Gaurav had to be the guru of the runners and a team leader by proxy. He was the one that planned and signed up for community runs such as these.

He cranes his neck to perform a routine headcount. One, two, three ... he counts to sixteen but wait, there is one more than there should be. There are seventeen heads. He starts over. Still seventeen. He looks to Brij. "How many did I say there were for today?"

"Sixteen including us both."

He re-checks his list and then examines each face in his group. It is hard to make out their features in the dim light of dawn. At best, it gives him sight like watching an old copy of a black and white movie.

He squints, turns his head this way and that before Gomez from Logistics, a feisty and fast sprinter with calf muscles so taut you could play a tune on them, approaches him with a stranger in tow.

"This is Barkha. Barkha, meet Gaurav, he's the boss of us today."

She is slender. Her hair is pulled back into a neat ponytail, accentuating her oval but sculpted face. She is tall for a woman, her eyes the same level as his. She wears trainers that glow yellow neon, the expensive variety. Barkha extends her hand. "Hi, Barkha Bindra. Sorry, I know this is last minute, but I just joined the company and only heard about this over the weekend. I love to run, so I couldn't resist."

Her last name has an effect quite like the grandfather clock in his house. He is startled. But he's also grateful that the sun isn't out yet so she cannot see the way his face has twitched awkwardly at the sound of her name. "Not a problem, I'll just run over and register you with the organisers. Be right back."

Brij follows him. "She's hot," he says as they near the registration desk, "you should have introduced us."

Gaurav whacks him on the back, "Oh please, don't even think about it. Her last name is Bindra. She must be related to my boss."

CHAPTER SIX

12th May, 1988

It is lunch hour, and the offices of Zinmac resemble a ghost town. Gaurav is the single unfortunate audience of an unpleasant choir of phones that ring in insistent succession at one work station after the other. On and on they chime, not to be answered till the clock turns two and their owners return. Less offensive pings and bings echo from the communications room where the machines are stationed; telex, facsimile, printers.

Gaurav cannot afford to take the full hour of his lunch break. He has a deadline to meet, so he has purchased a chicken puff from "Ali's Special Veg and Non Veg Canteen" on his way to work earlier in the day. With it, he got two paper towels, a plastic fork, and a packet of nowhere near enough ketchup.

He settles at his desk, tears a portion of the paper towel, divides it into two, rolls the two pieces into balls and plugs his ears.

Ah much better.

The other piece he unfolds and places over his desk to serve as both plate and table mat. He sinks his teeth into the pastry. There is no evidence of chicken, all he gets in his mouth is salty baked dough that leaves a thick layer of cheap plasticky butter on his tongue.

Scoundrels.

He bites deeper toward the middle and finally encounters a dry crumbly texture that he presumes is the mince. It smells dubiously sour and tastes nothing like chicken.

Bastards.

Fifteen good rupees for this glob of rubbish. He swears as he bins the remaining half of his lunch. Inflation has brought about a sort of muted despair in him. At this rate, he will never be able to afford the wedding he wants to give Asha. Not that she wants anything elaborate. *Something small at the temple perhaps. Just you, me and close family. No need for any frills. After all this is about us. I don't need anything other than you by my side.*

Still, he has been evading the issue of a final date for months now. Because even if it ends up being a small affair, he cannot serve coconut water and onion fritters, can he? There will need to be some basic arrangements. And flowers. He needs to fill up the venue with loads of flowers because Asha loves them.

He remembers now how he'd protested that day, "I

should think twice about giving you flowers for your birthday next year. You look at them with more love than you look at me."

"They're so selfless, don't you think?" she'd said with more beauty in her eyes than the bouquet of roses she was holding. "They exist only to give pleasure to others. They bloom, spread their fragrance and when they've given all they can, they wilt."

It is the things like this that catch him completely off guard and leave him reeling in love. He feels like the luckiest man in the world. Yes, the wedding must have flowers. Lots of them. And they are expensive.

But there is an even bigger worry which is for after the wedding. With this salary, he will have to move out of his parents' shoddy home into a shoddy home of his own. He and Asha will live happily ever after in the gentle breeze of the foul stench from the gutters below and the sweet sounds of the leaky pipes and faucets. And those damned rats. They'd be scratching away in the pipes too.

Recently, an idea has been fluttering about his head. He has been thinking about trying his hand at his own business. Surely it cannot be very hard. Bindra has built an empire, and they say his is a rags-to-riches story. Gaurav has stayed up nights wondering where to start, what kind of business to do, and where to find some capital. He has come up with nothing except empty dreams with invisible roadmaps.

He glances at the giant clock on the wall, the one that dictates what happens when at this office. It is a quarter past one. He clears the crumbs from his table and makes his way to the copy room.

The "summary report" is anything but that. It is a thirty-two page document riddled with squiggly graphs and numbers in fine print. It tracks acquisition, cash position, progress, and other such corporate phenomena. He has been tasked with preparing this complicated manifesto every month and his deadline hovers close.

From the doorway of the copy room, he catches a sight of somebody else. He'd thought he was alone. She stands with her back to him and he can hear the sounds of her fingers fumbling with a machine. She is dressed rather unusually, nothing like the women he sees around here; here in this office dress as though there is no one in this world worth impressing. They are unremarkable to say the least, even the young single ones. Their hair is in plaits, their clothes ill-fitting. There is a pitiful confusion in their minds, having mixed up frumpiness and modesty.

This woman is modern, slim and shapely and she wears a tastefully tailored navy pencil skirt. Her heels are high and pointed like pins. *It must be very difficult to walk in them,* he thinks. But she moves with swiftness and grace to the next machine. *Like a cheetah,* he thinks.

She turns around. He has seen her before. "Oh, hi!" she bubbles.

Barkha Bindra.

His smile does well to cover the flurry in his mind while he frantically tries to estimate the nature of the relationship between Mr. Bindra and this woman. Now that he can see her features in the bright fluorescent light, he notices the pronounced arch of her jaw. A bit like Mr Bindra.

"Can I help?" he offers, because she is struggling to do whatever it is she has come here to do. And of course, because she is the boss' relative.

She pouts. "Yes please, I was trying to get this thing to work, but I couldn't. I went looking for someone, anyone who can help but this place is deserted. Does nobody work at lunch hour?"

"They are all out having lunch, it is called lunch hour for a reason, you know," he says. "So what do you need done? Let me see if I can help."

"These," she holds out a stack of papers to him, "I need these faxed."

He takes them from her. "Oh. Then it would be wise to try with a fax machine instead of a copy machine."

Her cheeks turn beet.

"But not to worry because the fax machine," he points to it, "is right here."

He places the sheaf on the feeder, she hands him a scrap of paper with a number scribbled on it. He dials and they wait till the machine starts to eat.

"Thank you very much. For yesterday as well. I expected

it to be a little more uncomfortable with the Bombay humidity, but I guess once you get moving it is all the same."

He had already guessed she is from out of town.

"Where else have you run?" he fishes.

"I'd done the Brum Fun Run in the UK a couple of times when I was a student."

"Oh, how interesting."

What kind of a name was Brum Fun Run? He is careful not to seem too curious. There is the possibility that pursuing the topic will likely expose his own lack of travel experience. He does not need specifics on a world he hasn't and probably will never explore. He has not even been to Calcutta let alone another country. Hell, he had never set foot in an airplane, didn't even have a passport.

If indeed she is the heiress of this huge fortune and has lived overseas, he is puzzled at why she performs petty chores like sending faxes. Surely she must have a secretary like her Daddy does. And when had she started work in this office? He's pretty sure he hasn't see her here before.

The machine beeps its completion.

"Great, yours is done." He smiles cheerily. "If you will excuse me, I had better get started on these," he flicks through the thick stack of reports. "Please drop by if you ever need any help with these complicated, life-altering matters." He gestures at the machines. "I am right over there." He points to his cabin across the room.

"Thanks so much. I really want to get involved in what you're doing with the running club. I have many ideas. Have you tried yoga?" She eyes the reports he holds in his hands. "Oh I am so sorry, you said you had to go. Let's have lunch tomorrow?" she beams.

The pause in his head lasts much longer than the one that actually occurs in real life. He marvels at her bizarre forwardness. He has never known a woman to take the lead and it leaves him utterly confused. His mind says no, she seems too upper class. What would he have in common with her? These rich people are a different breed.

But his instincts kick in. She is a Bindra. She could be Bindra's daughter, or niece, or God knows. It would not bode well for him to decline and offend her. Would lunch be considered a date though? He doesn't want to go on a date, he's taken, engaged, in love.

But no, surely that is not her intention. Just look at the disparity in their class. Stupid of him to even think of it like that. She is new, she mustn't have many friends. If she did, she would be out to lunch right now with them.

"Yes, that would be nice," he replies politely.

"Madam, your father awaits you in the car." A tall, stocky mountain of a woman stomps into the room. Gaurav knows her to be the personal assistant of Mr Bindra. He is now firmly established in the knowledge that he will soon be lunching with the boss' daughter and this feels rather strange. Perhaps it would be good to orchestrate a nice warm friendship with her. It could clear up the road to a swift promotion. The wedding may happen sooner than he hoped. Well played Gaurav, he compliments himself.

"Great! I will see you tomorrow," she sings.

But she's left without her documents. The fax has gone out and the papers are partially strewn on the floor and partially dangling off the mouth of the fax machine. *Typical*, he thinks, *she is probably used to people picking up after her.*

He gathers them in a neat pile and scans the vicinity to ensure there is no one around. He looks through them one by one. The pictures, page after page, are in black and white and only clear enough to make out that they are photographs of houses. Well, four are of houses; another three are of buildings with either a balcony or a window circled in black marker pen. At the bottom of each picture is an address. In Bombay, Bangalore, Delhi, and London.

There is also a cover letter typed on Mr. Bindra's personal stationary addressed to a Messrs Arihant Realtors. It is peppered with the formal pleasantries one would expect to see in such letters. The paragraph articulating the crux of the matter reads:

Please find attached the properties from my portfolio that are currently vacant. I have been unable to find tenants for some time now, and your attention to them will be appreciated. Please do not revert with offers for sale because as I have mentioned before, I no longer have the autonomy to make any decisions for them. I am only ensuring they create fair revenue. The ownership of these assets was transferred after my health scare last year. They now belong to my daughter, Barkha.

CHAPTER SEVEN

24th June 1988

It is Gaurav's seventh lunch with Barkha in as many weeks. He was right, she doesn't have very many friends in the office. Sure, they are all nice to her and make small talk with her, but he knows it to be obligatory.

So when she comes to his desk every Tuesday and says, "Lunch?" he accepts. They are getting along well and have enough in common for small talk.

"The usual?"

'Yes, please. One."

She drops a teaspoon of sugar in his coffee before two into her own.

Their first meal together had been a short affair, they'd talked mostly about running. She is passionate about the sport and disciplined too.

Lately, they've been talking about other things; their

school and college lives, books, best friends and Bombay traffic. A couple of weeks ago, she had started to tell him stories that have kindled within him a sense of wonder. She has taken his mind on journeys to the villas in the south of France, to treks in the rain forests of Bali, to camps in the national parks in America, to the Louvre and the Leaning tower of Pisa, the Taj Mahal and the Niagara Falls.

He's had nothing much to share of his own adventures. But he is content to listen.

"Have you ever tried deep sea diving? It's like a dream, so surreal, you would never imagine the universe that exists beneath the ocean. It is a phenomenal feeling to be where men rarely venture. I'll bet it's as awesome as being in outer space," she enthuses.

"I don't much like diving," he says, determined to mask his awe. He stirs the reluctant coarse grains of sugar into his lukewarm coffee.

"But you have never tried it, have you?"

"Can't say I have, it just doesn't seem to be something I think I would enjoy," he sips.

"I'm doing Thailand in August next year with some friends. I insist you join, you could try with a coach."

He laughs. "Some of us have to work you know."

"Oh come on! I'm sure you can get leave."

Yes, and I will be needing it for my wedding. As will I be needing the money.

He marvels at how it does not even occur to her that in order for him to consider a holiday, he will have to jump through many hoops. Airfare, hotel expenses, gear. How easy it must be for her to just up and go without having to worry about money. Maybe she can't be blamed because she's never known anything different. With how well Daddy's company is doing, many a thriving money tree must be growing in her backyard. She probably has one right outside her thousand-square-foot bedroom. Wake up in the morning, open the window for some fresh air and oh look at that, pluck a few bills.

He has always, from the very first day he met Mr Bindra, admired him for his entrepreneurial spirit and sheer hunger to succeed. The man chases deals like his life depends on it. If only his own father had even an ounce of the same passion, he wouldn't be sitting here wondering what his half of the lunch bill is going to work out to.

"Never mind, we will figure it out. It is still a long way off. You know what's not so far away?" she asks before the waiter interrupts, clearing the empty plates and placing a small dish at the centre of the table. "Oh my god, fortune cookies," she says, "the last time I had these was when I was in the U.S. on holiday last year." She slides the biscuits toward Gaurav. "You pick."

"Ladies first." He smiles.

She tears open the plastic and reads the small strip of paper.

"Your fortune is as sweet as a cookie." She rolls her eyes,

"That's a cop out."

He laughs, impressed with the accuracy of the biscuit's astrological wisdom.

She crumples the strip, throws it under the table, and takes a bite. "What a dumb aphorism . . . at least it tastes good. What does yours say?"

Gaurav reads aloud, "*A smile is the shortest distance between two people.* Now that is a lame one."

"Well, it's true." Her eyes are fixed on his and it is making him very uncomfortable. Is he reading her right?

He holds her gaze for the briefest of moments before looking away and motioning for the bill. "You mentioned something coming up sooner than your great diving adventure?"

"Yes!" She claps her hands together excitedly and straightens up. "My birthday party. You have to come."

"Really? When's your birthday?"

"Next week, but the party is this Saturday. It's just a small dinner with some friends, and then maybe we'll head someplace for a drink."

"Let 's see. Today is Wednesday, so am I a filler? Did someone cancel?"

"No, silly, it is a last minute plan. My friends insisted. In fact, bring a friend."

What friend would he bring? He couldn't bring Asha, she doesn't even know he's been lunching with the boss' daughter every week. He hasn't told her because she would jump to conclusions, she'd think there was something going on and there wasn't. Was there?

He decides there and then that he will not go to her party. It just all feels wrong. But he can't tell her that, it would seem an insult. He decides to stall her.

"I will let you know if I can make it. A very happy birthday in advance and thank you for inviting me."

"I hope you can come." Her smile is flirtatious. "It's nothing too fancy. Piccolo Mondo at the Palace Hotel, 8 o'clock."

CHAPTER EIGHT

27th June, 1988

She'd checked with him the next day and he'd told her he wasn't sure if he could make it. On Thursday she'd come to his desk again. "Hey, I hope you're on. I have to give the restaurant the numbers." He couldn't say no. But he didn't want to say yes either.

Now he stands in front of the mirror in his bedroom, labouring over the decision of which shirt to wear. He tries on two and detests both. He then settles on a three-tone cobalt blue casual shirt which he wears with his slim-fit Lee Cooper jeans. He isn't entirely satisfied, but it is the best of what he owns and it will have to do. He can't hope to compete with that crowd anyway, no matter how hard he tries.

"This colleague of yours must make a lot of money. Who throws a birthday party at the Palace?" Brij says as Gaurav reverse parks into the basement of the Palace.

"It's not a him, it's a her."

"Wow, a woman is making more money than you? India is turning into America." Brij looks like a wolf when he laughs like he's doing now. "What does she do? Dirty secretary?"

"You're a male chauvinist pig. No wonder you can never keep a girlfriend. You will die single." Gaurav kills the engine and gets out of the car, lighting a cigarette.

Brij checks his reflection in the car mirror for deviant strands in his neatly waxed hair. "There is no shame in this. If one has something that the other wants, then a transaction is wise. Your boss's limp *danda* must be standing up seeing a young thing, and the young thing's mouth must be salivating when hearing the tinkling coins. And by the way, thank you for your great blessings. There is nothing I want more than to die single. I am not like you. I can't hide under one skirt for the rest of my life. Life is to enjoy! One day chicken tikka, one day mutton kebab, one day biryani. I don't know how you do this commitment nonsense. By the way, where is she?"

"Where is who?" Gaurav puts out his cigarette and pushes open the creaking door to the lift lobby.

"Asha *yaar*, who else? She must be busy with something important else why would you bring me as your plus one to a place like this. Not that I'm complaining—I'm always up for a free meal and who won't want to eat here. Remember all those fat roasting chickens in their kitchen? I can't wait to sink my teeth into them. Imagine the amount of butter and ghee on those things." Brij licks his lips and clicks his tongue.

"Please don't behave like you've been starved, eat slowly and don't stuff your face."

"Okay okay, calm down. I am not a kid, I also know how to act posh like these people."

"So you didn't tell me, where is Asha?"

The elevator pings open, letting out a gust of citrusy fragrance.

"She's busy tonight."

"So we are single and ready to do some *danda* pleasing."

"Brij, please no antics today. It's not some secretary, it is the boss's daughter's birthday. Behave, ok?"

"*Saala*, you got invited to the owner's daughter's birthday? You sly fox." Brij pauses, then sneers with a glint in his eyes. "Why would she invite a louse like you?" Brij pauses and tilts his head to one side, having his epiphany.

"Wait a sec. Your boss' daughter has invited you to her birthday party. And Asha I am sure knows nothing about this and you are dressed to kill. What is going on? Come on, spill the beans."

"Nothing Brij, now shut the hell up."

"I can only say one thing Gaurav, I know you're engaged to Asha and everything. But she's not here. Instead you brought me. Think about why you did that. If you play this well, you will never have to suffer another day in your life."

Brij adjusts his collar, fixes his hair and leads the way into the restaurant.

A delicate scent, absent of the pungent spices he is accustomed to fills his nostrils. Gaurav recognises it as the yeasty aroma of freshly baked bread and roasting garlic. He surveys the packed restaurant in search of Barkha's table while Brij stares agape with cow eyes. "This is like the restaurants in those fancy American movies, totally high class. Just look at the getup."

Massive crystal chandeliers twinkle above finely set oversized tables that are seamed with grand chairs upholstered in red velvet. A checkerboard tiled floor sparkles beneath their feet. There are large paintings on the walls that portray peasant life in a country other than India. The women in them wear no *sarees*. Instead they don long flare skirts, bodices, and muffin caps.

A waiter, brown in skin but Italian in speech, politely requests to pass, *Scuzi*, and he whizzes by balancing an impossibly enormous tray with impossibly enormous cloche-covered plates. In the background, behind the sounds of chitter chatter and clinking cutlery, Gaurav hears soft instrumental music. It is a tune he recognises from a film he had taken Asha to. His heart starts to sink. Panic, doubt and guilt tug at his chest, his conscience devours his heart. His mind fills in the words to the song.

My love,
There's only you in my life

The only thing that's bright
My first love,
You're every breath that I take
You're every step I make
And I
I want to share
All my love with you
No one else will do...
And your eyes
Your eyes, your eyes
They tell me how much you care
Ooh yes, you will always be
My endless love

He had surprised Asha with balcony seats for a matinee show at Metro Cinema just two months ago: tickets he was able to get only after a hefty black market price was paid to a crafty fifteen-year-old with a shrewd eye for loverboys looking to please their beloveds.

A full hundred rupees he'd paid for them. Each. And when he got home that night, he'd safely placed the tickets in an envelope and taken them with him the morning after for his run. He was going to make it special. It was the anniversary of their first date

That same evening as he and Asha strolled along Marine Drive, a beggar boy approached her as instructed. He carried in his hand a red rose and the sealed envelope.

"This is for you." He held them out to her.

"For me? From who?"

"Yes madam, for you. Last night while I slept on the footpath here, the sea arose in high waves, high they were I tell you, higher than the big buildings on Nariman Point and higher than the top of the Gateway of India. One of them stepped out and came right here. In front of me like you now are madam, God promise," he pinched the little flesh of his neck to assure her, "the big high wave stepped out and spoke to me in a thundering woman's voice. *I am the Goddess of the Sea*, she said. And then she handed these to me, dry as day old roti even though coming out of her hands. She said to tell you that not only does she sprinkle blessings for the both of you, but she also sprinkles gifts. She said your love is endless like her."

The boy then shoved the rose and the envelope in Asha's unwilling hands and ran away.

"What is this?" she asked Gaurav.

He shrugged his shoulders and smiled, "How would I know? You heard the boy. It's from the sea."

When she discovered the movie tickets, Asha swung her arms around him and kissed him on the lips, hard, right there on the boulevard. He had to pull away and remind her that they were in full public view.

He could taste that kiss now. He could feel her hand squeezing his own, her body huddling up next to him as they watched the movie. When they came out of the cinema the streets were flooded. It had rained. A light drizzle still fell and he removed his windbreaker and held it above her. They ate pizza for dinner in a restaurant nearby. They ordered one between them, plain cheese just the way she liked it.

Why has he decided to come anyway? Is it because he was so flattered to be invited that declining had never been a serious option? Is it curiosity? Is it to experience a slice of life from someone else's cake? Why does he feel like the biggest fool in the world?

"Come on Brij." He turns to leave, he'd make up some excuse on Monday.

"Hey, Gaurav!" Barkha calls out his name from the far end of the room. She is waving eagerly. "Over here!"

Too late.

"I can't believe you almost left. You should have at least walked about to look for us. Anyway, you're just in time, we just opened the bottle and Sanjeev is about to make a toast." She pecks him on the cheek, hands him a glass filled with red wine, and eyes the stranger. "I'm so glad you brought company."

"This is Brij."

"Nice to meet you, Brij." She pours a glass and hands it to him.

"We've met before. I would never forget a face like

yours," he winks. Gaurav wants to kick his leg, but she can see.

"Oh no. I hate when this happens. Please remind me."

"Don't worry, it was only a handshake. At the run."

"Yes I remember now." They clink glasses and sip. "Welcome, Brij."

The two men are led to the only two empty seats left at the table.

Cutlery tinkles against crystal, and a man's voice booms. "Everyone, may I have your attention please!" Conversations stall at tables nearby, heads turn, faces smile. It dawns on Gaurav that this dinner party is not so small after all. Her guests fill nearly half the restaurant and are seated separately in fours, sixes, and eights. His seat though, along with Brij's, is on the main table where Barkha is.

The man stands up. He is young and speaks with the ease and confidence that Gaurav has only seen in the rich. "For those of you who don't know me," the speaker looks directly at Gaurav and Brij, "I am Sanjeev. I would like to say a few words about our dear friend, Barkha Bindra. Everyone who knows Barkha knows that she is one of the kindest, friendliest women around." He flashes a warm smile at her and she blushes. The guests clap in agreement. "Today, she celebrates her twenty-sixth birthday, and I want to thank her for all the good times in all the years we've known each other. I will never forget our trips together, be it Bali or Barcelona, Mauritius or Manila. We have had some fun times together.

Please join me in wishing Barkha a happy birthday, and I hope we have many more years together." The guests raise their glasses and sing the birthday song as a two-tiered pink frosted cake is rolled out.

The Lair Bar is exactly that; a den. Albeit a posh one, with dim lighting, heavy drapes, dark timber panelling and plush leather sofas. It does not suffer, though, the same ruffian patronage as the Swigs Sports Bar and Grille that Gaurav frequents. No, this bar is for the more discerning consumer, the kind of consumer that can afford to make merry on a whiskey that costs as much as one day of Gaurav's pay, the kind of consumer that checks in upstairs in one of the guest rooms of the hotel.

Here at the Lair, they serve cashews instead of peanuts, have dainty glasses for martinis, and every glass served sits atop a leather coaster. They don't have a giant screen like Swigs, but their smaller TV screens are clear as reality and they don't flicker with static.

The entire bar has been booked out for Barkha's after-party. Gaurav was ready to go home after dinner but Brij would hear nothing of it.

"Are you crazy? Have you seen these people? They're bloody awesome. This is the time to network my friend. And Barkha was looking at you all night. She seated you right next to her. What the hell is wrong with you? You pray for opportunity and when it is smacking you in the nose, you walk away. Let's just fucking go and drink some good whiskey. Black Label baby."

At dinner, Brij was seated next to one Renuka. She wore a shiny silver nose ring and a permanent pout that made her look like she was ready to kiss anyone at any moment. The two talked through the entire meal, oblivious of the other guests at the table and now at the Lair Bar Gaurav can see them both on a loveseat in the corner. Their faces are jammed into each other's.

Gaurav was seated next to a doctor, Dr. Aditya. "Please Shal, stop doing that. Call me Aditya," the man had politely corrected when the woman across introduced them.

Gaurav learned many things of many subjects from this Dr. Aditya that he hadn't previously thought about in such depth; that the cure for cancer was no longer a distant dream but a certainty, and it was only a decade or so away. He learned why Congress lost the seats they did in the elections, and how black money leaves the country. They talked about the Americans and their space missions, India's place in the global marketplace, the caste system.

He was perturbed to learn the length and breadth of this man's knowledge. How is it that rich people know as much as they do? Is that what makes them rich in the first place; that they have the ability to learn and absorb things the poor don't even think about? And that could be, Gaurav thinks, because they do not have to exhaust their mental energy in the pursuit of the next pay check. They have all the time in the world to read and reflect.

But Gaurav did not hold it against the bloke. He respected him for it, even hoped some of it would rub off on him. Later in the evening, between the second course and the third, the two stepped out for a smoke together. A doctor who smokes, so he wasn't perfect after all. Gaurav learned during the course of their conversation that Aditya's father was the Director for Bombay General Hospital. He also received the awkward but kind offer of contacting Aditya (a business card was handed over) should he or his family ever need any help for any unfortunate emergencies that may arise. That was very kind of him, Gaurav thought.

The other guests at dinner were mostly Barkha's school and college friends. He was pleasantly surprised by how forthcoming and friendly they were. He had always thought the rich to be incapable of congeniality with anyone but their own kind. After a few glasses, everyone bonded perfectly.

Guests are scattered here, there and everywhere. Some stand at the bar and wait for their martinis to be mixed, others lounge on sofas, some have started moving on the dance floor. A slow song starts playing and a few couples are dancing very close together. In the corner sofa, he can see Brij's hands sliding up Renuka's dress.

Barkha stands with a group of women at the far end of the bar. Sanjeev is dancing with a pretty young thing in a slinky black dress. His hands are on her hips and their lips devour each other's necks. He is more than a little surprised. He'd thought Barkha and Sanjeev were together after that speech.

He orders a whiskey on the rocks at the bar while deciding how much longer he will give Brij before he leaves without him. The drink arrives, he drains it in one swig and orders another. May as well make the best of the free booze. He sips the second and glances back at Brij who is still at it.

He finishes his second glass and gets up to leave. There is a tap on his shoulder, he swivels the stool around.

"Hey." It is Barkha. She stands so close he can feel her breath on his face. "Shall we dance?"

The whiskey rolls around in his brain, he can feel her thighs touch his knees, she is tilting herself closer and closer. Her eyes are wild and hungry. She brushes her hand over his leg.

He is about to say no but before he can, her lips are on his. His body responds with fervour.

CHAPTER NINE

28th June, 1988

The sky is fresh red in places and dirty blue in others. The city is quiet; it is a Sunday. The streets are scant with people that don't rush. Nobody clamours, pushes or shoves. Bombayites change on Sundays, for the better. They become patient, they speak softer.

People change so easily. One minute they can be one person and the next minute another. It is all circumstantial, isn't it?

Gaurav sits at the table in his bedroom and watches the few cars lazily roll in and out of the driveway of the Palace Hotel. But today he feels different. He has tasted the bed that he now sees from his window, he has stretched his legs on the room's sofa, he has smoked in its balcony. The Palace Hotel is not foreign anymore. He has made love inside it. He has showered in its bathroom. Now he knows: he knows what it feels like.

It is impossible to unsee what one has seen, to unexperience what one has experienced, to unenjoy what one has enjoyed. Everything has changed. Everything.

When his lips had touched Barkha's the previous night, she received them with a terrible hunger. She tasted sharp like vodka, but her breath was fruity from the cherries on her cocktails. She kissed him long and she kissed him hard.

This morning he had awoken in the four-poster bed, covered with silken sheets and against her soft body. "I love you," she had breathed onto his bare chest.

He hadn't replied because he had never been a good liar. Asha had said so often. "Don't say you were waiting twenty minutes. You just arrived, you are late too. Now before you argue please know when you lie, it always shows on your face. Your eyes go all squinty and you play with your fingers and just... just... you can't lie to save your life."

So he'd turned his head away from Barkha and caught sight of his own bedroom window through the French windows of the hotel room. Such a short distance away his life waited, so near, yet so far. When they checked out from the hotel this morning, she said she couldn't wait to see him again.

He said, "me too" and left.

He will see her tomorrow at the office. Nothing will be the same though. How can it be when you have heard the sounds of each other's deepest pleasures, when you have touched each other in the most intimate of places, when you have shared bodies in the dark.

He sits on the real side of his life and looks into a terrifyingly possible one. He is so afraid to even imagine it, just in case it mutilates his soul. For if he pictures a life of comfort and luxury, he will have lived it in his mind. And if he lives it in his mind, he may do what he knows he can now do to bring it to life.

He has two choices, two roads. And one of them may change his life forever. It could lead to joys his mind cannot even conceive.

The other road leads to Asha.

Asha. He has been thinking of Asha. He will call her. Soon. As soon as he can figure out what he loves more, his dreams or his reality.

PART IV
FLIGHT
VA4625

CHAPTER ONE

MIRA

5th March, 2012

Remember I told you, these were stories of choices?

※

Mira decided to choose and so in this moment she is very different from the little village girl all those years ago. I still remember her wrapped against her will in yards and yards of red and gold, eyes wet with fear and irresolution, lips quivering in trepidation. Mira, the girl who grew up too soon.

She has never set foot in the hallways of a university or a library, never read literature or economic theory, but Mira is not illiterate. For it is the mark of an educated mind to know when to walk away and when to stay. When one is no longer welcome, no matter how heart-wrenching, one must have the courage to leave.

I see Mira now and I feel sorry that she waited this long to be happy, wasting away so much of me like water between fingers. But I console myself that at least she has managed to finally scavenge some years for herself. She is braver than the ones that die before they die, existing unconsciously day after day in the cycle of waking, working, sleeping.

She chose and so the entire universe conspired to carry her along to a more desirable place. It is synchronicity.

She has aged well. She is sixty-four years old and works twelve to fourteen hours a day. Files and folders, notebooks and ledgers litter her desk. She has many bills to approve; the *dhobiwalla's* for the clothes of all the hundred and some children, the *bhajiwalla* who delivers fresh vegetables by the kilo every morning, the *doodhwalla* for the litres and litres of milk these children guzzle. She also has to review the grocery requisition list and make sure there is enough petty cash in the float for Uma to attend to the shopping.

Uma. She could never have done this without her. And she didn't even have to ask; Uma volunteered to move to Bombay the minute she heard of Mira's plans.

That night, after Mira heard those words waft like vapours of poison from inside the bedroom of her son Jeevan and her daughter-in-law Maya, she sat on her bed alone and traced the lines of her life. When had she gone from being a naïve village schoolgirl, a silly child in love with her tutor, to a grandmother? Yes, she took all the steps—but who made all the decisions?

And what now? Was she to stay here in this house with this son that wanted her only for her wealth? Is this how she would meet her end?

A memory from decades ago swam to the surface of her mind.

She must have been six, maybe seven. She could see the hills, pale and green, the lush pastures ahead. She could feel the soft earth beneath her feet and the tall grass brush against her skin as it danced in the breeze. Behind her, hooves thumped as the cattle trundled lazily. She was happy, because these were the rare mornings she was allowed to go out with the farmhands. Her mother forbade it if the womenfolk didn't follow. But that day they were there, right behind her, she could hear the jingle of their bangles and the clapping of their long loose skirts in the wind.

There was this one particular cow; Bijli was the name Mira gave her because of the lightning bolt-shaped scar above her left eye. Every time the cattle grazed, Bijli would wander away. Mira would laugh and clap as the bewildered cowherds searched for her and then after hours find her behind the pines or near the river. She just never wanted to stay with the others. She wanted to go where she wanted to go and do what she wanted to do.

Then one day, an elderly farmhand, who didn't much go out, happened to join them and upon seeing Bijli misbehave, he took a long rope and tied her leg to a tree. Now Bijli could only graze in the area the length of rope permitted. After feeding herself, she would try to leave, tug and tug, then finally give up, accept defeat and sit down in the shade, her eyes forlorn and her head bowed in submission.

"Tie her like this a few times, she will get used to staying within this place only. Then it will become habit," he told the others. They did and for many days Bijli, bound by the rope around her hoof obeyed. Once, the boys forgot to bring the rope, but they coaxed her to graze by the same tree that she was used to being tied to. Lo and behold, Bijli fed herself, settled down on the grass and dozed.

"Wake up Bijli! There is no rope today. You can go. Then they will go mad looking for you. Walk away Bijli, go!" Mira pleaded, but Bijli, well-fed and well-trained, slept peacefully.

The farmhands never bothered with a rope again after that for Bijli was trained. She was never again tied but she forever remained bound.

That night in the house where Mira had bid goodbye to Karan all those years ago, where Jeevan was raised from boy to man, where she welcomed the joy and blessing that was her granddaughter, Mira hardly slept.

Before the morning flooded through the windows, her heart was already bubbling with joy, and when she heard the main door of the house open, she ushered the houseboy into her room in a hurry.

"Climb up and get me that suitcase, son. Help me fold these clothes. And those photos, take them off the wall and wrap them in newspaper, I don't want the frame to break.

Yes, like that. No old saris, please don't pack those. I can't wear them, they are coloured. Pack only the whites. And my prayer beads, don't forget to put those in. Here, my toothbrush and comb."

"Memsahib, the zip is sticking."

"Bring some ghee and rub over it, it will slide right open. Quickly go, I want to be ready before they wake up."

She went in to shower and when she came out, there it was, her entire future tightly packed and zipped shut in one large dark blue American Tourister suitcase—the same one Karan and she shared on their first trip outside India, the one to Singapore for which she had to apply for a passport. Yes, the passport! She slipped that inside her handbag, too.

By the time Jeevan and Maya emerged from their bedroom, Mira was fully dressed. She sat at the table, the last of her milk tea drained and her buttered toast almost finished.

"Up early Mama; going somewhere?" Jeevan asked as he took a seat beside her.

"I have been thinking for some time now. You are a growing family. You need your space and privacy."

Jeevan looked bewildered, but then she thought she saw a shade of guilt as he said slowly, "Mama why are you saying all this all of a sudden?"

"Saying what?" Maya asked as she came out of the kitchen with her steaming cup of coffee. How easily her body moved, how comfortable and reassuring youth was, but she knew how quick it tended to evaporate.

"Mama is talking about moving out," Jeevan said in a somewhat disturbed voice.

Mira wondered with sadness how he had come to that conclusion. Why did he assume with such readiness that it was her that would leave? Did he not think she may ask them to go? This was her house after all.

But deep down, her heart knew. Mothers know their children better than their children know themselves. For a mother sees from her heart, not from her eyes. She had known from the time he was a boy. There were so many signs that she pretended not to see; him hungrily taking the first roti off the fire for himself, closing the car door before she got out, always walking ahead, walking away. And the cards Amma insisted he make for her where there was never anything more than "Happy Birthday Mama". No message. Not even a "Love" before signing them. When he grew up and left her to study in Delhi, the only times they spoke was when she called him. He never called her. He seemed to be in a hurry to become himself, to become separate.

But she never dwelled on these things, she only held on to the little boy who would wrap his hand around her finger, would cuddle up in her bosom when he was shy and strangers spoke to him, the boy that stammered adorably when he was just starting to learn to speak. Even now, when she looks at him, she cannot see the morning stubble that has formed on his cheeks, she cannot see the manly features that make him handsome, she cannot see the broadness of his shoulders. She can only see the little boy that clung to her sari and slept in her arms.

"*Beta*, it is also good for me. All my life I have been with so many responsibilities. Maybe some alone time for me will be good."

"Mama, this is not right. Where will you go?"

"I am thinking of visiting Uma in Delhi. I haven't seen her in a year. She has been asking me to come, and I am also missing her. Then after that I will see. You all please continue to stay here. I will get Uncle Inamdar to organise the papers to transfer ownership of the house in Isha's name. It is too big for me anyway."

It was fleeting, but Maya's face twitched and Mira saw it.

"And you can still work out of the office. Nothing will change," Mira added before getting up and fondly running her hands through his hair like she did when he was a boy. She then smiled. "I will leave for the office since I am ready early. I will call the agent to make arrangements for my ticket."

The houseboy brought her bag out and loaded it in the trunk of the car. But before Mira left, she went into Isha's bedroom. The little angel slept soundlessly, her breaths deep and even. The birthday dress hung ironed from a hook on the wall. How beautiful she would look, how perfect she was. How much Mira would miss the joy of seeing her every day. Mira's lips touched Isha's forehead in the softest of kisses, and the girl stirred. She patted her, trying to sway her back into deep sleep but Isha wrapped her arm around Mira's and held on tight.

"*Beti*, Dadima is going for a holiday. You be good, okay?" she whispered into the half-asleep child's cheek.

"Can I come with you?" Isha mumbled.

"No. Your new school starts in a few weeks. We have bought all your uniforms and everything else. And that new pencil case, the one you were excited about. How will you use it if you come with me?"

"My birthday?"

"Dadima will be back for that."

Isha, only because she was half-asleep, let go and turned over.

The car moved along the busy morning streets, but strangely, the route she had been taking for years and years was blocked with orange cones and a huge truck, the kind used for construction works. Her driver was told by a man in uniform that because it had rained all night, the main artery was badly flooded, and no cars were allowed to go through till the mess was cleaned. The driver then detoured and they journeyed via unfamiliar back lanes where he quite expectedly lost his way.

And it so happened that the spot he stopped the car to ask for directions was the very same place Mira had been to years ago. Seva Dham. Where she had gone to give charity on the day of Jeevan's thread ceremony. Karan was alive then, and her parents too. A tear escaped her eye as she remembered her mother and father. She said a prayer for all of them, all who had curated a life for her that she hadn't had any say in.

Seva Dham, it was where she had seen the little girl that she still remembered clearly. She searched her mind for the child's name, that little girl with the tattered doll whom she had to persuade to come to the ice cream truck. What became of her, she wondered. How badly she had wanted a daughter then. She would have brought that girl home the very same day if it weren't for Karan.

Radha. Yes. That was her name. Radha with her tattered doll and the eyes of an angel.

Mira stood and stared at the padlocked gates of Seva Dham. Why was the orphanage shut? What happened to all the children?

A bored old watchman lingered outside, sucking on a cigarette and fiddling with a mobile phone. Mira got out of the car.

Yes, it has been closed for some time, the watchman said. *Very sad, very very sad,* he kept repeating as he shook his head. *Mrs Kamalnath was first to go and her husband, poor man, he was so distraught it was like the blood was sucked out of him. He grew pale and weak, listless. But they had stopped accepting children long before that. There were only a few young ones that were quickly placed in other orphanages and three older ones, all grown up, working at nice jobs and everything. They stayed on only to tend to the old man in his final days. Good children, responsible and kind, God bless them,* he said again and again. B*ut everyone has been gone a long time, years, and the place has been up for sale because there was some problem with the Trustees and no one cared anymore and no one filed papers with the government and so the government took over the property. Here, look at this notice for auction.* The watchman pointed to a frayed sheet of paper glued to the side wall.

There was a date and some legal looking paragraphs.

Mira returned to her car and told her driver to take her to the office. She had no concrete plans for her future when she left her son's house in the morning. Before this moment, before laying her eyes on the orphanage she didn't know what her next steps would be. But the path ahead was crystal clear now. Incidentally, the traffic on the highway had cleared too.

When Mira arrived at her office that morning, she immediately rung her accountant, Mr Inamdaar and instructed him to call as many brokers as he could find and he had five days to come up with an offer. She then checked into the Palm Hotel and Apartments and unpacked her suitcase, waiting for some leads.

He called three days later with the news that there was an interested buyer for the company. She wasn't entirely surprised. When Karan passed, she had received offers here and there. People assumed the village widow would not be enterprising enough to manage the small business. But she thought it her duty to keep Blooms & Blossoms alive. It had given her and Karan a good life. And it was in great health, turning handsome profits year after year.

"We are lucky Madam, it is a big multinational company, Zinmac Industries. They have many subsidiaries all over India and they also have branches overseas. They trade in commodities and construction and even shipping. Recently they have started an online company; they sell things on the computer. Everything from safety pins to teacups to motorbikes. They are constantly in search of new assets, small and medium businesses that are already up and running which they can acquire and add to their portfolio. Apparently, a lot of people will be interested in buying flowers online and Blooms & Blossoms has lots of potential. They say they know how to take it to the next level. They are eager."

Mira booked a flight to Delhi. There she stayed with Uma and told Uma of her plans. She needed to bounce her ideas off someone. Uma's eyes lit up.

"That is a great idea. It is both noble and timely. Your son will not run your business. He is a lawyer and after the way he and his wife have treated you there is no need to conserve the money for them. You have given them a house, that is enough. I think you should do it. I will come to the auction with you. We will do this together. I will help you run the school you want to build in the vacant lot next to Seva Dham. We will buy Seva Dham at the auction and then contact the owner of the lot next door. I will move to Bombay. I am old, retired. I am also lonely, Mira. I'll run the school."

Running Seva Dham is a demanding job but Mira is happier than she has ever been in her life. She and Uma live in a simple house behind the orphanage and school. There are three bedrooms in it, one for her, one for Uma, and one for when her granddaughter, Isha comes over and stays on the weekends. The little boy, Sham, never stays. He is only three and still looks for his mother. But Isha loves to spend the night. And when they play monopoly—Uma, Isha and Mira—they always let Isha win. But Isha's favourite is charades; she is good at that game.

Just as Mira is halfway through the paperwork on the table, there is a knock at the door. It is Uma. She places yet another file on Mira's overflowing desk. "These are last term's school reports. Some of them are doing much better, but many will need a talking to."

Mira smiles. "You are not going to settle for anything but straight A's, are you?"

Uma shakes her head and sits across her. "Why should I? Look at the opportunity they are getting. They must not waste it. I want to see this school's academic performance in line with the national average."

"It is only a primary school, Uma. Let them be children."

"You didn't bring the principal of a Delhi College all the way to Bombay for nothing, did you?" She checks her watch. "Look at the time. When is your flight? Shouldn't you be on your way to the airport?"

Mira gets up and hurriedly slings her handbag over her

shoulder. She glances at the piles of paper on the table. "I lost track of the time. There is still so much to do." She hands the keys of the safe to Uma. "All the documents, the deed to Seva Dham, the bank statements are in there. The petty cash is enough, I checked. And the cheque book is here." She slides open the bottom drawer of her desk.

"You're only going for few days. Actually I should be the one going. You with your bad back and all…"

"No Uma, it is best I go. The school needs you around. Term has just started. Besides, it is a cheque presentation, and my name is already on the programme flyers. Those people from Zinmac have been giving us donations every year and they are used to seeing me."

"Can't believe you sold them your business and are still getting money from them year after year. But then again, I guess these corporates have to show some charity and social service work in their annual reports. Anyway, I have asked Ramu to put your bags in the car. You have taken your passport?"

"Yes, and my ticket." Mira takes out her passport case and checks if everything is in order. It is; seat 18B, Vimaan Air VA4625 scheduled to depart for Delhi at 1225HRS.

CHAPTER TWO

GAURAV

4th March, 2012

Human existence is the result of a universe formed and fine-tuned by ingredients in perfect proportions. A little bit of gravitational force, a large pool of hydrogen, just the right amount of energy, matter, electromagnetism all in mathematical congruity, and you have a soup that allows life to exist. Things are in accurate order, the force of gravity just so, keeping the planet from spinning into the tremendous black nothingness of space; the distance of the sun from the earth precise enough so that the sun can lick but not consume it. Tamper with these coordinates even in the slightest, and the earth would fold into itself.

A perfect explosion of billions of stars trillions of years ago. And here you are, part star, part dust and perfectly whole—constructed from an atomic storm—living, sentient, breathing, conscious. Miraculous, isn't it, this experience of Life—because of or perhaps despite its joy, sorrow, success, failure, togetherness, separation, adventure and fate.

Do you believe in fate? Do you believe in destiny? Or are you one of those that believe in choice alone?

Do you make your choices or do your choices make you?

~

Gaurav has made some choices; you could say they were for better or for worse. He leans against the railings at the deck of HMS Gagan, the thirty-eighth vessel in the Zinmac-Xinmei Shipping Corporation fleet.

The bow cuts through the waters of the Arabian Sea, leaving behind a frothy scar in the heaving blanket of azure. Gaurav watches the waves, endless in number, as they agitatedly slap themselves against the hull of the ship. The afternoon sky is clear, white patches of marble against a silky brilliant blue.

He has a view of Marine Drive at the shores in the distance. How many mornings he had run the length of that concrete, how many walks he had taken hand in hand with Asha. Sometimes he still thinks of her. Asha, the woman who used to say the sprays of sea water are blessings from the Goddess of the Sea, gifts because the Goddess was happy that they were together. But this is not true, because now she is not with him, and yet he can feel the salty droplets speckle his face. Is the Goddess blessing him, or is she letting him know she watches him and disapproves?

That morning when he awoke in the hotel room beside Barkha, he knew by the way she had touched him, by the way her lips fluttered over his shoulder, the way her arms searched for him through the night that there was a strong possibility she was in love with him. He had been so drunk that night, but the morning brought with it the piercing reality and gravity of what he had done. There he was, engaged to a woman he loved but in bed with another, and terribly aware of the malleability of his future, aware that if he lost this opportunity someone else would seize it. In that moment, Barkha was his, laying against his chest, wrapped in his arms, breathing over his body. And the chart of his life would forever be defined by this opportunity, whether he took it or not.

This could either be a beginning or an end. Perhaps both.

He called Asha that night and mentioned nothing of his infidelity. When she asked why he sounded withdrawn, he told her he had had a late night at the company dinner and too many drinks with the boys. Her dim reply, he can't remember what it was, either a "hmm" or an "I see" or perhaps silence, was testament to his inability to lie to her.

In the days that followed, the phone calls and meetings with Asha were significantly reduced. No, he could not make it to the movies because he had a conference call with an associate in a faraway country whose day is his night. No, he can't talk now because he needs to get this or that report done. No, this weekend is not good, he is required to be in the office. No, he didn't hear the phone ring, his phone was on silent.

Finally, after two weeks, he mustered the courage to call her. He wanted to ask her if they could meet for a cup of tea, he had something important to talk about and that it is best they meet soon. But before he could, "Why don't you just tell me on the phone, Gaurav? It will be easier for the both of us."

It pained him to hear the voice that called his name so tenderly when they talked, so deeply when they made love, so fondly when he made her laugh, now turn stoic, cold, distant. Yes, his heart had sorrow, guilt even, but not doubt. His decision was made. He did not like himself for it, he had trouble sleeping, he longed and yearned for the comfort of Asha's presence. All those things were there, present, gnawing at him. But he also knew his future lay ahead, bright and promising, his dreams would no longer be dreams, he had the power to transform his life. He had the tools to rewrite his destiny. So he chose, consciously, painfully, guiltily he chose.

He thought he knew Asha well. He was wrong. She did not express shock and she was not broken. There was none of that. Even when he told her he was with someone else, Asha did not ask who. She simply said goodbye and hung up. Just like that.

"Hey, where is your phone? I've been calling you." Aditya

hands him a glass of champagne. "I've been looking all over the ship for you."

Gaurav pulls his mobile phone out of his suit pocket and checks it. "Sorry, it's on silent. You're slurring. Drunk already eh?"

"You bet I am. It is not every day I get to go on a cruise on my friend's ship."

"Yeah well, don't say it is mine in front of the Chinese—they get all upset."

"They wouldn't be here if it wasn't for you," Aditya says incredulously. He opens his arms and gestures at the freighter, "It is amazing what you have done with this company! Ever since you took over, there have been milestones every single year. And this partnership with the Chinese? Genius. Mr Bindra would have been so proud."

"He could have done this for himself years ago had he not been so conservative; I brought it to table in 1992, before he passed," Gaurav said with more than a hint of bitterness.

"Yeah he was a hard head. Hey, how are things with Barkha now?"

"Like father, like daughter." He laughs at his own joke. "Where is everyone?"

"The press are downstairs getting a tour of the captain's quarters. Just finished the boiler room." Aditya lights a cigarette and offers one to Gaurav. "You're the only runner I know that smokes."

"You're the only doctor I know that smokes."

"You have a bloody answer for everything, don't you? Hey before I forget, sorry we can't make it tonight for the awards. I'm on call and Sudha is knee-deep in assignments for her Masters. You know you have our best wishes. *Company of the Year*—Zinmac deserves it. Let's do dinner next week to celebrate."

The sound of clicking heels nears. Barkha is in a white lace dress to the knees; a string of South Seas pearls hugs her slim neck. She holds in one hand an ivory colour clutch and in the other a glass of champagne.

No matter how perfectly her dress fits, how well manicured her nails are, or how red her lips are painted, Gaurav never sees beauty. He used to see something, attraction or lust or some other such base feeling. But beauty? No.

Others do. They say she looks young, that she has maintained herself well, not at all like the mother of a fifteen-year-old. *You are so careful,* they say when she eats only leaves at dinners. *What do you use for your skin?*

The problem is that he has already glimpsed beauty, and he knows very well what it is. He has loved it and held it so close, as close as his own breath. He cannot be fooled like the others. Beauty is in the small carefree imperfections, the crease in a skirt, a missing button, the stray lock of curls from a tied ponytail.

Beauty is a sparkle in the eyes that comes from inside a pretty soul. It is the lightness of laughter, the simplicity of innocence, the gentle dignity of confidence. Beauty is the ability to talk to a stranger and smile, to sing when it rains, to skip when happy, to not cry when your heart gets broken.

"It is so hot. I told you that you should have scheduled the press tour for the evening," Barkha says. She stands beside him but there is a distance; their bodies never touch.

"That would not have been possible. The awards are this evening."

"Then we should have scheduled it another day." She drains her glass.

If one is intelligent and attentive, one can quickly sense a storm brewing, and in such inopportune times it is wise to seek cover. Dr Aditya reaches his hand out to Barkha and takes her glass. "Let me get you another."

The couple are alone, and so there is silence.

But Gaurav is now in a foul mood. The date and time for this tour were dictated by the visit of their business partners who are on a tight schedule. She knows this and yet. He finally mutters with some bitterness, "You didn't have to come, you know."

"Wouldn't you just wish," she replies with scorn.

The horn blares as the ship drops anchor on to shore.

✦

Gaurav considers the two bowties against his shirt in the mirror. He likes the contrast of the dark orange one and the specks of silver on it match the white of his starched shirt.

He had bought it on his last trip to London and has never worn it. But the muted beige one may be a better choice for tonight; it is less flashy and nicely understated.

Their walk-in closet is a thousand square feet in size, cut in the middle by a three hundred square foot bathroom. Barkha's own area houses eight doors of closet space for her clothes, a glass display cabinet at the centre of the room for her accessories, and some custom-made drawers for her collection of shoes. There is also a vintage vanity table and stool where she sits now in front of the mirror, taming her hair.

Like most of their social engagements, tonight's dinner is both convenient and burdensome, because although these superficial events can be painfully lifeless, staying home with only each other for company is a far bleaker option. So they spend their nights in the loneliest places of this world; inaugurations and openings, launches and anniversaries, award ceremonies and ballroom parties filled with hundreds of soulless breathing bodies.

"Where is Vikram?" he calls out over the roar of the hairdryer.

He hasn't seen the boy in days. Vikram's ability to converse with his family and behave acceptably is inversely related to his age. Last year, he turned fifteen, and Gaurav spent a total of six mornings in the principal's office at his school. Truancy, backtalk, inattentiveness and late homework have been the charges.

He spends his time either locked up in his bedroom or

out with his friends, and any attempt by Gaurav to speak to him is met with unwilling, monosyllabic responses.

It had not always been that way. When he was a young boy, they got on well, went on holidays and picnics and road trips. But as he grew, Vikram seemed to withdraw into himself and his world; he disconnected. Barkha lets him be; she does not share Gaurav's concern that if left alone he will drift further away. She does not worry about where he goes, or with whom, or even what he does. Last week, Gaurav smelled alcohol on his breath.

"Where is Vikram?" Gaurav repeats with simmering impatience.

"Why are you shouting?" Barkha retorts. "He's out at a friend's party."

Gaurav storms into Barkha's section of the dressing area. She sits at her table in her bra and underwear. Her body is lean and supple, unmarred by age and motherhood. It is perfect, like the imported fruits and vegetables that come from China and Japan, injected and sprayed with chemicals to keep them fresh, expensive . . . but they never taste quite as good as they look.

Silk, lace, and beaded gowns lay crumpled on the floor, tried and rejected. Expensive branded handbags are strewn, pairs after pairs of high-heeled shoes in disarray. He scowls at the mess, inhales deeply, and controls his urge to scream. "I have told you before, he is to ask my permission for going out at night."

"You weren't home," she responds to his reflection in the mirror.

"I have a phone. It is because of your spoiling that he has become belligerent. How much money did you give him?"

She is silent; she cocks her head to the side and dabs the rouge on her cheek, checking if both sides of her face are evenly made up.

"I asked you a question." His jaw is clenched, the words escape one by one, slow and deliberate like a threat. "How much money did you give him?"

She gets up from her table, leans closer to the mirror and wipes the smudged eyeliner from the corner of her eye. Then, leaving him standing there, she goes into the bathroom to put on her dress. He follows her.

"Neither do you care nor do you let me care," his voice echoes off the marble floors and walls. "Look at this place, bought with hard-earned money that you don't value, expensive clothes crumpled like rubbish."

Barkha advances toward him, glares and breaks into a sardonic smile. "I don't see why it bothers you. It's not your money." She shoves him slightly as she squeezes past him out the door.

The next morning Gaurav wakes up before the sun and spends thirty-five minutes on the treadmill in his home gym. His overnight bag has been packed the night before. He checks the contents. The last time he travelled, to

Bangalore it was, the houseboy had inadvertently forgotten to pack his pyjamas. Today they are there along with his bathroom slippers. He bathes and dresses, checks his briefcase for his passport and ticket, laptop and wallet. It is nine o'clock and she still sleeps, oblivious to the world that has already been reborn and is alive with purpose.

He has a flight to catch. Every year Zinmac participates in a Corporate Social Responsibility conference organised by the Delhi state government. India's largest companies attend and hear presentations by both government and non-government organisations. They hear about programmes for rural development, sanitation, waste management, education, health and vaccination, institutions for the destitute, the aged, the disabled. And they contribute funds as well as assist in kind. Gaurav will present cheques to five organisations tonight, and because of his generosity, he will also be seated on the main table with the minister of education.

Morning traffic on the highway is bumper to bumper. Gaurav surmises there must be some sort of a hold-up in front, an accident or a broken down vehicle or the damned road works people fiddling with something again. Whatever it is, it has caused all engines to be switched off as everyone waits for it to go away. Some drivers have already stepped out and wandered into the sea of cars and trucks to find out more. Ten minutes pass, then twenty. Horns blare, fumes rise from old lorries, windows roll down and abuse is hurled.

"Sahib, what time is your flight?" Param the driver asks.

There is a good chance Gaurav will miss his flight. He

arrives two hours later, at 11.15 am and there are only forty minutes for him to get to the gate. It's well past check in time and an ominous sign stares back at him from the business class counter of EasyFly. "Sonia" as her name tag reads, is behind the desk locking drawers and shuffling papers into a neat pile.

Gaurav edges forward and offers her a smile of sincere appeal. "Ms Sonia, can you help me check in please?"

"Where to, sir? This counter is for EF756 to Delhi; we are closed."

"Yes, I know." Gaurav points at the sign. "The traffic this morning was unexpectedly heavy; it took me three hours instead of two. Can you please check me in? I have a ticket and no check-in luggage." He hands her his passport and ticket, lifts up his cabin bag for her to see.

She inspects his papers and hands them back, genuinely sorry. "Sir, there is nothing I can do. This flight was shut out of the system ten minutes ago. Even if I wanted to, I couldn't help you. There are a couple more flights out to Delhi around now, you could enquire and purchase a ticket at counter twelve."

Gaurav flounders through the crowd of travellers and their cumbersome trolleys, down the length of steel and glass. He waits in queue to buy his new ticket on the next available flight. A pool of sweat collects under his collar. He removes his jacket and reaches for his wallet from his briefcase. When he looks up, the world has vanished. There is only her.

His breath stops. She hasn't noticed him. She speaks to a young man that Gaurav is certain he knows but has not met. She hands the man two passports and is saying something to him, but Gaurav cannot hear because his mind whirls with madness and her words are like leaves swept away. She turns, sees him, sees him looking at her.

"Asha?"

She has recognised him, he knows even though she does not reply. Instead, she fusses with the strap of her handbag, with her sweater, moving it from right arm to left and then back. He knows, because the instant she saw him she flinched, and when he said her name she couldn't bear to look at him anymore. But the silence is awkward.

"Asha?" he says again, this time his voice shakes.

She looks up and responds with a smile he has seen her give the clerk at the Bank of Baroda when requesting a spare copy of her monthly statement; it is the smile she would give his friends when she met them for the first time. It is a polite smile of courtesy, obligatory. That is the smile she gives him, and it is one that crushes his heart.

"Hello, Gaurav," she says, barely audible.

There are no signs of age in the deep black of her hair, no lines around her eyes, no tiredness in her complexion. She is as she was; uncomplicated, natural, and innocent. But there is an otherness to her, a dimension he cannot name or describe like strokes of a painting that are too abstract, meaningful yet inexpressible. She wears an off-white cotton *salwar khameez* instead of the jeans he is used to seeing her in, and the bright red *sindoor* in the parting of her hair tell him a story. He is relieved to know by these signs that she must be married, for this oddly extricates him from his own misdeeds. Still, there is a pang of guilt that rushes through him as he remembers the evening years ago at the temple when together they stood at the threshold of the inner sanctum of Shiva and he rubbed the red paste in that very same spot, and made promises he never kept.

The man behind him in queue nudges him. "Eh, *aagey*, front, front." The line has moved leaving an empty space, but they stand still. Gaurav gestures to Asha to move ahead. She steps forward with the boy; Gaurav follows behind them.

"Hello, I am Gaurav." He extends a hand to the young man with Asha. He is neither a teenager nor a man. He is dressed well, his blue shirt neatly tucked into his khaki trousers. He smiles politely and his handshake is firm. "Aryan Dubey."

A chill runs through Gaurav's spine upon hearing his own surname. It cannot be. Can it? His mind races back years, twenty-one to be exact, that was the last time he saw Asha. He studies the boy's face desperately, searching for any hint of himself. It is not in the boy's face that he finds the truth, but in Asha's.

"How do you and Mom know each other?" Aryan asks politely.

"Aryan, *beta* come it is our turn. Give the passports." Asha is at the counter now, her hands shaking as they fidget with her purse.

"Nice to meet you, sir." Aryan joins his mother at the counter.

Gaurav is left standing there, his world now unrecognisable. Then, just as suddenly as she appeared, she is gone without as much as a backward glance.

"Next please."

Gaurav says something to the lady at the counter; some words come out of his mouth but they are floating far away beyond his reach. He cannot hear them.

"Yes sir, there is a seat on Vimaan Air VA4625 scheduled to depart for Delhi at 1225HRS." She glances at her watch. "That is in an hour. You can make it."

He nods, handing her a card from his wallet.

"Sir, this is your driver's license. I will need a credit card."

He gives her one. He then follows the men clutching briefcases, the women with babies in their arms and diaper bags on their shoulders, the aged fragile passengers being pushed on wheelchairs, the children, the families, the young, the old. Like sheep, he follows the torrent of travellers, going where they go. An officer checks his ticket, another his passport, another scans his bag, another his body.

He makes it to the aircraft, even though he is absent.

"Welcome aboard, sir. Business class passenger? Let me see your boarding pass, sir. Here sir, may I get you something to drink before take-off? Oh, I think we are closing the doors now. I will come back to you after take-off. Please fasten your seat belt. Here, let me take your jacket."

There is an announcement, and the pilot says something about flight time and poor weather and turbulence.

But Gaurav is not paying attention. This soft seat is swallowing him, this wine tastes of poison, these clothes prick like thorns. As the wheels screech and leave the earth, he is crying. He wishes he were dead.

CHAPTER THREE

RADHA

5th March, 2012

Babaji has taught Radha that the body is ephemeral. He has taught her to detach from this fickle spouse that plays the part of a loyal mate but is sure to betray, decay, and die. She can hear him now, his voice thinned by the last breaths of life. "Do not fear letting go. Loving is letting go. Love never dies. I am not dying. It is this body that dies. And because this body has lived for something, it is not dying for nothing. It will perish, it will disintegrate, it will cease to be. But me? I live on in your heart as memory, I live on in the words I have spoken to you, I live on in the love that has blossomed in your heart. When you feel the wind gently kiss your cheek, when you hear the raindrops surrender to the earth, when you see a flower blossom in the wilderness, when you smile from within your heart and that smile reaches your eyes for all to see, when you go within and seek the truth inside, know I am with you, know I am alive, know I am and will always be. I am. I am. I am."

But watching Champa lay shrunken, a ghost of the woman who fed her and bathed her, who sung her lullabies and braided her hair, who played music like the angels in heaven, is not easy. Her eyes are sunken and translucent, Radha can glimpse into her mother's soul through them. And in this moment, Radha does not feel like a yogi clad in orange, a detached renunciate. She feels like a five-year-old girl. She wants to cuddle up inside of her mother's bosom. She wants to hear her love-soaked whispers of reassurance. She wants her mother not to die.

"How beautiful you look. You have an orange dress too, a dress—not a sari like this. Papa took many photos of you in it. They are in the album, you ask papa to show you. Wear that dress." Her mother's speech is like sludge.

Mohan lays a hand on his wife's shoulder, "Dear, that was when she was nine, that dress won't fit her now."

Champa knits her brows and blinks her eyes, her mouth slackens. "Oh," she mutters before her eyes glaze over. She turns her head to the window. A little yellow bird is perched on the pane, pecking on grit and dust.

Radha wipes the dribble from the corner of her mother's mouth. Champa has drifted away into a world where she cannot be reached. It will be a while before she returns. Radha kisses her forehead. "I love you, Mama."

Her father gently shuts the bedroom door and they step out into the living room. "She is too thin," Radha tells him.

"Yes, the difficulty in swallowing is getting worse. The doctor says we may have to start feeding her through a tube."

"Are you ok, Papa?"

He smiles feebly. "I am well, well enough to look after the woman I love. I consider that a blessing." He pours sweet milk tea from a thermos into two cups. "I am glad you came to visit. I know the disease is winning, but I like to believe she will be around long."

Radha places her hand over her father's. "Papa, she is lucky to have you."

"No, I am the lucky one. She has been the joy of my life. She taught me what it is to love."

"And you both taught me," Radha says.

"There really is nothing else to learn."

"Babaji used to say that."

"Yes, your Babaji and the book. What time is your flight?" He glances at her passport and ticket laying on the table. "You're on Vimaan Air. It says 1225 Hrs. I thought they only had two flights a day. I have taken the morning flight once, I think I was going for a conference but that was few years ago. Then there is one in the evening. They must have added this on. Anyhow, you haven't much time. Let me guess, no check-in baggage?"

She smiles and shakes her head.

"I still wonder how you travel with as little as you do."

She laughs and adjusts his glasses that have slipped down a little on the bridge of his nose. "Because I am not a photographer that needs a whole suitcase for my tripods and lenses and cameras."

"Now come on, that is equipment, it doesn't count. But how do you survive with just three sets of clothes?"

"Papa, the less there is to look after, the better. I am free."

"Yes but your tickets and travel expenses aren't. I was surprised when you said you did not need me to send you money for your airfare. Where do you get the money from? Surely people mustn't be donating very much."

"Some do. Babaji had some people who loved him dearly. They continue to visit the house to pay their respects and they send money for the work that goes on. He touched many lives."

Mohan cocks his head sideways and nods. "Well, it is both surprising and reassuring that even in this day and age, people are charitable. You had mentioned something about a soup kitchen; how is that going?"

"We just started operations. Babaji had an old friend, someone who grew up with him and knew him from before his spiritual quest. I have never met this man but Babaji was fond of him. It was at his company that Babaji was working and that was where Babaji made lots of money and travelled the world. Of course he renounced everything when he started his journey. This friend of Babaji's never came to visit, but he would write and call every now and then. He is wealthy with planes and ships and factories to his name.

One day, he called to speak to Babaji but Babaji was no more. I have never heard anyone cry the way this friend of Babaji's cried that day. It turned out Babaji never told many of his illness and this gentleman had no idea he was so sick. He told me he'd always planned to come visit but never hurried thinking someday soon he would be able to find the time to make the trip. But it was too late. He said he wanted to start something in Babaji's name, a charity of some sort. I told him there are many hungry mouths in Varanasi and thus the idea of the soup kitchen. He has paid for the whole project and has even started a small trust for it. He calls every now and then checking to see if anything more is needed. He sends me a donation every month even though technically I am supposed to own nothing."

"It is impossible to live in this world with nothing."

"So it is. But it is also impossible to live with everything."

"You really sound like a wise yogi. So tell me, do you get lonely there? You don't want to come back to Bombay?"

"Papa, my life is at the river, at the feet of my master and in his teachings."

"But he is no more."

"Physically he is no more, but his work goes on. The soup kitchen, the temple, I must look after them. And this book. His memoir, his story, his writings are finally published. Now

I must create awareness."

"When is the launch?"

"There is no launch, Papa. I am going to be doing a reading tomorrow at the biggest bookshop in Delhi. It will be very special. Hundreds of city folk will hear his words, will know him, will know of his message."

Mohan brushes the back of his hand over his daughter's cheek. "How deeply you have fallen in love. You left the whole world behind."

"Yes papa, I left the world, but I found my universe. And I didn't fall in love. I rose in it."

He picks her small suitcase and escorts her out the door. "Take care of yourself. I am happy you have found the path to your happiness."

She hugs her father before the elevator doors open. "Babaji says there is no path to happiness. Happiness is the path."

And then she is gone.

PART V
AND THEN...

EPILOGUE

If you are reading this, you are alive. This is, of course, a good thing. It means that you still have me, you still have Time. You have to your name seconds, minutes, hours, perhaps years worth of breaths yet to come; blank canvases that you can fill with whatever your heart desires; summer skies or clamoring confusions, whispered gratitude or embittered curses, unbridled laughter or hopeless dejection. You can dance in ecstasy, love and be loved, swallow the sunshine and set the night on fire; you can smile at the stars, you can be, because you live. You are.

Some aren't so lucky. Their time is up even as you read this sentence.

There weren't many details at first; all that was known was that an airliner had disappeared into the clouds and scattered like rain over the farms. But there were so many unanswered questions, a state of chaos really. Who were the people on board? What had happened and how? Was there a passenger manifest? A transcript from the control tower? What about the black box? Were they looking for it? Television screens flashed images of Vimaan Air aircrafts, aerial views of the land between the two cities, graphical depictions of the route, visuals of 737 planes from every perceivable angle. They regurgitated these over and over again with no respite, and people sat glued to their screens devouring the dread and gloom, letting the images roll around in their minds, savouring fear and anxiety like delicacies. But some weren't aware, they heard the news in the cruelest of ways.

"There you are!" Uma hollers at nine-year-old Ganpat. She pulls him out from under the bunk by his ear which turns red as a tomato.

"Aaaahhh you're hurting me!" his bawling bounces off the walls of the large empty bedroom of Seva Dham. All the other children are away at school but Ganpat is running a fever and even though he looked well enough to go this morning, the policy is adhered to.

"We have been looking all over for you! Come here, come out!" she scolds.

Jairam, their homeless youth-turned-assistant warden appears. "There he is!"

Uma turns to Jairam. "Can you believe it? He was here

all the while, hiding." She glares at Ganpat. "You had us worried sick. Is this why you didn't go to school today? You think you can get out of studying? Get your books! You know the rules, fever or not, books must open."

Snot, tears and bits of saliva glisten on his face. His body jerks. "How can I get my books when you are holding my ear? I want Aunty Mira!"

Uma grits her teeth and tries to stay calm. Ganpat is an especially difficult boy. Last month, he picked a fight with an older orphan twice his size. After all those years as principal of a college, she cannot seem to get used to the absurd tantrums of young children. But running the school is much easier than the duties of manning them at home. Thank God Mira and her divided their duties suitably, heaven knows how Mira has the patience she does. Kids are so much noisier and uncontrollable outside school, she thinks. But thank God again that she only has to do this for a few days. Mira will be back and she can then go back to the more disciplined environment of the school.

Jairam places his hand on Ganpat's forehead. "Madam, he is still having fever."

"Yes, that is what I came here to check. I have so much work still at the school. But this boy has wasted a whole hour of mine."

Ganpat is sobbing quietly now, defeated. She lets go his ear, kneels down and waves a finger at him. "Listen now," she says softly, "you are sick. But you have to study. You failed the last Maths test, didn't you? Now you go with Uncle Jairam.

He will give you something to eat and then he will give you your medicines. Be a good boy and take them. After that you revise your multiplication tables. When I come back from school, I will test you, ok?"

He looks up at her with his watery eyes and nods with sincerity.

Jairam leads the sniffling boy by the hand out to the the verandah.

Uma has to rush, recess will be over and she has a class to take. She is on the way to the gate when Jairam comes after her, running and holding her phone in his hand. It is ringing. "Madam, madam, you forgot this."

She glances at the blinking screen. It is an unknown number.

"Hello."

"Hello, Uma?"

"Yes, who's this?

"It is Rimi, Mohan's sister. Champa's sister in law."

Why would Champa's sister in law be calling her? They must not have seen each other in years. When was the last time? Yes, it was supposed to be at Champa's house on Radha's birthday but Uma never made it to that party. She can't remember why. Oh yes, Mira was visiting. Mira had come to Delhi to visit her son Jeevan, the same son that turned on her.

"Yes, Rimi. How are you? Are you in Bombay? Can I

call you back after school?"

"Can you come over, Uma?"

Uma's blood turns cold. Champa... has something happened to her?

God, please don't take her yet.

Pangs of guilt run through her and her heart feels like it is going to explode.

I should have spent more time with her. Dear God, don't let it be too late.

Uma thought that after moving to Bombay they'd meet often but that never happened. The building and setting up of the school took so much out of her. But ever since she learned that Champa had cancer, she's been over to see her every couple of weeks.

Jairam is still in view at the verandah, about to enter the building. She calls out to him as she pushes open the gates. "Inform Mrs Bannerjee I won't be in today. Tell her to get Mr Inder to sub for me."

Rimi is still on the line.

"Is she alright?" Uma asks.

"Yes. But I think you should come."

"I'll be over right away."

Uma could not have picked a worse taxi to ride in. The driver won't stop talking and in spite of her monosyllabic acknowledgements the man does not get the hint. She is not even listening to him but knows vaguely that he is telling her all about his family and work and the gossip he hears while driving strangers around.

Her mind is on her Champa whose voice now rings in her ears.

You're coming to Bombay? What? You're moving here? That's great news. Are you going to work here? Oh, a school? What school? You're building one? Orphanage? Where?

Champa had been so excited to learn of Uma's move. And what a surprise it had been for the both of them to discover that the orphanage Uma's friend Mira was out to buy and rebuild was the very same one that Champa had adopted her daughter Radha from. Such a small world they had both said at the same time.

She will never forgive herself if she doesn't get bid Champa farewell. But Rimi said on the phone that Champa was ok. Then what could it be? Perhaps she is teetering at the edge of death, and the doctor has asked the family to gather all the loved ones to bid her goodbye. The thought makes her stomach churn.

She hopes this isn't true. But if it is then the whole family will be there. Radha will be there. She hasn't seen her in years, ever since Radha left home to live at the river with her teacher.

What a shock that turned out to be. Uma still can't believe she chose the path she did. Never saw the faintest glimmer or inclination in the girl. Pity, she thinks. She had a great acting career going for her. Uma still remembers the day Champa called to tell her they had adopted a daughter. Uma had gone to the biggest department store in Delhi and bought a doll house so huge that she could barely fit the box in the car.

"Which block madam?" the driver is speaking to her but it takes a moment to come out of the depth of the past. "Madam, block? Which block?" he repeats, this time louder.

"Block A."

The taxi forges on through the gates of Shireen Society and Uma hands the driver a hundred rupees even before it stops. She dashes out without waiting for the change.

Let it not be too late to say goodbye.

The ride up the elevator takes forever and when the door to flat 5E opens, Uma is met with a tense and tearful Rimi.

"Say something, Rimi. How is Champa?"

"She is OK."

Uma's body relaxes, she breathes a sigh of relief and Rimi steps away from the door, opening it fully and letting Uma in.

"Is everything alright? You asked me to come over."

Rimi says nothing. Instead she closes the door behind them and leads Uma into the living room. It is crowded with people; some neighbors she has seen before at this home, relatives, Mohan's brother Subhaash, Rimi's husband, Champa's second cousin Anita whom she has met once before. Why is everyone upset? Why are a group of women in the back of the room huddling and whispering, wiping their tears?

She spots Mohan. He is sitting on a dark blue sofa. It used to be grey just a few weeks ago. They must have changed it. Why is Mohan's head bowed, in his hands? His other brother, she can't remember his name but she has met him before, has an arm around Mohan's shoulder. Is Mohan crying? His shoulders heave. She can't see his face. Why are they all looking toward the television?

"What is going on?" Uma turns to Rimi who is standing behind her. "You said Champa is alright? She's alive isn't she?"

Rimi only replies with one word but tears are streaming down her face.

"Radha."

Uma sits down at the sofa, on the other side of Mohan, and watches the news with the rest of them.

Poor weather. Disappeared from radar. Search parties mobilised. Lost contact with control tower. Sixty-four passengers and five crew. Unconfirmed reports of two government officials and a shipping magnate on board.

She is numb with confusion. What does this have to do with Radha? Surely Radha wasn't on this flight? Why would she be flying anywhere? Where was she going?

The thought of Mira doesn't even cross Uma's mind. But the newsreader continues to report the news.

Took off earlier today. 1225HRS. Bound for Delhi. Vimaan Air flight VA4625.

A kind of mental paralysis occurs in Uma. Then violent waves of terror cut through her every cell.

Mira....

The tears burst out of her like water from a dam.

⁓ ᴏᴄ ⁓

Sanjeev is already seated at their regular table at the coffee shop of the Oberoi Hotel. She will want the herb grilled chicken but he won't order for her as yet because sometimes she goes with just a salad and a soup.

He looks at his watch. She's running late. Lunch time traffic perhaps, or the awards ceremony may have ended late last night. He picks up his mobile phone to check if she's messaged. There's nothing from her since the last message a couple of hours ago.

Lunch? Same time, same place?

Same time meant one-thirty but it is a quarter to two when Barkha enters the restaurant. She is dressed immaculately as always, in a pair of slacks and a pastel pink blouse. Her oversized sunglasses sit atop her head and on her ears dangle a pair of pear shaped solitaire diamonds.

"Hey!" Sanjeev gets up to greet her. They peck at each other's cheeks and she sits down across from him, placing her maroon leather handbag on the empty chair at their table for four.

"You look great! White or Red?" he offers as the waiter appears at the side, pad in hand.

She grimaces. "I'm still hung over from last night. I knocked back quite a few out of sheer boredom. Hate these formal affairs."

"A diet coke then, I'm guessing?"

"Just a club soda would be nice."

Sanjeev places the order for the drinks and dismisses the waiter. "So how'd it go?" he asks.

"How do you think it went? Gaurav was loving it. Went up on stage to get the award and everything. He was lapping it up."

"Did he make an acceptance speech? Lots of press?"

"Yes he said the usual. Thanked my father for starting the company and having the vision. Thanked his people for all they've contributed. Thanked the partners for their trust and commitment."

The waiter returns to serve their drinks and takes their orders for lunch. Sanjeev was right, he knows her well. She only wants a salad today. He orders himself a grilled fish with a side of potatoes and tells the waiter not to return until the food is ready.

"And you?" Sanjeev asks with a smirk.

"Me what?"

"He always mentions you too."

She smiles gingerly. "Yes he does. He thanked me for being by his side and for all my support. If only he meant any of it."

Sanjeev places a hand over hers. "I know it's hard. And I know you go to these things to honour the memory and hard work of your father."

Barkha gives him a wry smile. "How come you weren't so understanding and tender when we were together?"

"*Were* together?" Sanjeev winks.

"You know what I mean. I wish we got along then like we do now."

"We always got along. Even after we broke up, we got along. Ok, so I swayed just a little, but you were tough on me, Barkha," he complains and sips his wine.

"*I* was tough? You couldn't keep your pants on. We were in Barcelona and you were banging the waitress right under my nose. Did you think I would never come back to the room from the pool?"

"Oh, come on we were young."

"Yes we were but if you needed to cheat you could have at least done it discreetly. Then I wouldn't have caught you and maybe we would have never broken up."

"Those were some good times we had, Barkha. I wish things had worked out. I wish we never broke up. We would have been great together. Remember that trip to Maldives? That villa was just out of the world…and the view. If I close my eyes, I can still see those mountains in my head today, can still feel that warm breeze. We should go again."

"Gosh I haven't been to Maldives in so long. Last time I went was with Gaurav years ago and what a rubbish time I had. We had a fight the first night there and that mood sort of lingered the whole trip."

The food arrives and Sanjeev has been hungry for the last hour. Eagerly he digs into his lunch. Barkha is flicking the leaves in her salad, tossing them around with no intention of actually eating.

She finally speaks, words pouring out of her laced with hurt. Sanjeev puts down his fork and listens to her, waits till she finishes saying what she has to say.

"We have nothing in common. I often wonder why he married me. He doesn't seem to love me. He only does what is absolutely necessary, says what is expected to be said. You know what I mean? Its like his mind is on someone else, somewhere else. But there is no one, I know that for sure. It is so different with him. When you and me were together, we laughed, we wanted to be around each other. And even though we are both married to other people, we still have that bond, you know."

He has heard different versions of this before.

"I never really saw what you saw in him. That night on your birthday, after we'd broken up and you'd told me you were seeing this guy at work, I was looking forward to meeting him. Wanted to see what you'd found."

"I wasn't seeing him then."

"Yes but you were clearly interested."

"I don't know. Maybe it was a running thing. We had that in common. But he was so nice when we met at the office. I guess I watched too many romantic movies those days. Or maybe I was on the rebound from you."

"Wait, you're blaming me now?" Sanjeev teases, trying to change her mood. "Tell you what. I will make it up to you. I'll come over after work and I'll stay till the morning. Promise. I'll tell Kareena an urgent business meeting came up out of town. He is away, isn't he?"

"Yes. He left this morning for Delhi. Yes, come over. I could do with some real company."

Sanjeev sets down his glass of wine. His brows furrow with worry. His face has turned white.

"What's the matter?"

"Did you say he's gone to Delhi?"

"Yes, why?"

"When did he leave?" Sanjeev leans forward. There is panic in his tone.

"I don't know, some time this morning. Why are you freaking out like this?"

"Barkha, I heard some of the girls talking in the office, just before I left to meet up with you. A Vimaan Air flight bound for Delhi has gone missing."

Barkha reaches for her handbag, fumbles around for her phone and dials the office. There is no answer, she tells Sanjeev, must be because everyone is away to lunch.

"Call his secretary's mobile, don't you have her number?"

Barkha doesn't have her number saved but she remembers a message she received a few days ago, something about coordinating her calendar dates for a dinner that Gaurav wanted her to go with him to.

Helen, Gaurav's secretary picks up at the first ring.

Sanjeev waits, studying Barkha's face for signs of shock or sorrow or disbelief. But instead he sees her breathe a sigh of relief.

"What did she say? What flight was he on?" he asks as soon as Barkha hangs up.

"He wasn't booked on Vimaan Air. He was booked to fly on East Air. Helen knows about the missing flight. And she was crying when she told me that she almost booked him on Vimaan but Gaurav wanted an earlier flight out."

"That was close," Sanjeev says. "Can you imagine?"

"No I can't," Barkha states, as though having an epiphany. "I can't imagine it. You scared me."

Sanjeev swallows uncomfortably and looks away. "Sorry, I really didn't mean to. It's good to know you still love him. I guess that's why you're still with him."

Barkha goes quiet, lost in her own thoughts. "Love is too big a word."

They finish their lunch in silence. Before they part Barkha stutters a little when she tells him not to come over. Vikram may be home tonight she says. Plus she has a hangover. And she's not sure if she asked a girlfriend out to dinner tonight. He interrupts her by gently kissing her cheek. "It's alright, honey. I get it. Some other time."

~~~

Varun is at the Epic Bookshop in Delhi. His fingers hover over shelf W2-065 of the thriller and mystery aisles. He holds in his hand a copy of the book for which he is here today. He has taken the day off work and he feels like a schoolboy playing truant. But he would not miss this for the world; Radha has always held a special place in his heart. She was his first ever girlfriend. And perhaps also the first girl he loved. He still has his half of the jagged edged heart he gave her on the rooftop that day, her sixteenth birthday.

They broke up soon after but it did not come entirely as a surprise. Deep down, he never really expected their relationship to work out although he always hoped that it would. She was too beautiful, too vast for him. She was the weightless sky and he was the trembling sea beneath. She was the flowing wind and he was the rooted tree. She wanted to be a song and he wanted to fade into the quiet. She was out of his league and he could just tell that she was meant for something bigger, something unearthly.

She was always searching, but he had never imagined she would find what she craved in the arms of the holy river. For this is where she lived now. He had heard from the friend of a friend who had heard from yet another friend, in the customary route all gossip travels, that Radha had lost the plot, that she had moved to live by the Ganges and renounced all things material, including her budding acting career. He knew better. Radha had not lost anything—she had found her purpose.

It had been years since he'd connected with her, and so after some asking and checking and poking around, he managed to get an address and a phone number. There were no romantic intentions at all—far from it. He was a married man, a happy one at that, and he was well settled in Delhi with a secure job, a two-year-old daughter, and a son on the way. He had always loved Radha more as a friend than a girlfriend. She was not an ex. She was Radha. And she was coming to Delhi.

For the first time in his life, Varun cannot find a book he wants to buy. His mind is occupied with fond memories of his friend and he cannot wait to see her. Time and distance have added a glaze of deeper respect and love for her, untainted and pure. He advances to the cash register to pay for the book he holds, the book that she is going to read from today, the book she has compiled, "Tablets of Love: Inspirational thoughts of My Master."

Her photo is at the back of the hardcover, beside that of a somewhat aged man with a short grey stubble. They both wear saffron. Her face, even without the enhancements of makeup or jewelry, is beautiful. Now there is a new dimension to it: her features glow, her eyes burst with joy, her smile is pure happiness. It is as though she has blossomed.

"Sir, that will be one hundred and sixty rupees," the cashier says. He pays with cash and climbs up to the first floor of the bookshop where he has heard many authors read from their work before. He has invited Radha over to his house tonight after the reading. She will meet his wife and child. He is sure she will like Shalini, even though the two haven't met before. Radha is easy with people, she takes to them without preconception or judgment. And Shalini has been intrigued from the moment Varun told her about his friend.

The reading corner is only half full with attendants, and Varun feels a little disheartened on Radha's behalf. He thought she would have a good turnout but there are still fifteen minutes to go and he is hopeful. He sits down beside a middle-aged lady in a bohemian skirt and a loose-fitted kurta. Her spectacles are thick and her sense of dress unconventional. She could be an artist or an author herself. She looks up from her book, smiles at him, and goes back to Albert Camus.

He waits patiently, flipping through the book he has bought. Perhaps he will get a glimpse of her mind in these pages, he will be able to see her thoughts and her beliefs, and what she has given herself to.

A thick voice drones out of the speakers on the ceiling in the corner of the small hall. Today's author signing and reading is cancelled. The invisible woman with the man's voice then pauses. "We apologise for the inconvenience caused. Please do browse the store and remember you can enjoy a fifteen percent discount on all romance and YA titles today through till Friday."

The woman next to Varun looks up from her book again. "Oh no," she sighs, "I was looking forward to meeting her."

"Me too," he replies, bewildered. Shalini will be disappointed. But what could have gone wrong? Perhaps her flight was delayed. Wouldn't she have called to inform? He does not know the answer to that, he doesn't know her like he used to, so many years have passed.

"I came all the way from across town only to meet her and tell her how much I love this book. What a shame! I hope they reschedule."

"Me too. Have you read the whole thing?"

"Yes, I have. So many gems in there, I tell you. Uplifting. Here, let me show you."

She takes Varun's copy and turns to a random page, her finger slides over the print, her eyes search. "Here, read this." She points to a paragraph.

Varun reads.

We are only alive because we love. Even if we love nothing else, we love our own life. And Love is that which keeps us alive. But loving only your own life is such a waste of love and of life.

Chairs are pushed back, people rise to leave, and the crowd disperses because the author is not coming anymore. Varun is the last to stand up because the words are still seeping through his mind like water drenching dry earth. When all others have left, he too leaves to go.

On the way home, he passes a flower shop, Blooms & Blossoms. He has fond memories of when he used to work at one of their first few branches in Bombay as a young boy. Amazing how they have branched out to every city in India.

The roses in the window are a lovely deep shade of red. Shalini likes roses. He can't remember the last time he bought her some.

We are only alive because we love.

What a beautiful thought. He selects a dozen of the freshest ones and has them packed to take home for his wife.

L.M. Valiram is a blogger, writer, entrepreneur, globe trotter, wife and mother. She writes in multiple genres including suspense, mystery, thriller and literary fiction. She hopes to one day write a timeless romance. *Part Star Part Dust* is her debut novel. She was born in Bombay and raised in Hong Kong. She resides in Malaysia with her husband Sharan and two sons Neerav and Divesh.

www.lmvaliram.com

ACKNOWLEDGEMENTS

This book would not have been possible without:

My mother and father who turned me into a princess.

My husband, my biggest advocate.

My children, it is for them that I continue to strive to be the best version of me.

Mahesh and Reyna, my ardent supporters.

My best friend, Swamini Supriyananda, who reminded me that I once loved to write.

H.H. Swami Chinmayananda whose words are quoted in parts of Babaji's letters.

The Valiram family (Mom, there is even a character named after you) who gave me my wings.

The many writing instructors who have trained me to string words with patience and battle the blank screen with bravery.

My friends, my beta readers (Swaminiji, Simi, Ria), my forum mates and my critique group partners.